THE
MAGICIAN MURDERS

Nothing up his sleeves. Nothing but murder...

Jason West, hot-shot special agent with the FBI's Art Crime Team, is at the Wyoming home of Behavioral Analysis Unit Chief Sam Kennedy, recuperating from a recent hit-and-run accident, when he's asked to consult on the theft of a priceless collection of vintage magic posters.

But before Jason can say "presto change-o," the owner of the art collection turns up murdered in a National Forest.

When the dead man is revealed to be the Kubla Khanjurer, a much-hated part-time magician accused of revealing the highly guarded secrets of professional illusionists, it seems clear this is a simple revenge killing— until Jason realizes an earlier suspicious death at the trendy magic club Top Hat White Rabbit might be part of the same larger and more sinister pattern.art collectors. A killer whose calling card is a series of grotesque paintings depicting the murders.

THE MAGICIAN MURDERS
Art of Murder Book III
April 2018

Copyright (c) 2018 by Josh Lanyon

Cover by Johanna Ollila
Cover and book design by Kevin Burton Smith
Edited by Keren Reed

ISBN-13: 978-1-945802-82-9
ISBN-10: 1945802820

Published in the United States of America
JustJoshin Publishing, Inc.
www.joshlanyon.com

This is a work of fiction. Any resemblance to persons living or dead is entirely coincidental.

THE
MAGICIAN
MURDERS

ART OF MURDER BOOK III

Josh Lanyon

JUST JOSHIN'
PUBLISHING INC.

To Johanna— thank you so much for regularly working your own magic on my behalf.

Chapter One

Rain flicked against the apartment windows in random, off-beat splash and dissolve.

It was sort of soothing, and Jason had not had much sleep the night before, but he could not afford to drift off in the middle of a phone call with his boss.

"If the legendary West charm has failed to convince Ursula Martin to file charges against Fletcher-Durrand, maybe the DOJ should take a swing at her," Karan Kapszukiewicz was saying.

Kapszukiewicz was chief of the Major Theft Unit of the Criminal Investigative Division. She oversaw the Art Crime Team agents from her Washington DC office, which was where she was calling Jason from. Jason was on his cell phone, lying on Sam's sofa in Sam's apartment in Stafford, Virginia. The apartment was not far from the training academy where Jason was attending routine in-service refresher training.

"Respectfully, I don't think that's the approach we want to take with Martin," Jason replied. "I think there's still a good chance she'll ultimately come through for us, but not if we push her. Her situation is complicated."

"Isn't everybody's?"

Jason waited politely.

Karan sighed. "I had a feeling you'd say that, so…okay. I'll let you make the call. She's your complainant. Or was."

Jason winced. The collapse two months ago of charges against the Fletcher-Durrand art gallery was still painful. He had worked his ass off building a prosecutable case of fraud, grand larceny, and forgery—only to have the rug yanked out from under him when his original complainants had agreed to settle out of court with the Durrands.

There had been a hell of a lot more to it than that, of course, but the bottom line was the US Attorney's Office would not be filing charges against Fletcher-Durrand at this time. Especially since the Durrand most wanted by law enforcement and everyone else seemed to have vanished off the face of the planet.

Not that Jason was so naïve as to imagine hard work and determination alone ensured the successful prosecution of every case—luck always played a role, and his luck had definitely been out. At least as far as the Durrands were concerned. In other ways…

His gaze traveled to a large Granville Redmond painting of California poppies beneath stormy skies, hanging on the opposite wall.

In other ways, his luck had been very much in, which was how he came to be lying on Behavioral Analysis Unit Chief Sam Kennedy's sofa, waiting for Sam to get home. Two months ago, he'd feared his relationship with Sam had run its blink-and-you-missed-it course, but against the odds, here he was.

"All right," Karan said more briskly, her attention already moving on to bigger or more winnable cases. "Keep me posted."

"Will do."

She was clearly about to ring off, but Jason being one of her protégés, Karan asked suddenly, "How's training? You're still at Quantico?"

"Yeah. I fly out tomorrow night. Training is…training."

"Always," Karan agreed gravely. "Okay. Have a good flight home." She did hang up then, and her timing was perfect. Jason heard Sam's key in the front door lock.

He clicked off his cell and rose as the front door swung open. The scent of April showers and faded but still slightly jarring aftershave wafted in.

"Hey."

Sam was a big man, and he filled the doorframe. Instantly, the quiet, slightly dusty rooms felt alive again. Occupied. The stale, centrally heated air seemed to break apart as though before a gust of pure, cold oxygen.

"Hi." Sam looked tired. He always looked tired these days. His short blond hair was wet and dark, the broad shoulders of his tan trench coat splattered with rain drops. He was not exactly handsome—high cheek-bones, long nose—hard mouth—but all the pieces fit perfectly in a face that exuded strength, intelligence, and yes, a certain amount of ruthless-ness. His blue eyes looked gray—but they warmed at the sight of Jason coming toward him. He dropped his briefcase and took Jason into his arms, kissing him with full and flattering attention.

Sam even tasted tired—too many cups of coffee, too many breath mints, too many conversations about violent death. Jason kissed him back with all his heart, trying to compensate with a sincere welcome home for what had probably been a shitty day.

Not that Sam found a day of murder, rape, and abduction as depressing as Jason would. Sam wouldn't be so very good at his job if he did.

As always, the softness of Sam's lips came as surprise. For a guy who was rumored to have a heart of stone, he sure knew his way around a kiss.

They parted lips reluctant. Sam studied him. "Good day?"

"It is now."

Sam smiled faintly, glancing around the room, noting Jason's coffee cup and the files and photos scattered across the coffee table. "This looks industrious." His pale brows drew together. "It's hot as hell in here."

Jason grimaced. "Sorry. I turned the heat up. It was freezing when I got in."

Sam snorted, nodding at Jason's jeans and red MOMA T-shirt. "You could always try putting on a sweatshirt. Or even a pair of socks."

"True, I guess."

Sam grinned. "You California boys."

"Known a lot of us, have you?" Jason was rueful. At forty-six, Sam had twelve years and a whole hell of a lot of experience on him.

"Only one worth remembering." Sam pulled him back in for another, though briefer, kiss.

Jason smiled beneath the pressure of Sam's firm mouth.

When Sam let Jason go, he said, "Sorry I'm late. Any idea where you want to eat tonight?" He absently tugged at his tie, probably a good indicator of what he'd prefer. Jason too, for that matter.

"We don't have to go out. Why don't we eat in?"

Sam considered him. "You've only got another day here."

"I didn't come for the nightlife. Well." Jason winked, but that was just in play. He suspected it was going to be a low-key night. Sam pushed himself too hard. There wasn't any good reason for it because the world was never going to run out of homicidal maniacs. There was no finish line in this race. "Anyway, it's not like I don't get to eat out enough."

The corner of Sam's mouth tugged in acknowledgment. "Yeah. But you must've noticed there's nothing to eat in this place."

Jason shrugged. Sam's fridge reflected the state of his own—the state of anyone whose job kept them on the road most of the time.

"I did notice. Not a problem. We can get delivery. Or I'll run out and pick us something up."

Sam opened his mouth, presumably to object, and Jason said, "Let me take care of dinner, Sam. You look beat."

"Why, thank you." There was the faintest edge to Sam's tone.

He didn't like being reminded he wasn't Superman. Jason had learned that over the past ten months. Sam worked hard and played—when he did play, which was rarely—harder. He had the energy and focus of guys half his age, but part of that was sheer willpower.

"You know what I mean."

Sam grimaced. "I do, unfortunately."

"So? You must have a favorite Chinese restaurant." Jason was smiling because he didn't take Sam's flickers of irritation all that seriously—and because the first meal they'd shared had been Chinese food.

Ah, memories. They'd pretty much detested each other back then. Which had made the sexual tension that flared instantly between them all the more—and mutually—exasperating.

"Sure. But..."

Sam didn't finish the thought. Weariness vying with his sense of obligation. Their relationship was such—the nature of their jobs was such—that there was not a lot of time for dating as most of the world understood it.

Jason got it. Anyone in law enforcement got it. But Sam still suffered these occasional bouts of guilt. Or whatever. Sam's obsession with the job was always going to be a challenge to their relationship. Initially, Jason had figured it had to do with losing Ethan, but for all he knew, Sam had always been like this.

And maybe that single-minded drive had been an issue between Sam and Ethan too. Ethan had been Sam's boyhood love. They'd grown up together, planned to spend their lives together, but Ethan had been murdered while they were still in college. That was about all Jason knew because Sam was not informative on the topic of Ethan.

"Delivery and staying in is actually what I'd prefer," Jason said.

"Yeah?" Sam scanned his face, then relaxed. "Well, if that's the case, the China King restaurant on Hope Road is pretty good. There's no delivery, though. Tell me what you want—"

"Nope. You tell me what *you* want. I've been sitting around here for a couple of hours. I need to stretch my legs anyway."

Sam hesitated. "You sure you don't mind?"

Jason half closed his eyes, consulting his memory of that first night in Kingsfield. "Hot and sour soup, shrimp with lobster sauce... What else? Steamed rice or fried?"

"Steamed. Good memory."

"You need it in my line of work." Jason wiggled his eyebrows as though he was involved in some nefarious occupation and not just another cop with a fancy title. He hunted around for his shoes, locating them beneath the coffee table. His leather jacket was draped over the autumn-colored accent chair in the corner of the room.

He was pretty sure Sam had taken this "apartment home" furnished, because the décor had a definite Overstock.com vibe. Comfortable, attractive, generic. Other than the four paintings by Granville Redmond that decorated his living room, office, and bedroom walls, the place could have doubled as a very nice hotel suite.

"Hope Road, you said?" He checked his wallet.

"Go north on US-1. It's less than a mile." Sam was shrugging out of his raincoat, preparing to get comfortable, and Jason smiled inwardly.

"Got it. I'll be back in a few."

"West?"

Jason glanced back. "Mm?"

Sam grinned. "Don't forget the fortune cookies."

"Roger that." Jason touched a finger to his temple in mock salute and stepped outside.

* * * * *

It was tough, no question. Not knowing when, after tomorrow, he'd see Sam again. Not anytime soon, that much he did know. And Sam didn't—couldn't—offer any promises that things would get better. Sam was one hundred percent committed to the job. That's what Jason had signed on for, and it was still easier, at least for now, knowing that eventually he *would* see Sam. Easier than the alternative. He'd had to face the alternative two month ago, and it had been hell.

For now, he would take what he could get because when they were together, it just felt…right.

These were Jason's thoughts as he pushed out through the glass door of the China King restaurant. It was dark at seven thirty. The rain was coming down much harder now, and he ducked his head, tucking the white paper bag of fragrant-smelling food beneath his arm, feeling in his coat pocket for his keys. He jogged toward his rental car. The damp air smelled of wet brick, wet cement, wet trees, and car exhaust. The parking lot was a large one and reasonably busy on this Thursday night, though it was a relatively rural area. Well, compared to Venice.

There had been a line inside the China King, anyway.

Should he stop and pick up a six-pack? Sam would drink whisky sours all night, but Jason had training the next day, followed by a long-ass flight home. Beer might be the better choice.

Originally the plan had been to stay the weekend, but duty called. Duty called Sam, to be precise. He was flying out tomorrow afternoon to Seattle. So the much-anticipated weekend together would have to wait for another time. Another city.

The blue pickup was still parked on the passenger side of Jason's rental car. A black Porsche had pulled into the slot next to the driver's side, close enough that it made getting into Jason's vehicle awkward. The hood of the Porsche's trunk was popped and wide open. The driver did not appear to be about.

Someone just figuring out he—she?—didn't have a spare tire? Or a jack?

A black sports car had pulled out after him when he'd left Sam's, but had continued down the highway when Jason had pulled onto Hope Road.

He unlocked the passenger side of his rental car to deposit the bag of takeout, absently considering that memory. He was not really on guard. Why should he be? The world was full of black sports cars—as well as people who didn't carry spare tires. He bent down to set the food on the seat.

"Agent West?" The voice was male, a little high, a little strained. It seemed to come out of nowhere, and Jason backed out of the car, straightening.

There wasn't even time to look around. He caught swift—aggressive?—movement out of the corner of his eye, and instinctively reached for his weapon...which was still lying on the nightstand in Sam's bedroom. He'd taken it off to grab a quick nap when he'd arrived back from training.

What the fuck—

A dark figure crashed out of the barrier of trees hemming the nose of the rental, shoved the passenger-side door into Jason, and pinned him for a crucial split second.

A burning bite at the base of his neck. He cried out in shock and pain. Jesus, had he been stabbed?

Not happening. This can't be happening…

But it was happening. Happening so fast and so violently, he barely had time to react. Which is how it always happened. To everyone. *The predator always has a plan.* He could hear Sam's voice in the back of his brain.

He jammed his car keys in his assailant's face, but everything was going wrong. Terrifyingly wrong. His strength drained away with the suddenness of a cut power cord. He felt weak. So weak. His vision blurred, blackened at the edges. There was no muscle in his punch. His knees gave. The stink of rotting onions seemed to permeate the air around him, making it hard to breathe.

Jason fought the weakness, the sudden overwhelming lassitude, somehow shoving the heavy car door back, sliding free. He stumbled away from the rental car, lurching across the asphalt.

It felt like running through water. His feet were sliding out from under him. He couldn't see through the blur of rain and lights from the restaurant windows. *Bokeh. The word is bokeh.* Red, blue, white streaks. An out-of-focus dazzle…

YES, WE ARE OPEN glowed the neon letters.

People. Safety in numbers. In people.

He had to get to the restaurant. Any business. Anywhere there were people.

He staggered on. Just a couple of steps but it felt like he was trying to cover miles. Felt like he was not even moving. He could hear footsteps behind him. Not running. Walking briskly, with purpose.

"Agent West," the voice called again, sounding weirdly muffled. Hand clamped over his broken nose maybe? *Hopefully, you bastard.*

Did he *know* that voice?

He staggered, managed another faltering step toward the black outline of the building.

A white glare loomed out of the rain, bore down on him. Headlights. A car. Coming straight at him.

He couldn't stop. Didn't want to stop. Was more afraid of what was behind him. But he was going down anyway. Everything falling apart inside him. Two lights as big as twin suns swam toward him. For an instant he was ablaze, caught in the supernova.

Impact was a distant, dull thing.

He felt himself flying—and then nothing.

Chapter Two

Before he opened his eyes, he knew he was in a hospital.

He'd been in the hospital a lot as a kid. Asthma. He'd outgrown it. Still. There was no mistaking that antiseptic smell, the hushed beeps and buzzes of constant monitoring, the crackle of tension that permeated the temperature-controlled air. He'd been hospitalized after getting shot in Miami, and it had been just the same.

Had he been shot again?

He couldn't think of any other reason he'd be lying in a hospital bed.

He didn't remember being shot.

He didn't remember...

Wait.

He'd been back at Quantico for in-service training. He'd been staying with Sam. He'd...

What?

What had happened to him?

His heart jumped at the sudden flash of memory: *a dark figure bursting through a wall of wet leaves and dead branches.*

"...the hell?" Jason's eyes flew open. He blinked a couple of times.

Yeah. A hospital room, all right. Neutral walls, luminaires, acoustic ceiling panels...a lot of monitors, some in use, some not...and *Sam.*

Sam rising from a chair near the window and coming to lean over the bed railing. He wore jeans and a black sweater. He was smiling, but it didn't warm the wintery glitter of his eyes or soften the hard, almost harsh lines of his face. It was not a reassuring smile. "Hi. How are you feeling?"

"Hi…"

How *was* he feeling? Not great. He began to take quick, worried inventory. Fingers, toes, hands, feet, arms, legs…everything was still there and seemed to be working…some parts more painfully than others.

"You're okay," Sam told him. "You're going to be fine."

Was he? Because the expression in Sam's eyes was more assessing than reassuring. Not that Jason didn't believe him. He did. He knew he was not dying. He had nearly died in Miami, and this did not feel like that. It did not feel good, though. And he suspected painkillers were masking the worst of it.

"What happened?" He tried to read Sam's face.

Why didn't Sam kiss him? Or if he couldn't manage a kiss—*since when?*—how about a pat on the hand? Or one of his famous shoulder squeezes? Something. Why were they—Sam—being so… So formal? Jason felt more confused by the minute.

A muscle moved in Sam's jaw. "That's what we need to figure out. Feel up to answering a couple of questions?"

Kind but brisk. As he would be with any victim of violent crime. Getting down to business. Was that the real reason for the bedside vigil? Sam had been waiting to interview him?

Well, hell.

It hurt. Jason did not want a lead investigator; he wanted—embarrassing to admit, but the truth—his boyfriend. The guy who had once told him he was "irreplaceable." The guy who had once said he wanted him—and only him—all the time. The guy who presumably gave a fuck what happened to him, and not merely in his professional capacity as BAU Chief.

"Sure," Jason said stiffly. Not like he couldn't be a professional too.

Sam's gaze flickered, registering whatever he heard in Jason's tone, but remained steely, as intent as if he was trying to skip the middleman and scan Jason's brainwaves for himself. "How much do you remember?"

Now there was a question.

Jason closed his eyes, tuning Sam out, forcing himself to focus.

Night. Cold. He remembered the rain and the smell of the parking lot, the smell of Chinese food... No. No, rotting onions.

His stomach roiled with unexpected nausea. He swallowed the sourness, opened his eyes and faltered. "Can I— I need a glass of water."

"Of course." Sam pressed the button to raise Jason's bed and poured water from the plastic pitcher into a plastic cup with a straw. He seemed ready to hold the cup for Jason too, but Jason took it from him and sipped a couple of mouthfuls of flat water.

"Take your time." Sam sounded gruff. Awkward.

Jason ignored him.

The water helped. So did having a minute or two to pull himself together. He belatedly noticed he had an IV stuck in one arm. The knuckles of both hands were scraped and cut. Was that it? Had he been in a fight? Had someone tried to mug him?

He began to be aware of a myriad of aches and pains. His lower back hurt, his knee, his elbow, his right shoulder—granted, his right shoulder always hurt. His right ankle was propped up and tightly taped. He could wiggle it, but it was painful.

He was bewildered and hurting. He wanted time to process. He wanted Sam to stop asking questions. No, more than anything he wanted Sam to—well, it didn't matter because it was clearly not going to happen.

He glanced up at Sam, who was still regarding him with that intense, unblinking stare—no doubt evaluating the victim's credibility as a witness.

Victim.

No. No way. He did not like that word. Did not like thinking of himself as a victim. He was a special agent with the Federal Bureau of Investigation. He was not a civilian. He was not a victim. Hell, he'd rather be a suspect.

"Sorry. I'm fine." Jason handed the plastic cup back to Sam, who set it on the bed table.

Sam could see Jason's distress, but he did not say, *We can do this another time.* The interview was going to happen regardless of how lousy Jason felt. And Jason understood the reason for that. A crime had been committed, the clock was ticking, and law enforcement needed whatever help he could give them.

He stared beyond the foot of the hospital bed to a metal-framed photograph of a lighthouse on a rocky point. It was not a great photograph, but it did capture the way sunlight looked on water and the sparkle of foam. Sea and silence. He let out a long breath, forcing himself to calm down, and tried again to remember.

The chill air scented with exhaust…cooking from the nearby restaurants…the wet green fragrance of the trees next to the parking lot.

"He was waiting in the trees," he said.

Yes, he remembered now. A black Porsche parked too close to his own car, making it difficult for him to get inside. The hood of the trunk had been raised. Why had he not recognized that as a warning sign?

"He?" Sam repeated. "Did you get a look at him? Did you see his face? Could you identify him?"

Jason moved his head in negation, but he was uncertain. He thought male was correct. It felt correct. He *must* have seen the guy. *Why* couldn't he remember?

"How tall was he?"

The question snapped his concentration. He was trying to remember the sequence of events. Sam was trying to get a workable description of the unsub.

"Tall."

Sam was patient. "Was he taller than you?"

"I…"

"About your height? Was he taller than me?"

"Tall," Jason repeated slowly. It was like trying to see through murky water. He remembered the sensation of looming darkness. Was that the setting or the assailant? Was it even accurate, or was it an effect of the drugs he was on? They had definitely pumped him full of something. Even lying back against the mattress, he felt woozy.

"Were you able to see his hands? Did he wear gloves?"

Jason shook his head again, and again it was *I don't know.* It was embarrassing because he was trained to remember this kind of thing.

An image came to him then. Sharp, horrifying. The sting of a needle. He had been stuck in the neck.

He stared at Sam, reached up automatically. There was a small but tender lump at the base of his throat, right above the clavicle. Not a dream.

"What did he inject me with?" he asked.

Sam's expression was hard to interpret. "Thiopental."

Jason's eyes widened. "Sodium Pentothal?"

"Yes. Correct."

Weird. Or was it? Famed on 1970s TV as a truth serum, Sodium Pentothal was a swift-acting barbiturate which, in large doses, resulted in almost immediate—and prolonged—unconsciousness.

So...the intent had not been to kill him. Not immediately. What, then? He thought of the raised lid of the trunk. Abduction.

He swallowed against another surge of sickness.

"He would have had to get right up in your face." Sam was circling back. "Try to visualize. Was he wearing a mask?"

Jason closed his eyes, but the picture... Would. Not. Come. "Maybe."

"Did he speak? Did he say anything? Address you by name?"

Jesus Christ, you asshole. Can you give me a minute here?

But as Sam's words registered, Jason's eyes jerked open. "Yes. He called me by name. *Agent West.* I remember."

Not a random attack, then. But hadn't he already known that? For one thing, fully grown men were rarely abducted off the street by anyone other than the mob. Or maybe the CIA. He was pretty sure he had not been targeted by the mob. Or the CIA. No, he had been the intended target of some private citizen. Someone who knew he worked for the FBI. Someone bold and ruthless as fuck.

His heart sped up in angry—and yes, no point kidding himself, alarmed—response. Sam glanced at the monitor over the bed.

"You're doing great," he said.

Jason's laugh was terse. "Sure. Aside from the fact I can't remember anything. Didn't notice I was followed. Wasn't carrying my weapon."

"Thiopental acts instantly and causes unconsciousness in thirty-five to forty seconds. Had you pulled your weapon, there's an even chance you'd have shot yourself."

"Right."

"You're not required to be armed at all times."

Jesus. If Sam was making excuses for his complete stupidity, he really did view Jason as a victim.

He opened his mouth, but Sam cut in. "Do you know for sure you were followed?"

Jason rubbed his forehead, trying to recall. "I had to have been. We didn't plan on getting takeout."

He was silent, still massaging his temples. Chinese takeout and a night at home with Sam seemed like another lifetime.

Sam said nothing.

Finally, Jason looked up. "I think so. I think I remember a black sports car following me when I left your place." He corrected, "Behind me. I don't know if it was following me."

"Go on."

"When I came out of the restaurant, a black Porsche had pulled up next to me. The trunk was open. I figured the driver was getting out the spare." He added curtly, "If I thought about it at all."

"That was a reasonable assumption."

"Sure. Anyway, he'd parked too close, so it seemed easier to go around to the passenger side and put the food on the seat. That's all I really remember. That and getting jabbed with a needle. Everything else is a blur."

And getting blurrier. He desperately wanted to close his eyes and sleep again. He felt sick, cold, shaky.

Sam's voice snapped him out of his miserable self-preoccupation. "Did you recognize his voice?"

Jason forced himself to think back. "Not…exactly. There was something. He was excited. His voice was shrill. Nervous. Maybe tense?"

A novice? First try at abduction?

"Good," Sam said. "That's good."

"Is it?" Jason asked shortly.

"Yes. Anything distinctive about his voice? Do you think he had an accent?"

Jason sighed. "I don't think so. I can't…" All at once he had reached his limit. His heart was thudding, perspiration breaking out over his body. Pride kept him from asking for a break, but he was starting to hate Sam.

"I know," Sam said, and his tone was unexpectedly gentle. "I'm sorry. Just a couple more questions. Can you think of anyone who might want to harm you?"

Jason gave him a long, hostile look.

Sam met it, unfazed. "Yes, you work for the FBI and hard feelings come with the territory, but this is the public assault and attempted abduction of a federal agent. Who wants you out of the way that bad?"

"No one. I'm on the Art Crime Team, for God's sake. Nobody tries to take out members of the ACT."

"You were shot in Miami."

"Heat of the moment."

Sam grunted acknowledgment. "What about Shepherd Durrand? He had a nice thing going before you came along. What about the brother? Barnaby."

Jason summoned energy to refute this. "Getting rid of me isn't going to stop the investigation into Fletcher-Durrand, which is at a standstill anyway. Getting rid of me would be the worst move they could make—for this very reason. It refocuses attention on them."

"All right. What about your personal life? Anyone you can think of with a grudge?"

"You're my personal life," Jason said shortly, and he couldn't help the note of bitterness that crept in.

That seemed to give even Sam pause. He pressed his lips together, said, "Your family is politically connected. It's possible—"

"I know it's possible. I don't think that's what this was—and you don't think so either."

"No? What do you think this is?"

"My pen pal. Jeremy Kyser."

"It's a possibility," Sam said.

"He'd have to be fucking nuts."

"Maybe he is fucking nuts."

Over the past few months, Kyser, a witness in last summer's disturbing Kingsfield case, had mailed Jason a succession of increasingly troubling handmade greeting cards. Initially, Jason had been inclined to brush off those unsolicited communications—until he saw what a dim view Sam took of them. Though Sam had been the one to point out the cards in themselves were inconclusive.

Uncertain, Jason studied Sam's impassive expression. "*Is* that what you think?"

"It's too soon to form a theory."

"Last time I heard from him, he was in the Richmond area. And I seem to recall he owned a black Porsche."

"Kyser is on my list."

"Are you seriously not going to tell me what the hell ha—"

The rest of it was cut off as Sam bent to press a quick—too quick—hard kiss to his open mouth. "You did great. Try to get some rest. I'll be back as soon as I can."

It was like a shot of much needed adrenaline. Brief as that kiss was, Jason's mouth seemed to tingle as he listened to the sound of Sam's footsteps disappearing down the hallway.

Chapter Three

He was not on his own for long. A petite nurse in flowered scrubs soon appeared to congratulate him on regaining consciousness.

"What the hell happened to me?"

She looked surprised, but instead of answering, assured him Dr. Taggert was on his way, and presented him with a small paper cup of medication as though it was a special gift—and judging by the way he felt without the distraction of Sam's presence, it probably was.

He and the tiny nurse had a brief difference of opinion as to whether he was allowed to use the toilet, but after Jason assured her he had plenty of experience unhooking himself from IVs, she surrendered. Jason was released from his various leashes and permitted to hobble painfully into the cubby-sized restroom on his own.

In the harsh light of the mirror over the sink, he got a good look at himself, and the sight was not reassuring. His left eye was turning purple-black. His good eye was bloodshot, though not quite as gruesome, and he had a red scrape across his forehead. He probably had an assortment of nicks and scratches beneath the dark stubble on his jaw. All in all, he looked pretty disreputable, but his teeth were intact, his nose did not appear broken, so that was the good news.

He lifted up the blue and white hospital gown and got another shock at the vision of ugly bruises and contusions covering his torso and buttocks.

Jesus Christ. He steadied himself on the edge of the sink. Had he been beaten? Hit by a Mack truck?

It seemed like something Sam might have mentioned.

Except Sam had been at his bedside to get information, not give it.

Okay, that was a little cynical. The last twenty minutes had not been particularly heartwarming, but he knew Sam did sincerely care for him, even loved him in his own way. It was just that the job always came first—even when the job was his boyfriend.

Why the hell was no one willing to explain what had happened to him? Why the hell could he not remember?

Jason brushed his teeth, splashed some cold water on his face, used the toilet. The basic necessities seen to, he shakily returned to his bed— more grateful than he wanted to admit at lying flat again—swallowed his meds, had a brief and unsuccessful look for his phone, and shortly after fell deeply back asleep.

His final thought was the hope that Sam would wake him if he did stop by again before flying out to Seattle.

* * * * *

He woke to the unmistakable scent of Escentric Molecules Escentric 03 men's cologne—ginger, white pepper, lime, and vetiver made a welcome change from disinfectant and bleach—and the warmth of strong fingers wrapped around his own.

Jason lifted his eyelashes. Sam sat beside his bed, holding Jason's hand in both of his. Sam's thumb made small soothing circles on the back of Jason's hand. His blue eyes regarded Jason, but there was none of the steely determination of earlier. He looked serious, sympathetic.

Jason offered a crooked smile.

"More questions?" he could almost joke about it now that Sam was sitting there looking so concerned. Plus, he felt a little better than the first time he'd woken.

"Only one. How are you feeling?"

Jason grimaced. Not at the question, but because he knew Sam understood that he had been upset by their earlier interview.

"I'm fine. Mad at myself for walking right into...that." Whatever *that* had been. It was still really hard to believe someone had tried to snatch him right there in an open parking lot.

"It could have happened to anyone." Not in Sam's nature to make excuses for people, so see? He really *was* fond of Jason.

"Let's hope," Jason muttered, and Sam made a sound that could have been agreement or even grim amusement.

Funny thing. Jason had never been a guy for handholding, so it was a revelation how comforting Sam's touch was.

Sam's voice broke into his thoughts. "I hear you've been giving the nurses a hard time."

"Me?" Jason was genuinely startled, then remembered the argument over, well, stuff. He flushed. "I just wanted to get back to feeling like normal."

"I know." Sam let go of Jason's hand. He leaned over the low hospital bed and slid a muscular arm beneath Jason's shoulders, cradling him to be kissed. It was a nice, leisurely kiss. Sort of sweet and sort of sexy. Exactly what Jason needed right then, really, to feel...appreciated.

He kissed Sam back, opening his mouth to Sam's tongue, which slipped inside, leaving Jason instantly hot and aching and flustered. Sam kissed him with gentle ruthlessness before settling him back against his pillows.

It was like the earlier interview had never happened. Now that Jason was waking up a bit, coming back to himself, he began to wonder why it had.

Wasn't the attack on him the jurisdiction of Stafford County Sheriff's Office? Even if the Bureau was asking in on the investigation, surely Sam would not be taking lead? Wouldn't be included at all. Not only were they personally involved, Sam was a Behavioral Analysis Unit chief. He didn't waste his valuable time on ordinary run-of-the-mill violent crime.

Furthermore, wasn't Sam supposed to be on his way to Seattle?

Jason glanced at the windows. The drapes were drawn, but he could see the dark shadow behind the yellow fabric. Nighttime, then. He looked toward the large LED clock on the wall next to the door.

Seven thirty.

Hell. Sam should be mid-flight by now. Not that he wasn't glad Sam had postponed his trip, but...

"What time are you flying out?"

"I'm not," Sam said.

"You're not? What about Seattle?"

"Seattle can wait."

"Since when?"

Sam frowned. "Do you honestly think I'd fly out under these circumstances?"

"Well... No."

Sam said drily, "You could sound a little more convinced."

"I mean, if I was at death's door. But I'm not. And we both know the job takes precedence."

They did both know it. They'd had one particularly memorable conversation on this very subject, so why Sam should look almost pained at hearing Jason acknowledge it was puzzling. He ought to be relieved that Jason was—so far—still accepting the terms of engagement.

Sam said brusquely, "Anyway, it's Saturday now."

Jason tried to sit up. "It's *Saturday*?"

Sam put a big hand on his shoulder and pushed him back against the mattress. "Yes. So relax."

"How the hell long was I— I was out *two* days?"

"Roughly."

"*Jesus Christ.*"

"You're okay," Sam said. "All that Thiopental floating around in your system is what caused the prolonged unconsciousness. It's also why you weren't injured more badly."

Huh? That was kind of confusing. But there wasn't a chance to question it because Sam was continuing, "I've spoken to your doctor. You're going to be fine. They'll probably discharge you tomorrow. You just need to take it easy for a bit. Give yourself a chance to—"

"But I don't even know what happened," Jason broke in. He was unexpectedly indignant. "You questioned me and then charged out of here—"

"Okay." Sam looked pained. "Jason—"

"The only thing I know for sure is I was shot full of sodium pentothal. Which, for the record? Not pleasant." He could add a splitting headache to his list of miseries.

"I realize that."

"Were there witnesses? How did I manage not to get thrown in the fucking trunk of that Porsche? I look like I was hit by a semi."

"If you'll let me get a word in, I'll be happy to answer any questions you have."

The flash of resentment was already fading, not least because Jason still didn't have the energy for prolonged outrage. He pressed the heels of his hands to his eyes, trying to squish the steady throb in his skull.

Watching him, Sam said, "I'm sorry I 'charged out.' I promised Stafford SO they'd have your account of Thursday night ASAP."

Jason lowered his hands, started to speak. Sam said, "And I'm sorry there wasn't time to…help you fill in the blanks. Obviously, I needed to get your version of events before I risked contaminating your memory with eyewitness accounts."

"Obviously." *Fill in the blanks* was a careful euphemism if there ever was one. He had been confused and in pain and, yes, a little shaken—and Sam had recognized and dismissed his distress as low priority.

As though reading his thoughts, Sam said, "It wouldn't have been my first choice either."

Hopefully that was true.

"I still don't understand. Why would you be in charge of this investigation?"

"I'm not."

"Then why the *hell*—"

Sam said quietly, "Keep your voice down. It's a hospital."

"Yeah, I *know* it's a hospital." Jason kicked impatiently at the sheets and then winced. His propped right ankle was definitely sprained. He lowered his voice. "Then what the hell were you doing in here interviewing me?"

"You really want to go into this now?"

Meaning Sam didn't? No surprise there.

"I really do, yeah."

"I pulled in a couple of favors from the Stafford Sheriff's Office. I thought it would be easier on you and it would guarantee me getting the information I wanted."

Jason's jaw dropped. This sweeping obliviousness, of course, was an example of why Sam, unlike himself, had a whole list of people dying to throw him in car trunks and permanently dispose of him.

There was so much to say in response, Jason wasn't sure where to begin. Aggravatingly, the first thing that bubbled out was, "Easier on *me*? Easier having *you* interview me?"

"Yes. Of course."

He really believed it too. Really believed that it had somehow been more pleasant for Jason to be questioned by Sam as though he was an unknown victim—a stranger—in a criminal investigation rather than be questioned by the local sheriffs.

"You really think that's what I needed most from you right then?"

Sam's frown deepened. He did not answer.

"Sam…" Jason stopped. "I just don't understand how you're so good at your job when you're so *bad* at dealing with people."

Sam reddened, looking both startled and offended. "Meaning?"

"Forget it. If you're not in charge of this case, why was it necessary to interview me? What information were you after—and why?"

Sam appeared not to understand the question.

"If this is a matter for the local police—"

"I don't know that," Sam said. "It's too early to know that. You brought up the possibility of Jeremy Kyser. He's been stalking you for several months and can't be ruled out. But you're also working something like twelve cases per day."

"More like fifteen."

"Right. And every one of those open and ongoing cases has to be examined. Correct?"

"Yes."

"The Sheriff's Office will pursue their investigation as they see fit. I intend to monitor the situation."

"You?"

"Hell yes. Who better?"

This...arrogance...this attitude of law-unto-himself was why ten months ago Sam's career in the FBI had been hanging by a thread.

Jason wasn't even sure how to answer—*maybe an investigator not personally involved with the victim?*—but in any case, a nurse—older and about four sizes larger than the morning's model—bustled in on her nightly rounds. She checked Jason's vitals, assured him he was doing great, and commiserated over his once again having missed Dr. Taggert.

"He hasn't had anything to eat today," Sam interjected.

The nurse assured them that was impossible, Sam assured her that he'd been sitting next to Jason's bed all afternoon. The nurse assured them Jason's meals had been delivered, Sam assured her Jason had slept through his meal times. She seemed skeptical but finally departed, promising to see if she could hunt up a stray sandwich.

The debate over his meals defused a lot of Jason's frustration. Now that Sam had mentioned it, he was kind of hungry. In fact, maybe some of his physical discomfort was partly due to hunger.

Like it or not, Sam operated by a different set of rules. It didn't mean he didn't care. Jason was disarmed by Sam's casual mention of sitting beside his bed all day. He remembered how comforting it had been to wake up and find Sam there—and how nice it had felt to have Sam holding his hand.

It was kind of like dealing with someone on the high-functioning end of autism. Though more likely Sam was just an arrogant bastard—but that didn't mean he didn't have a lot of good qualities too.

Sam had followed the nurse to the door, which he closed after her.

"Does my family know I'm in here?" Jason asked as Sam reseated himself in the uncomfortable-looking chair beside his bed.

"Yes. I spoke to your father. I let them know you were recovering quickly and would likely be released before they could make the trip." Sam looked braced for Jason's ire, but Jason sighed wearily.

"Thanks."

His parents were elderly. He did not want them—or either of his sisters—flying across country if they didn't have to. In fact, thank God Sophie was back in California right now and not in Washington, or nothing on earth would have kept her from showing up to tell the hospital everything they were doing wrong.

Sam studied him for a moment. Nodded.

They were silent for a few seconds. Even at night, even with the door shut, a hospital was always humming with activity. Through the closed door he could hear a Dr. Harmon being paged. And from down the hall, someone was crying.

"Listen." Sam's voice sounded slightly strained.

Jason turned his head to meet Sam's glinting look.

"I don't know any other way to say this. You're important to me. Too important to take chances with." Sam seemed about to add more, but instead simply shrugged. "That's all."

That was all—and it was kind of everything.

Jason reached for Sam's hand, and Sam's fingers instantly wrapped around his in a hard, reassuring grip. "It's okay. I'm just...rattled. Sorry."

He understood. Sam had not been able to protect Ethan. That perceived failure drove him in his professional life. Naturally, it would be a driver in his personal life too.

Sam said in a flat, impersonal tone, reminding Jason of their earlier interview, "There were no witnesses to the attack on you. A couple of people saw a black sports car racing out of the parking lot after you were hit. Nobody got a license plate. All attention was on you—and the driver of the car that hit you."

"The car that..."

"Our best guess is the unsub followed you to the restaurant, waited for you to come out, and injected you with Thiopental. Somehow you got away and tried to make your way across the parking lot. You were hit by a vehicle entering the fire lane. Fortunately, the car was only traveling about ten miles per hour, and it was a glancing blow. Even so, it knocked you into the trees and shrubs of the street frontage. That attracted immediate and considerable attention. We believe the unsub was forced to abandon his plan and flee."

Well, he'd asked. That accounting seemed to line up with the little he did remember.

Sam said, "You're trained to memorize details even under the most stressful conditions. I think your recall of those missing minutes will return. Part of the problem now is the Thiopental still floating around in your system. It can affect memory."

"I hope you're right."

That was the good news. The bad news was only now really sinking in. Someone had planned to abduct and perhaps—probably?—kill him. He had been too groggy earlier—and there had been so much to think about—that he had not had time to really consider what this meant. He had not had time to be afraid.

He was afraid now.

Chapter Four

"**N**o way."

It was the next morning, and Jason, having been cleared for takeoff by Dr. Taggert, was hobbling slowly and painfully around his hospital room as he prepared to be officially discharged.

Sam said, "Hear me out."

Jason squared his jaw. "I heard you. The answer is no way."

"Maybe you heard, but you're sure as hell not listening."

"No? Then maybe you should try listening to *me* for once."

Yep, what they had there was a failure to communicate, that was for sure.

Sam opened Jason's carry-all and handed over Jason's shirt, watching grimly as Jason slipped on the shirt and slowly did up the buttons. Sam handed over his jeans. Jason had to sit down for those. He wriggled awkwardly, wincing his way into the soft denim, trying not to open any cuts or tear any stitches. Lying in bed, he hadn't quite realized how banged up he was. He hurt. A lot.

His mood was not improved by the suspicion that Sam was letting him get a good feel for just how limited his mobility was—how difficult it would be to protect himself if simply getting dressed required this much effort.

Sam produced his brown leather belt, which Jason shakily fed through the loops of his jeans. He fastened the buckle with a pretense of briskness. Then he stared down at his feet. His right ankle was still too swollen for shoes. Bending, stretching, squatting were all excruciating, so maybe he'd be walking—rolling—out of the hospital in bare feet.

"You're on sick leave," Sam said. "That's nonnegoti—"

"I can be on sick leave at home. That's what home is for." Jason managed not to yelp reaching for his sock, and reconsidered the best angle of approach. Maybe if he lay back and lifted his leg à la chorus-girl kick?

Sam made a sound of exasperation, took the sock from him, and knelt. He lifted Jason's good foot on his knee, rolled up the sock, and pulled it over Jason's foot. He slipped the left of Jason's Converse Chucks on and laced it up.

Jason made a sound in the back of his throat that was supposed to be…well, who knows. It was hard to stay irritated with a guy who was willing to do up your shoes as if you were nine years old.

The thing was, he'd had a horrible night. The pain meds had failed to work their magic, and he had slept badly. Which meant Sam, who had insisted on staying with him, had also slept badly. When Jason woke freezing in the middle of the night, Sam had gone in search of extra blankets. When Jason woke thirsty, Sam had been there to pour water and steady the cup. And when Jason woke gulping and gasping in the wake of a dream where Dr. Taggert had turned out to be Jeremy Kyser, Sam had been there, quiet and calm and steady as a rock. He hadn't even laughed at the idea of Dr. Taggert—who was short, squat, and resembled a cartoon genie—as an alias for Jeremy Kyser.

Sam was a candidate for sainthood after the night he'd spent, but if he thought imminent canonization meant Jason was simply going to fall in with all his plans, he was in for a rude awakening. Another rude awakening.

Sam lifted Jason's swollen foot to his knee and gently, very gently eased the sock over Jason's discolored and puffy toes, smoothing the soft cotton over the elastic ankle brace.

"Thanks," Jason muttered. There was nothing erotic in Sam's actions, but it still gave him a funny feeling in the pit of his stomach.

Sam lowered Jason's injured foot to the floor and rose. "Consider the Bureau's perspective. We've got an unsub out there brazen enough—or crazy enough—to attack a federal agent, not just in a public parking lot, but within a stone's throw of Quantico."

That would be quite a throw. Quantico was about fifteen miles from Stafford. But, okay, close enough. Stafford was essentially a bedroom community for Quantico, populated with military personnel and various employees of the FBI.

"I remember. I was there. I'm not going into hiding. The idea is ridiculous!"

"But that's the problem," Sam returned. "You *don't* remember. You don't remember most of what happened, and you don't remember who came after you."

"I'm missing a couple of minutes. At most."

"Crucial minutes."

"Okay. Say they are crucial minutes. There's no guarantee when I'm getting those minutes back—or if I'm getting them back. I can't hang out in a safe house indefinitely."

"Of course not."

"I'm not the first agent to have threats made against him. For God's sake, I'm not the first agent to have an attempt made on his life."

"No, unfortunately you're not. And in those cases, the endangered agents were offered protection for themselves and their families."

Jason smiled sardonically. "And how many of those agents accepted protection for themselves? How many agents went to the safe house with their families?"

"You're the one who keeps talking about safe houses. I'm suggesting something different. Something I would think you'd like."

Jason stopped smiling. "Wyoming."

"Yes."

"Your home in Wyoming."

"Technically my mother's home, but yes."

"And you'd be staying there too?"

"That's what I said."

"Right," Jason said.

"I'm lost." Sam did seem perplexed. "What is it you don't like about this plan? I was under the impression you wanted to spend a little more time together."

"I would. Of course."

"Well?"

Jason glared at him. "We both know it's completely impractical. You only came up with this solution because you know how much I want that—to have a little time to ourselves."

"Yes. I did. Of course. What's wrong with that?"

"Because. Because you're profiling me."

"*Huh?*"

Sam's astonishment was kind of comical, and it flustered Jason— who was already uneasily aware he was neither at his best or most logical. He said defensively, "You're exploiting what you see as my weaknesses to manipulate me into doing what you want."

Astonishment gave way to amusement which, to add insult to injury, Sam belatedly tried to swallow. He said gravely, "That's a little, er, operatic, don't you think? 'Exploiting your weaknesses'? Does it not occur to you that I also want a little time together? That I see this is a way of giving us both what we want? Maybe what we both need?"

"You're saying that once we're in West World, you're not going to find urgent cause to return to Quantico or fly out to Seattle?"

"I give you my word." Sam said it with perfect sincerity.

Jason raised skeptical eyebrows. "And what will you be doing while I'm resting and recuperating?"

"I haven't had a vacation in seven years. Nobody's going to give me a hard time about taking some personal leave."

"Seriously?"

"You don't believe me?"

"It doesn't sound like the Sam Kennedy I know."

Sam studied him. "Aren't you the guy always telling me I need to learn to trust the people under me? That I need to stop micromanaging my team? That I need to learn to delegate?"

"Yes. Aren't you the guy who said I didn't know what I was talking about?"

"I'm sure I phrased it more diplomatically."

"Actually, n—"

"Anyway, maybe some of what you said is starting to sink in. As you keep pointing out, the other BAU chiefs don't fly around the country at the drop of a hat. There's no reason I can't monitor most of these situations long-distance."

Jason was torn. In normal circumstances there was nothing he'd like more than a chance to spend extra time with Sam. But these were not normal circumstances. Even putting aside the stress of knowing that someone was out to get him, the timing was not great. He was buried under his current caseload, which included the acquisition—again!—of looted antiquities by a private museum in Los Angeles, a faked-art heist at the home of a well-known film director, and the reopening of the 1973 cold case robbery at the Natural History Museum. Frankly, Fletcher-Durrand was the least of his headaches. As one of the only two ACT agents on the West Coast, he was never working less than fifteen cases a day, but art crimes were on the rise, mirroring the jump in legitimate art market prices.

"Look." Sam's tone was almost—and uncharacteristically— coaxing. "You need time to rest and recover. Stafford SO and the Bureau need time to figure out what's going on. We need time together."

Even knowing he was being maneuvered, it was all but impossible to refuse Sam this. Not least because he wanted it so much himself.

"For how long?" Jason asked unwillingly. "I can't just dump my caseload on Donovan while I hide out in the Badlands."

"The Badlands are in South Dakota."

"Still."

Sam knew he had won. He didn't go so far as to smile, but Jason saw the infinitesimal relaxing of his shoulders, the satisfied gleam in his eyes. "Two weeks. The length of your sick leave."

"I just don't see the point," Jason protested, but he was just bitching to bitch now, and they both knew it. The sad truth was he'd lost this battle the minute Sam had said, "We need time together."

Because it was true. Ten months in—and about that many days together. Who were they when they didn't have the structure and routine of the Bureau as a framework for their relationship?

"Suppose at the end of two weeks, Stafford SO and the Bureau still don't know who came after me?"

Sam's smile was humorless. "Leave that to me," he said. "I think we'll have our answer."

Despite his mild tone, it sounded more like a threat than a promise.

After Sam departed—with unneeded admonishments not to reveal their plans to anyone—Jason had another look for his cell. What he found instead was the remote control for the TV. He flicked it on, and the parking lot of the China King restaurant flashed on. A reporter in a trench coat stood in front of the restaurant, animatedly describing something that probably had nothing to do with wontons. The chyron at the bottom of the screen read: FBI AGENT TARGET OF ATTEMPTED KIDNAPPING?

He hit the Unmute button.

"…there are still no leads. Back to you, Bart!"

Bart's big smile and bigger hair replaced the guy in the trench coat on the small TV screen. "Thanks, Ed. Cloak-and-dagger stuff for sure!"

Jason hit the Mute button again and reached for the phone beside the bed.

It took a little longer to figure how to call out than it should have—proof that the pain medication was working even if it didn't feel like it—but at last he got through to the Los Angeles field office. His immediate boss, Supervisory Special Agent George Potts, was on another line, but Jason didn't have long to wait.

"Jason!" George's voice was warm with concern. "How are you feeling? I wasn't expecting to hear from you so soon."

"I'm fine," Jason said. "I thought I'd better let you know I'm not going to be in on Monday."

"Well, no." George sounded slightly amused. "Of course not. Don't worry about that. We're up to speed on the situation there."

"That makes one of us."

"Is there anything you need? Anything we can do on our end?"

Jason rubbed his forehead. "No. I thought maybe I should talk to Russell, run over a few things regarding our ongoing—"

George cut him off with cheerful briskness. "No, no. Don't worry about any of that. You just focus on getting back on your feet, okay?"

"It's only one foot."

"Sorry?"

Yeah, shut up now, Jason. But he couldn't shut up.

"I feel like this is all being blown out of proportion. I really *am* okay."

"Sure," George said. "That's natural. But here's the thing, Jason. Look at it from the Bureau's standpoint. Your situation is a little unusual. Your family is politically connected. And you—your work—tends to generate media attention. Some of the things that make you a such a valuable asset would leave the Bureau vulnerable if something were to, well, happen to you." George delivered his bad news with the firm kindness that made him so good at managing his squad. "Something that we could prevent. You see what I'm saying?"

"Yes," Jason said reluctantly.

"Of course you do," George said bracingly. "That's why you're such a good agent."

Yeah, right. Jason sighed. "Okay. Thanks, George."

"You take care of yourself, buddy."

Next Jason tried to phone his eldest sister, Charlotte. Infuriatingly, he couldn't remember Charlie's cell-phone number and ended up having to use directory assistance to reach her at Le Cottage Bleu.

"Oh my God," Charlotte exclaimed, hearing his voice. "Are you all right? Where are you? Wait, don't answer that!"

"I'm still at the hospital," Jason replied. "It's not a secret. I just saw it on TV."

"You sound stoned. How are you feeling? Sam said you were banged up but otherwise okay."

"I'm fine. Just—"

"Sophie's right. You've *got* to quit that job."

"I'm not quitting my job!" Proof that he probably *was* a little stoned, Jason was instantly distracted from his reason for calling. Actually, what had been his reason for calling? He wasn't sure.

Charlotte was still rattling on. "This kind of thing doesn't happen to college professors."

"It doesn't happen to FBI agents either. Usually. Anyway...I just wanted you all to know that I'm okay."

"We know you're okay," Charlotte said. "Sam's keeping us up-to-date. I *do* kind of like him. I admit I was skeptical at first, but... Anyway, you know we love you and we're thinking of you. Now get off the phone. Your call might be traced."

"It's not a secret that I'm in the hos—"

Charlotte hung up.

Chapter Five

When he saw the three poodles, Jason knew he'd made a mistake.

Granted, he'd already decided he'd made a mistake about ninety minutes into the flight from Virginia when they'd hit a wall of turbulence and his back, hip, knee, and ankle had all begun to throb in syncopation. The thirty-minute drive from Cheyenne to Wild Horse Creek and the little house on the prairie hadn't helped.

The poodles clinched it.

Not that he didn't like dogs. He did. But these yapping white fur balls in rhinestone collars and tiny bows did not, in his opinion, qualify as canine. More like rodents with attitude.

"Ma, can you call off the hellhounds?" Sam requested tersely as the dogs circled them, darting at their ankles and then away again.

"Adele! Esme! Remy!" The woman scooping up the fluff balls one by one was probably in her sixties. She was short and trim with spiky brown hair. She wore an oversize blue denim shirt, skinny jeans, and red cowboy boots. She looked about as likely to have produced BAU Chief Sam Kennedy as a scallop shell was likely to serve up the goddess of love.

"I was beginning to think you boys changed your minds!" she called over the hysterical barking of the dogs. Blue eyes, the same shape and bold, bright shade as Sam's, raked curiously over Jason's face—and widened.

"Our connecting flight was delayed in Denver," Sam said. "Jason, this is my mother, Ruby Kennedy."

Ruby said automatically, "Nice to meet you, Jason," and offered a small, sturdy hand over the heads of the lunging, snapping dogs.

"It's a pleasure." Jason shook hands, narrowly managing to avoid being bitten. "Thanks for putting us up for a few days."

He wasn't sure she even heard him. She said to Sam, "He looks like a ghost, Sam." Her ruddy face grew pinker. "I mean, he's white as a-a sheet. This boy should be in bed!"

Sam said curtly, "I know."

In fact, Jason did feel like death warmed over. It was surprising how much damage a little tiny collision with a moving vehicle could inflict on you. Being stuck in a noisy, crowded airport for a few hours hadn't helped his nerves either.

Hard to believe that very morning he'd been arguing with Sam in a Virginia hospital room and tonight he was standing in Sam's mother's living room and being snapped and yapped at by three French poodles. The rest of the day was pretty much a daze, but maybe that was the good news.

They had gone straight from the hospital to the airport, Jason hustled out the back by Special Agent Jonnie Gould while Sam—playing decoy—had strolled out the front. Right there was a pretty clear indicator Sam had known which way Jason would ultimately jump on his proposal. The plan was already in place: Jonnie ready to move on Sam's go-ahead, Jason's bags packed and waiting for him at the airport.

Until he'd seen the uniformed police officer standing watch outside his hospital room, Jason had managed to downplay the seriousness of the threat against him.

Maybe he hadn't wanted to know. All this cloak-and-dagger stuff on his behalf probably should have been reassuring, but...not so much. He was torn between unease over the realization there was a credible threat and frustration that no one seemed to think he could take care of himself.

He got it, of course. George had spelled it out for him. The Bureau was understandably skittish about the health and safety of an agent with both a high media profile and political family connections. Jason served as a kind of poster boy for the new inclusive and culturally diverse environment the Bureau was hoping to foster.

Sam was saying, "It's been a long day." His large, capable hand gripped Jason's elbow as though he thought Jason was liable to keel over any moment.

Jason was not about to swoon away on Mrs. Kennedy's beige shag carpeting, to be eaten by poodles, but he did want to lie down and be quiet for a while. Like immediately.

"Is the guest house ready?"

"Everything's ready." Ruby's gaze returned to Jason's almost surreptitiously. Like she feared to be caught staring? His heart sank. Oh, right. The fact that he looked a little like Ethan. Or was it more than a little?

"I made chili, if you're hungry," she added.

Jason's stomach seemed to curl into itself and knot. He murmured politely and noncommittally.

Sam translated without effort. He said briskly, "We'll get settled, and I'll be back."

As the door to the main house closed behind them, the dogs threw themselves against it in yip-yapping fury.

The cold, crisp night air steadied Jason. He drew in a couple of woodsmoke-scented breaths. The moon hanging above them, shining into every dark corner of the farmyard, was commemorative-plate-sized. The stars too were so big, they looked garishly ornamental.

They walked across the creaking wooden deck, and floodlights blazed on, illuminating their rental car and what looked like a smaller house, a dairy barn, a poultry shed, and a farm utility building. A tumbleweed the size of a cow rolled past and vanished into the shadows.

"This is where you grew up?" Jason asked as Sam helped him down the steps. Between his sprained ankle and his stiff knee he was feeling a spry thousand years old. He'd seen mummies that could move faster.

"God no," Sam replied fervently. "I grew up in Cheyenne. Her parents were from around here, and she had this idea she wanted to move back and recapture her roots, so I bought her this place."

"Is it a working farm?"

"Terrifying thought. No. She grows a few vegetables and keeps a blind pet donkey and a flock of chickens. That's plenty."

The ground was hard and frosty as they crossed the yard to the smaller house. Sam stooped, felt around in the eye socket of a bleached buffalo skull, sighed, and drew out a key. "She hasn't changed the hiding place in ten years."

Jason smiled faintly, waiting as Sam unlocked the door and let them inside.

He was too tired and in too much pain by then to take much notice of his surroundings, but he could feel that the heat had been turned on. The rooms were comfortably warm and smelled like cinnamon-scented candles. It was a nice little guest house. Hardwood floors, eggshell-white walls, taupe furnishings. There were no pictures, but a couple of Federal-style mirrors offered dispiriting glimpses of his hollow-eyed and battered face from every angle.

"The bedroom's back here." Sam steered him on. "I use the second bedroom as an office." He added grimly, "I always stay out here when I visit."

"She seems nice." Jason was simply answering Sam's tone. He had no idea how Sam's mother seemed in the two minutes it had taken to be introduced, but that's what you said in these circumstances. Granted, he didn't really have a lot of experience in these circumstances. He'd never been brought home by a boyfriend to meet the parents or parent. Had never had any interest in such things.

"She's a handful," Sam said in that same stern tone, and Jason gave a tired laugh.

Sam glanced at him in surprise. His gaze softened. He said lightly, "Sure, but don't turn your back on her, West. Mark my words."

He pushed a partially open door wide. "Here we go."

There was probably other furniture in the room, but all Jason really noticed was the bed, which was queen-size and, beneath a fluffy white duvet, strongly resembled a square and sturdy cloud.

Sam guided him to the bed, and aggravatingly, by now he needed that helping hand. "Take it easy for a minute. I'll get our bags from the car."

Jason nodded, sat down on the edge of the duvet, which felt cloud-like too. "God." He fell back and was engulfed in downy whiteness.

"Are you hungry?"

He shuddered, and Sam said, "Okay. Hang on. I'll be right back."

Jason closed his eyes.

He didn't think he had fallen asleep, but suddenly he was meeting Mrs. Kennedy all over again—only this time Ethan was waiting there too.

"Who are *you*?" Ethan frowned, reaching his hands out to touch Jason's face. His eyes stared past Jason, and Jason realized with a jolt that Ethan was blind.

"Jason?" Sam said quietly.

Jason's eyes jerked open.

He was lying on a strange bed in a strange, brightly lit bedroom. Sam sat beside him, stroking his forehead, which was the strangest part of all. Maybe he was still dreaming. Dreaming about a guy he'd never met. A guy who had died before Jason had reached his teens.

Sam said, "Let's get you out of these clothes."

"Gah." Jason sat up and scrubbed his face. "You were a while."

"She made you hot milk." Sam's tone was resigned. He nodded at a vintage Hazel Atlas aqua and white Dutch Treat mug sitting on one of the white oak night tables.

"Hot milk? Really?" Jason wasn't sure if he was touched or repulsed. "I didn't know people still drank hot milk. Is that a Wyoming thing?"

"It's not a Wyoming thing," Sam said. "It's a mother thing. There's probably a slug of booze in there, given that it's my mother we're talking about."

What did that mean? Maybe Sam's mom had worked as a bartender as well as a waitress? Maybe trying to raise Sam had driven her to drink?

Either way…what the hell. Jason reached for the mug and sipped the hot liquid cautiously.

"Hm. Not bad." Sam was right. There was definitely brandy in there. There was also honey, vanilla, cinnamon, and nutmeg. It was unexpectedly delicious. His gaze wandered as he drained half the mug in one long, hungry gulp. A framed photo of a dark-haired man sat on the bureau.

Without looking at Sam, Jason said, "Do I look that much like him?"

The dream had been disturbingly vivid, even without the physical reminder that Ethan—or at least his death—continued to be a prime motivator in Sam's life.

He could tell by the small sigh Sam gave that Sam followed his thoughts easily. "No, not really. More like he looked in photographs than in real life."

Jason met Sam's eyes, and Sam added, "I didn't even see it at first. That's the truth."

That ought to be a relief—except Sam had disliked him when they'd met.

"Am I like him in other ways?"

"No." Sam was adamant. "You're very different types. Not least of all, Ethan was twenty-three when he died. He was practically still a kid. You're a grown man."

Who was probably acting like an insecure teenager? Jason winced inwardly. Sam's mother's reaction had thrown him a little, that was all.

He looks like a ghost.

Jason drained the mug and pushed to his feet—nearly toppling over. If he'd thought he was stiff after the drive from Cheyenne, he was nearly crippled now.

Sam steadied him, helping him undress and pull on his sleep pants and a long-sleeved T-shirt. It was managed with a comforting minimum of fuss, and in a couple of minutes Jason was in bed with his injured foot resting on a stack of pillows.

"Before you get too comfortable…" Sam dug into his jacket pocket, pulled out an ancient-looking white jar, and unscrewed the lid. The scent of wintergreen, juniper berry, and something peculiarly reminiscent of horse liniment wafted out.

"What the hell's that?" Jason asked suspiciously.

"I have no idea, but it works. Trust me."

"Uh, yeah, but..."

"It's called Medicine Man Salve."

Jason's brows shot up, and Sam said, "I know, but like I said, it works."

"Do I drink it or rub it in?"

"*I* rub it in. Roll over."

Jason scooted over onto his belly. Sam pushed the white cotton T-shirt out of the way and scooped out the liniment. Up close it was even more potent-smelling, and Jason ducked his head into his folded arms.

Sam rubbed his hands together and touched Jason with cool, oily fingers. Jason jumped, forced himself not to tense as Sam kneaded the bunched muscles of his shoulders.

At first, between the fumes of the salve and the strength of Sam's hands, it was kind of unpleasant, but then Jason began to relax. He sighed wearily and closed his eyes as Sam worked the oily cream into his shoulder blades and down his spine.

"Okay?" Sam murmured.

Jason moved his head in assent.

Sam's strong fingers poked and prodded all the little knots and kinks as he slowly worked his way down Jason's back to his hips, the backs of his thighs, his knees. His hands were large, and he had a powerful grip, but his touch was gentle.

"Feels good..."

Sam made a sound of acknowledgment.

He wasn't doing anything particularly erotic, but the massage was increasingly sensual, and Jason gave a little moan of pleasure.

"Better?"

"God, yes."

"You want to roll over?"

Was that supposed to be a question? Because of course he wanted to roll over. Of course he wanted more. Blood pulsing in his ears and cock. He'd have to be dead not to want more. He eased onto his side, his cock reaching up to Sam like a wand homing in to a magician's hand. And there *was* a kind of magic in the feel of Sam's hard fingers wrapping around warm, aching flesh.

Sam's grip was comfortable and comforting, sliding from the base of balls to the tip of prick.

Jason thrust hard into that hold, with a strength he hadn't thought he possessed five minutes earlier. Sam coaxed and chivvied him along, and one, two...abra-fucking-cadabra...*three*! He groaned softly, woundedly, spilling hot white seed over Sam's fingers, his own belly, and the folds of flannel sheets and fluffy cloud duvet.

"That's the way. All those nice endorphins doing their work." There was a smile in Sam's voice.

Jason smiled too, floating and drowsy in the aftermath, his thoughts continuing to wind lazily, slowly tumbling like paint through water.

In the distance he heard a long eerie howl that seemed to float in the air before fading into silence.

He opened his eyes.

"What was that?"

"Wolf."

"Seriously?"

"Sure."

Jason laughed. He had reached the point of exhaustion where everything was funny. His own weakness. Sam's unlikely tenderness. Wolves.

Sam made a quiet sound of amusement, drawing his face toward him and kissing him still. He whispered, "Sleep well, West."

Jason smiled and closed his eyes.

Chapter Six

"I want to see that security footage for myself."

Sam's work voice drifted through the not-quite-closed bedroom door, worming its way into Jason's dozy dreams.

He blinked awake, remembering abruptly where he was, and lifted his head, listening, frowning.

"No, I'll call them." Sam's tone was uncompromising.

Silence.

Not complete silence. In the distance a donkey was braying. Loudly.

"I'm not ruling anyone out at this stage—" Jason's jaw-cracking yawn muffled the rest of that. Sam concluded, "That's exactly the kind of thing I want to know about—and before anyone else. And I do mean anyone."

Present company included? No doubt.

Jason muttered under his breath and sat up, swinging his legs over the side of the bed. He examined his ankle, pleased to see that the swelling—even after the strain of the flight—was greatly reduced. He tentatively flexed his foot. Ouch. But still, way better than it had been.

He half closed his eyes, trying once again to remember. *Shadows of tree branches falling across the hood of his rental sedan like the painting on an art car. The smell of rain and exhaust. The crack and rustle of dead leaves and dried twigs as something—someone—pushed through the winter-bare trees—*

Then nothing.

Goddamn. *Why* wouldn't the picture come?

He expelled a long, frustrated breath.

In the next room, Sam's conversation had clearly reached the chit-chat phase. "He's all right. It was a rough flight…"

No lie there, and it would have been rougher had Sam not done his best to minimize the strain on him. Jason had wanted to die by the end of that flight—and he'd wanted to kill Sam for dragging him halfway across the country.

But that was yesterday. Today he felt like a fever had broken. Maybe it was those nice hardworking endorphins. Maybe it was the inappropriately named Medicine Man Salve. Whatever it was, now that he was himself again, he realized how totally out of it he'd been. The last couple of days felt unreal, a bad dream fading away with the return of daylight and normalcy.

God knew he had to have been out of it to ever give in to this bizarre plan of Sam's to hide out in cowboy country. For one thing, he was not critically injured. For another, going into hiding solved nothing. It was a Band-Aid, not a cure for his problem.

From the other room, Sam concluded his call.

Jason straightened as Sam opened the bedroom door. He'd had a shower and was dressed—in business casual—looking alert, if not actually rested. As always, Jason felt that surge of physical awareness. Even in these circumstances, there was something larger than life about Kennedy. Something broad and dangerous—leashed power.

They studied each other, and Sam said approvingly, "Well, that's better."

"No argument here."

"Did the phone wake you?"

"Maybe. I think I was already surfacing. Was that Jonnie?"

"It was. She says Stafford SO got a line on that black Porsche."

"That's great!"

Sam grunted. "Yes and no. The Porsche belongs to a newly hired manager for an insurance company in the complex. She was carrying boxes from her car to the office. That's why the trunk of the car was open."

Jason gave a disbelieving laugh. "You're saying she wasn't involved?"

"Looks that way."

"But why did she tear out of the parking lot?"

"Apparently she was alarmed by the commotion of you getting hit."

"That's…quite the instinct for self-preservation."

"So it seems."

"She's going to be formally interviewed, right? You don't buy her story?"

Sam shrugged. "People behave unpredictably when they perceive threat. But yes, she'll be interviewed. And then Jonnie's going to take a crack at her. She may have seen more than she's willing to admit thus far."

Jason had been so sure the driver of the black Porsche was his assailant, he couldn't quite make sense of this. He'd had the scenario of being followed from Sam's and jumped in the China King parking lot all worked out.

As though reading his confusion, Sam said, "You may not have been wrong about being followed from my place, though. Security cameras picked up a second black sports car parked on the other side of the building. The car exited the parking lot after the ambulance left with you."

"When did the car arrive?"

"Shortly after you."

"Were they able to get the make? The license plate? Is there footage of the driver?"

"A couple of frames. Unfortunately, it's the usual grainy, low-quality resolution. The lab is working on getting the images blown up."

Jason considered this, admitted reluctantly, "It could be another coincidence."

"It could," Sam agreed. "But whoever that driver is, it sounds like he was aware of and deliberately avoiding the security cameras."

Now that was interesting. The average law-abiding citizen tended to be oblivious of security cameras. "Is that so?"

"According to Stafford SO. I want to see that footage myself."

"You and me both." Jason glanced around the bedroom. Their bags and suitcases lay open on the floor. Aside from the iron bed and the matching nightstands, there was the tall bureau—now minus Ethan's photo—and a wooden valet stand with a single tie draped over it. He recognized the gray tie as the one Sam had worn in Los Angeles to his birthday party, and the memory of that evening—and the night that followed—comforted him.

"What time is it?" he asked.

"Eight thirty. I didn't think you'd be up this early. I'm going to take a run into town and stock up on groceries. I think it'll be easier on everyone if we do most of our own cooking."

Jason suspected that meant easier on Sam. He smiled faintly. "Sure."

"You want anything?"

"Do you know what I did with my phone?"

"It's in the living room. In your coat pocket."

The mystery of his missing cell phone had been solved on the flight to Wyoming when Sam had handed it over to him. He'd feared he'd lost it during the assault—and he hadn't been a whole heck of a lot happier to learn instead that Sam had confiscated it, had been controlling the flow of information to him.

Jason rubbed his bristly jaw. "I think I'll have a shower. I need to get rid of this beard."

"Nah. I'd leave the beard for a while."

Jason considered that silently. Sam thought the beard afforded him some camouflage. He said, "Are you planning to check in with the Cheyenne satellite office?"

"I thought I might mosey on by there."

Jason made a face. Sam's casual tone didn't fool him.

"Do you think we were followed?"

"No. I don't. I went to a lot of trouble to make sure we weren't."

Jason nodded noncommittally.

Sam started to speak, then changed his mind. "We'll talk it over when I get back, okay?"

So much for hiding his feelings. "Yeah. Of course. Sorry if I seem unappreciative. I just…"

"Don't like being on the outside looking in." Sam's smile was wry. "But the truth is, you're on sick leave. So whether we stayed in Virginia or you flew home to LA on your own or we spend the time together here, you're on the sidelines."

"True. I guess."

"You guess right."

"You're going to keep me updated on the investigation? You're not going to shut me out just be—"

"You'll know everything I know. Okay? That's a promise."

Jason nodded. Sam wasn't lying, but Jason knew full well he also wasn't promising to share information as he received it in real time. That wasn't the way he worked. And it sure as hell wouldn't be the way he worked if he thought Jason was better off not knowing something.

It was aggravating, but Jason knew to pick his battles. Sam was already making concessions he would not make for anyone else.

"I just don't know what we're supposed to do for two weeks."

Sam said mildly, "I bet we can come up with some ideas. If we put our heads to it."

"Ha."

"I thought I was supposed to be the workaholic."

"It's you I'm thinking of."

Sam laughed. "I see. Well, among other things, I plan on working on my book."

"Your *book*?"

Sam nodded.

"You're writing a book?"

Sam's brows rose. "It's not like I've never written a book before."

No. True. Sam had written *the* book on hunting serial killers. *Shadow on the Glass* was practically required reading at the academy.

"Sure, but in ten months you've never mentioned working on a new book."

"Because in ten months I haven't worked on the new book. Now I've got some time."

Okay. Fair enough. Over the next two weeks Sam would work on his book and Jason would...what?

Meeting his gaze, Sam's mouth twitched in private amusement. He kissed Jason, but all he said was, "I'll see you in a little bit."

When the rental car had disappeared down the long dirt driveway, Jason showered, dressed in jeans and a sweatshirt, and limped over to the main house.

He could hear the dogs barking before he was halfway across the farmyard. That was what you called old-school early security vulnerability detection. Chickens poked and picked at the hard ground with their yellow beaks, flapping their wings and clucking as he mounted the deck.

It hurt climbing the steps, and he hung on to the rail, trying to keep his weight off his bad ankle. He reached the back door and rapped on the glass.

The dogs went nuts. He heard Sam's mother yelling, "Remy! Esme! Adele!" The door swung open, and the homey scents of cinnamon, apples, and coffee wafted out.

"Hi, Mrs. Kennedy," Jason said. "I'm praying you've got coffee in there."

"Well, howdy!" She pushed the door wide. "Come in, come in. I've got a pot on now. And call me Ruby, honey. Mrs. Kennedy was my mother." She wore jeans and a baggy white sweater. Her blue eyes, so like Sam's, raked him over. "I'm surprised to see you. I figured you'd be down for the count today."

"No way," Jason said. "I'm a fast healer."

"You must be." She had to raise her voice over the yapping poodles. "You looked sicker than a dog last night. How about hot cinnamon rolls to go with that coffee?"

"Thanks!" Jason called back.

"Have a seat." She nodded to a small table covered by a yellow and white cloth featuring smiling rabbits hunting for Easter eggs. "I saw Sam drive out."

The killer poodles were falling over each other in their effort to keep him ringed and at bay. With a mutter of exasperation, Ruby scooped all three of them up and tossed them into what appeared to be a laundry room off the kitchen. She closed the door on their outraged protests.

"Shut up, you mutts," she called without heat. To Jason, she said, "Sam thinks I should get a police dog, but they're good company. How do you like your coffee?"

"Black." Jason gazed around the cozy kitchen. There was an abundance of dishrags and tea towels featuring cute barnyard animals, canisters and jars following the country-kitchen motif, and ivy and herbs growing out of copper tea kettles and creamers. Several framed photos sat on the corner shelf of the island. Even across the room, Jason thought he could spot Sam, though it was hard to picture Sam as a toothless baby. More easy to recognize him in that skeptical-looking second-grader with the cowlick.

A small television sat on the end of the sink counter. Fox News was on, and as usual everything was the previous administration's fault.

"How's the ankle?" Ruby asked, pouring coffee into another of those vintage Hazel Atlas mugs.

"Okay," Jason replied absently.

She followed his gaze to the television. Her sideways grin reminded him a little of that tiny twitch Sam's mouth made when he was privately amused. "Keep your friends close and your enemies closer," she said.

"Ah." He took the plate of cinnamon rolls she offered. "Do you bake these yourself?"

"It's my recipe. They bake 'em over at the Cactus Café."

A newspaper lay on the table. The mention of the official opening of a new magic club called Top Hat White Rabbit caught Jason's eye. Once upon a time, like a lot of boys who felt they didn't quite fit in, Jason had been interested in magic. And, like a lot of boys—and girls—he'd been disappointed once he realized the prosaic solutions behind most of the baffling illusions that fascinated and thrilled him. He still appreciated a great magic show, though nowadays he refrained from performing his own card tricks unless very, *very* drunk.

Ruby was asking, "How'd you sleep?"

"Like a log. That's a very comfortable bed—and a very comfortable guest house you have. You don't try to rent it out?"

Ruby laughed. "No. I keep it ready for Sam. I keep hoping he's going to visit more. Maybe when he retires." She made a face and swallowed a mouthful of coffee. "If I'm still alive."

Mandatory retirement for brick agents was fifty-seven, but the Bureau had limited discretion to keep agents on until age sixty-five. When it came to legendary BAU Chiefs? Who knew? Jason suspected Sam privately intended to leave feet first.

He took a bite of one of the cinnamon rolls. *Mm.* Soft, fluffy, melt-in-your-mouth goodness. Not too sugary and just enough cinnamon. He chewed, swallowed, took another bite. "This is great."

She nodded in agreement. "You work with Sam?"

"I have in the past." Jason explained how he'd first met Sam in Massachusetts, working the Kingsfield case. He didn't tell her how he and Sam had disliked each other at first or how personal that case had been for him. Mostly he stuck to describing his role on the Art Crime Team.

Ruby listened politely. "So you live in Los Angeles?"

"Yes."

Her thinly plucked brows rose in some private doubt, but what she said was, "Do you just protect other people's work, or are you an artist too?"

"No. I gave up the idea of being a painter early on."

She nodded thoughtfully. "Well, you're the first you-know-friend Sam's ever brought home. I'm naturally curious."

You-know-friend. Was that a euphemism, or was she fishing? Fox News had raised some questions in his mind.

He kept his expression impassive. "I think the job keeps him pretty busy."

"Sure," she said. "And times have changed."

Okay. She knew. He relaxed a little. "Yes. True." When Sam had joined the FBI, there was no question of an agent being out. Back then the closet was everyone's default. Certainly, everyone in law enforcement.

Ruby added in a thoughtful tone, "Not counting Ethan, of course."

Boom! And there it was. Jason said nothing.

Behind the laundry-room door, the dogs had settled down to muttering scurrilous things about the company Ruby was keeping.

Ruby scrutinized him. "I guess he told you about Ethan."

"Some."

Despite his curiosity, he was pretty sure Sam would not be okay with the direction this chat was going. At the same time, he did not want to offend Sam's mother.

"I'm not surprised. He doesn't talk about personal things. Even when he was a little shaver."

"No. Well." *Repartee. We haz it!* To direct the conversation into safer channels, Jason asked, "What was Sam like as a kid?"

"Shorter." Ruby gave a curt laugh at Jason's expression. She sounded like Sam in that instant. "Single-minded."

"Was he a good student?"

"Oh, sure. Always got As. Didn't even have to try, I don't think."

"What was he interested in?"

"Oh, a lot of things, I guess. He liked to read. He was always kind of a know-it-all."

She said it with pride, though, and Jason grinned. Ruby grinned back.

"Some things never change," she added.

"It doesn't help that he's usually right."

She cocked her head, considering him. "I guess it's lucky you think so."

"I wouldn't tell him that."

She laughed. "No. I wouldn't advise telling him that."

He nodded at the newspaper and said at random, "So you're getting a new magic club?"

"I guess so. They're having some kind of conference here for magicians next weekend. It's going to be good for business. Were you injured in the line of duty?"

"Not exactly. It turns out fast food really *is* bad for your health." She chuckled, but he thought he knew what she must be thinking. "Sam's job keeps him pretty much out of the line of fire nowadays."

"Oh, Sam." She seemed further amused. "Sam can look out for himself."

Which was surely true. Suddenly Jason couldn't think of anything to say. He drank his coffee and ate a second cinnamon roll.

"I think we'll get some rain tonight." Ruby was gazing out the window.

Jason murmured politely.

"Ethan was an artist," she said suddenly, turning her gaze on him once more.

"Was he?" The idea had never occurred to him, and he was surprised to find he didn't like it. Which was irrational. What the hell did it matter what Ethan had been or hadn't been?

"Pretty good too," Ruby said. "You look through that door, you can see one of his hanging over the fireplace."

Jason's heart sank. He did not want to discuss Ethan. He did not want to see Ethan's art. He did not want Ethan to be any more real than he already was. But Ruby was obviously waiting for him to admire Ethan's work—or maybe just acknowledge Ethan's part in Sam's past—so he obligingly turned his gaze to the door leading into the living room, and then rose, limping into the living room and over to the fireplace, studying a large oil painting of pine trees, rocky outcrops, and moonlight.

Ruby had followed him into the other room.

"Where is this?" he asked, because he had to say something. "Somewhere around here?"

"Vedauwoo. It's a campground off Interstate 80."

Jason hmmed. He really didn't have much to say, and after a moment of silence, Ruby added, "'Course, I'm not an expert."

"No, but you're right. He was talented."

That was the truth. There was genuine talent there. Raw talent. Not genius. This kid had not been a prodigy like Lucius Lux, Jason's wayward protégé. He'd had some training, clearly, but he wasn't a craftsman at the peak of his skill. No telling what he would have ultimately become with time and experience.

Jason peered at the signature in the lower right-hand corner. EO.

"What was Ethan's last name?"

"Ogilvie. His father still lives in Cheyenne. He's the only one left."

One of these days he was going to bite the bullet and do some looking into what had actually happened to Ethan. Not today. Not tomorrow. Not anytime soon.

However, having gone this far, he might as well go ahead and ask. "Was Ethan's killer ever brought to justice?"

"No. Never."

He nodded, again at a loss for the right thing to say. *I'm sorry?* He was certainly sorry about all of it. Disturbing to think that without

Ethan's death—murder—he and Sam would never have met. Sam had only gone into the FBI because Ethan had been murdered.

He couldn't quite get a handle on Ruby or on Ruby and Sam's relationship. Why had Ruby brought up Ethan to him? She had to know Sam would not appreciate his personal life being discussed behind his back. Was there some message she was trying to convey? Was she simply prone to gossip? She didn't appear to have any neighbors as far as Jason could tell. Maybe she was hungry for conversation—and it wouldn't be surprising if Sam was her favorite subject.

He knew Sam did not travel back to Wyoming very often. That must be hard on Ruby.

He said briskly, "Well, thank you for the rolls and the coffee. I should probably get back and make some phone calls."

She nodded, accompanying him to the back door. "If you need anything, let me know."

"Thank you, I will."

He went carefully down the steps and started across the barren, windblown yard. Before he was more than a few feet away from the house, he could hear the dogs throwing themselves at the porch door.

Chapter Seven

Special Agent Shane Donovan was Jason's Northern California counterpart and the only other Art Crime Team member on the West Coast. Though they didn't regularly work together, they were in the habit of brainstorming their cases and bouncing ideas off each other. Jason's assigned partner, J.J. Russell, was a first-office agent, just starting his third year on the job. Russell and he were not what one would call simpatico. Russell felt his abilities were being wasted paired with someone who spent so much of his time online checking art databases and national registers, meeting with museum curators, and haunting auction houses and art galleries. If there was a bright side to being placed on sick leave, it was not having to listen to Russell bitch about the pointlessness of Jason's mission for the next two weeks.

It took a couple of tries to reach Shane that morning. When Jason finally managed to get through, Shane was friendly but not encouraging.

"Hey, what's this about? You're supposed to be on sick leave, West."

"I know. I am. But I'm kind of worried about Ursula Martin." The one case where Jason and Shane did coordinate their efforts was Fletcher-Durrand. Partly because the Durrands had a home in NorCal, though they spent little time there. Partly because the potential scope of the case was so vast.

"What about her?" Shane asked.

"I'm afraid F-D might try to intimidate her." If by some crazy chance the Durrands were behind the assault on him, Jason feared anything was possible—including going after a witness and potential claimant.

"I don't know why they'd bother," Shane said ruefully. "She's not talking."

"All the same," Jason said. "I'd feel better if you touched base with her." Martin lived in Bodega Bay, which made it more than reasonable to hand this off to Shane rather than J.J.

"You sure you want to nudge her? Last time we spoke, she was intimating harassment."

"No, I'm not sure," Jason admitted. "But like I said, I'm concerned. I'd rather risk irritating her than have her come to harm."

Shane's sigh was resigned. "Okay. I'll do a welfare check. See what her mood is these days."

"Thanks."

"And," Shane added, "that's the last I want to hear about Fletcher-Durrand until you're back from sick leave. I got plenty of forgery, fraud, and felonies in my own backyard to keep me busy, thank you very much."

They chatted a couple of minutes more, then Jason disconnected and phoned Russell at the LA office.

Russell was even less thrilled to hear from Jason than Shane had been. With sour satisfaction he delivered the news that Fletcher-Durrand was hinting about suing Jason and the Bureau for everything from trespassing to harassment following the events on Camden Island two months earlier.

"What total bullshit!" Jason exclaimed.

"Also, all of our current cases have been pulled by the Stafford County Sheriff's Office."

He'd known that was coming. "Right," Jason said. "I don't think they're going to find the answer in our caseload, but they've got to look, I guess."

"I'll tell you what I told ADC Ritchie. With the exception of Fletcher-Durrand, I can't see how taking you out would help any subject in any of our current investigations. And it wouldn't even help F-D."

"I agree."

"Fletcher-Durrand wants to crush you through the courts."

"They can try."

"And if Eric Greenleaf wanted anyone out of the way, it would be *me*."

"Probably, yeah."

J.J. said, "I told Ritchie it's Kennedy's case files they should be looking at."

"*What?*"

"The BAU is where they need to focus their attention. Think about it. Think about Kennedy. *There's* a guy a lot of dangerous people would like to hurt. What better way to hurt him than take out his only friend in the world?"

Not an angle Jason had considered, and given the kind of perps who populated Kennedy's case files, it was a little bit of a kick in the guts. He said lightly, "Only friend is a bit much."

"Yeah? Well, in my opinion, eliminating you would be a big distraction for Kennedy. Maybe somebody needs a big distraction."

There was a certain crazy logic to it, emphasis on crazy.

Jason said reluctantly, "It seems kind of *Criminal Minds* to me."

"Sure," J.J. said. "But psychopaths watch TV too."

"I got a key made for you. In case." Sam was pulling goodies out of paper sacks like a magician producing bouquets. *Chili con carne! Beets! Potatoes! Cream! All out of a hat!*

"Thanks." Jason picked up the silver key lying on the white tile counter.

It had been nearly noon by the time Sam returned from town. As well as several bags of groceries, he'd picked up a couple of sweatshirts and a flannel shirt for Jason. That was classic Sam. He was not a guy for candy hearts and valentines, but he knew Jason had only packed for a weekend, so Sam bought him things he felt would make Jason's stay easier, more comfortable. Like vodka and Lays potato chips and wool socks and fleecy sweatshirts.

And Sam was right. Wyoming in April was *cold*. The sky was almost purple-blue, and the edges of sunlight had a sharp, icy glitter.

"Magic City of the Plains?" Jason yanked off the price tag and pulled the black sweatshirt with the buffalo graphic over his head. The right fit too. Sam was nothing if not observant.

"Supposedly the town sprang up so fast after the railroad was built that it seemed like magic." Sam drew a bottle of Canadian Club from the brown paper sack of groceries. It looked like he anticipated being stuck together for two weeks would drive them both to drink.

"What exactly are we eating?" Jason unloaded a sack that contained limes, lemons, and a lot of chicken. "Or are we starting a new religion?"

The sound Sam made sounded indulgent. "You want breakfast or lunch?"

"Lunch? I had coffee and breakfast rolls with your mom."

Sam's smile was wry. "That must have expanded your horizons."

Jason didn't quite get it. He shrugged.

Sam seemed to come to a decision. "Pan-seared steak and roasted beets, then."

That sounded pretty awful, but Sam was a more than decent cook when he had to be. It had initially surprised Jason how conscientious Sam was about trying to eat right—not easy given theirs was not a job with regular meal breaks. It was all part of fighting the tide of time. Sam worked hard to stay in top physical shape, and a good part of that battle was nutrition.

Now he turned on the sink taps, dropped the beets under the flow of water, and pulled a chef's knife out of the drawer next to the sink.

"What can I do to help?" Jason asked.

Sam said absently, "Stay out of the way."

In cooking as in everything else? Jason snorted, and Sam maybe heard his words through Jason's ears. He glanced up from chopping the tops off the beets, and said, "How's the ankle?"

"It's holding up."

"Yeah? Well, good, because I brought you a present."

"*Another* present?"

"How would you like to consult with the Cheyenne RA on a stolen art collection?"

The Cheyenne Resident Agency was one of Denver's nine satellite offices. Like a lot of satellite offices in these days of severely reduced federal budgets, they had to try to cover five counties with a skeleton staff, so it was reasonable they might need help with something specialized like art theft.

"What kind of stolen art collection?"

"I didn't get the full details. Art and antiques relating to magic and magicians."

Jason's interest quickened. "You're kidding. Really?"

"I'm not a kidder, West. You know that. Cheyenne's got one rookie agent trying to work this thing while the rest of the team's aiding local authorities searching for the unsub who robbed a federal bank last Wednesday."

Despite the not-a-kidder comment, there was the faintest gleam of amusement in Sam's gaze. "I take it you like the idea."

"I do like the idea. A lot."

"Okay, I thought you would. But you're still officially on sick leave. This is strictly *consulting* on another RA's case."

"I do that all the time. I'm happy to do that."

"You don't have to be quite *that* happy." Sam sounded rueful.

"Yeah, but you're going to be working on your book. What am I supposed to do? I can't nap for two weeks. I should be on limited duty, not sick leave."

"Don't push it. This is off the books. Nothing has been cleared through the Administrative Services Division."

Jason grimaced. "Got it."

Sam returned to preparing their lunch. He peeled, halved, and cut up the beets, dumped them on a baking sheet, drizzled them with olive oil, and shoved them in the oven. He heated more oil in a heavy iron frying pan and deposited the steaks on the shimmering surface.

Jason pulled a chair out from the table by the window and sat down, propping his sprained ankle on the chair opposite. He said, "I talked to J.J. Russell this morning—and before you say it, no, I didn't mention where I was."

"The thought never occurred to me." Sam, mixing tarragon, shallots, and garlic into a small bowl of butter, paused to lick some of the mixture from the edge of his thumb. Jason was momentarily distracted by the memory of Sam's tongue at other times and in other places.

He collected his thoughts and said, "Apparently Fletcher-Durrand plans to sue me for everything that happened on Camden Island two months ago. Me and the Bureau."

Sam's brows shot up. "Excellent."

"Uh, not the word my SSA or my SAC or the Assistant Director in Charge are using, unfortunately."

"No? But it's always excellent when the subjects of your investigation trot out the lawyers. It means you're getting to them."

Jason grinned and shook his head. He wasn't smiling when he said, "Russell had a theory. I don't know if you've considered it."

Sam was no fan of Russell's. "Let's hear it."

Now that he had to put it in words, Jason felt awkward. "Is it possible someone you're investigating might try to distract you by getting rid of me?"

Sam's attention returned to the ingredients in the small glass bowl. "It's not impossible."

"You'd considered that?"

"Yes. I'm considering all possibilities."

"Is it likely?"

"Very few people outside the Bureau are aware of our relationship. No, I don't think it's likely. But like I said, every avenue is being explored."

I don't think most people inside *the Bureau are aware of our relationship.* But Jason did not say that.

Sam turned the steaks in the pan. He pulled the roasting beets out of the oven. No, he did not need Jason's help. He had it under control. Of course. He always had everything under control.

"Want to go to a magic club this Friday?" Jason asked. "There's a new place opening up in Cheyenne."

"A magic club?" Sam looked taken aback. So taken aback, Jason found it funny.

"Why? Don't you like magic?"

"I don't believe in magic."

"Now *that's* disappointing." But Jason was teasing.

"Next you're going to tell me you collect energy drinks and dead batteries."

Jason laughed. "Didn't you ever try to learn any magic tricks when you were a kid? Sleight of hand? Invisible writing? Pulling coins out of littler kids' ears?"

"Are you telling me you *did*?"

"Sure." Jason pretended to preen. "I'm pretty good at card tricks. And at getting out of handcuffs."

"I've seen that last one for myself." Sam's tone was dry, but he was smiling quizzically. "Card tricks, huh? You're full of surprises, West."

"You don't know *any* card tricks?" Jason raised an eyebrow as though card tricks were some naughty talent—in fact, he *had* used card tricks as come-ons in his day.

"The only card trick I know is always winning at poker."

"I think that's called cheating."

"I think magic is another name for cheating." But Sam was still smiling that half smile.

Jason made a face. "Still. Want to go to the opening of Top Hat White Rabbit on Friday?"

Sam's expression grew regretful. "No. I don't want to go anywhere there are liable to be cameras or reporters. Not till we have a better idea of who came after you—and why."

And that pretty much took the fun out of that.

Chapter Eight

"Special Agent West? I'm Special Agent Abigail Dreyfus."

The woman—agent—standing on the cement stoop outside the guest house's front door was tall and broad-shouldered. She had big blue eyes in a round baby face and wore her long, wheat-colored hair in a ponytail. She had to be in her mid-twenties, but she looked about seventeen.

"You're right on the dot." Jason shook the ice-cold hand Dreyfus offered. He assumed that was the temperature outside and not nerves. "Nice to meet you. Come in." He stood back, and Dreyfus stepped over the threshold.

From across the yard, Jason could hear Ruby's dogs barking inside the house.

"Thank you." She did a double take, her wide eyes trained on Jason's bruised and battered face. "Is that— Was that— Did that happen on the job?"

If Sam had reported the reason for Jason's presence to Cheyenne's Resident Agency's Special Agent in Charge, word had not trickled down to the rank and file. That was a relief.

"Uh, no," Jason said. "I have an, er, strenuous social life. We can talk in here." He led the way to the dining room, sparing a glance for the closed door to Sam's office.

That door was not closed to give Jason privacy. Or so that Sam could concentrate on writing his book. Maybe Sam was working on a book, but judging by how often Jason had heard Sam's quiet voice on the other side of that plywood, he was pretty sure writing was not all Sam was working on. Sam being Sam, he would be in close communication with Stafford

County Sheriff's Office. He would downplay his involvement, though—either because he wanted to protect Jason or because he didn't want to have to waste time considering his feelings or listening to his theories.

Jason deduced the latter. Sam would figure he'd already handled the former by landing Jason in the middle of nowhere and giving him a nice, new art theft to keep him busy.

Dreyfus was saying, "I appreciate your making time to see me when you're on sick leave. There really isn't anyone local I can consult on a case like this."

"I'm glad to help, believe me. Would you like some coffee?"

"Coffee would be great. Cream and sugar if you have it." Dreyfus opened her briefcase and pulled out a thick file. She glanced around uneasily, seeming relieved to find Jason on his own, by which Jason deduced Sam had gone to the usual lengths to exert charm at the RA that morning—namely nil.

He returned with two mugs of coffee and studied the colorful spread of photos on the polished wood of the table.

Dreyfus watched him, saying, "Altogether, the collection is valued at $3.5 million. Honestly, I had no idea these things could be so valuable. The posters alone are supposedly worth thousands of dollars."

"How many items are missing?"

"The entire collection. One thousand and three separate line entries on the insurance policy. They didn't leave him so much as a silk handkerchief."

He nodded absently. The photos appeared to be taken for insurance purposes. They offered an overview of an impressive collection of magic art and memorabilia. Everything from autographed photos, sheet music, and performance programs to spirit cabinets and a Rudiger Deutsch wooden mind-reading machine. Wands, alarm clocks, prop pistols, coins, turnover bottles, light bulbs, all kinds of fans and small boxes and bells. Straitjackets, Selbit blocks, and Sands of the Nile...there was something for everyone. Best of all were the dozens of gorgeous old vintage posters.

The vivid colors and ornate script, the fantastical images of fanged monsters and lovely assistants, the grave visages of long-dead magicians instantly brought back the old delight of a time when Jason had still believed in magic—even as he tried to master the tricks and fakes of the trade. He recognized the painted faces as long-forgotten friends: Carter the Great...Thurston the Great Magician...Master Mystifier Houdini...Alexander the Man Who Knows...Bernardo...Kellar...Blackstone...oh, and the blandly handsome face of George the Supreme Master of Magic. That last one had always cracked him up. Something about a Supreme Master of Magic named George...

"These were all originals?"

Dreyfus replied, "According to the victim, Michael Khan, everything in his collection was original and of both historical and cultural significance."

Jason continued to examine the photos. He murmured, "Maybe so."

"Really?"

At the astonishment in her tone, he looked up. "Sure."

"It's mostly junk. Old milk bottles and fake coins. And, they're *magic* posters," she said, as though he might have missed that point.

"Right."

"How can they be significant?"

He said patiently, "Significance assessment is a qualitative technique to evaluate the relative importance of cultural heritage items for management purposes."

"Yes, I realize some of these items are valuable, and I realize Cheyenne PD doesn't have the resources to investigate the theft of such unique items, but—"

"It's not about that, though," Jason cut in. "It's not about commercial value. It's about cultural heritage, and these items meet that criteria."

Dreyfus actually looked dismayed. "They have devils and demons on them. They're advertisements for trickery and...and deception. Levitation and mind reading and decapitation and fortune-telling."

"Chicanery and shenanigans," Jason supplied, smiling. "Yes. But they also meet two of the four fields of value."

"What are the four fields of value?"

"Historic, aesthetic, scientific, and social. These posters are historic, and they're beautiful. And I think a case could be made for social value since that's always changing and subjective anyway. You could almost argue science given the ads for levitation and decapitation. Regardless, you only need to find significance in one field. You also have to take into account context, history, practical uses, and the item's social and spiritual values."

Her brows rose in polite doubt, probably thinking again about those tiny red demons and devils. She didn't argue, though. She said, "Here's the situation."

Dreyfus gave a quick and summary accounting of the robbery that had taken place at the home of Michael and Minerva Khan nearly seventy-two hours earlier.

At five o'clock on Friday evening, Michael Khan had left his home in Cheyenne to have dinner with his agent. His wife, Minerva, was performing that evening. The Khans had no children, and the servants were not live-in. When Khan returned home late that evening, he found the front door standing open and his entire collection of art and memorabilia gone. "Vanished" was the word he used.

"Was the door broken or the lock picked?" Jason asked.

"The door was unlocked. There was no forced entry. Minerva Khan left the domicile after her husband. She insists all doors and windows were locked."

"Was there a security system? Cameras? Anything like that?"

"There are cameras, but they were just for show. They're not hooked up to anything."

"You're kidding."

"No."

Jason said, "What about neighboring security cameras? Maybe someone caught something."

"Cheyenne PD is working on that. The best bet are the security cameras from across the street, but the owners are away on a skiing trip. The Khans do have a security system, but Minerva didn't arm it. That's not unusual, though. Both husband and wife agreed she often forgot. She told the detectives she had problems remembering the codes."

"Uh-huh. What about the other neighbors?" Jason asked. "This is a sizable collection, and some of the items like the guillotine, the trunks, chambers, and tables would be pretty heavy. It would take a crew—certainly more than one person—a few hours and a moving van to remove everything. Are you saying nobody saw anything?"

"Neighbors reported seeing a white, unmarked moving van parked outside the house around eight o'clock. No one thought anything about it because moving vans are a common occurrence at the Khans."

Jason's brows drew together. "What does that mean?"

"The Khans get a lot of deliveries. It sounds to me like Mr. Khan was a compulsive hoarder. Also Mrs. Khan is in the process of moving out of the house."

Now that was interesting. "They're separating?"

"Yes. Michael and Minerva Khan are in the middle of a hotly contested divorce. In fact, each of them has suggested the other is involved in the burglary and theft."

It wouldn't be the first time.

"You said Khan was meeting with his agent? What is it he does?" Jason asked.

Dreyfus shook her head as though the very idea pained her. "He's a professional magician."

Jason smiled. "Is he?"

"Yes. So is Mrs. Khan."

This was getting better and better. Jason considered. "Hm. Minerva. There was a famous 19th century female escape artist called Minerva the Handcuff Queen."

"I don't know about that, but Minerva Khan was a professional magician in Vegas before she married. She still does occasional shows for charity. Michael Khan is a regularly employed magician, if there is such a thing. He's known as the Kubla Khanjurer."

The name meant nothing to Jason. "Quaint."

"In fact, Khan's other theory is that his collection—and he does insist the collection belongs to him and is not community property—could have been stolen in reprisal."

"Reprisal for what exactly?"

"The Kubla Khanjurer is primarily famous for going around exposing the secrets behind other magicians' magic tricks."

Jason's gaze went automatically to a poster lavishly decorated with tombstones and dancing skeletons holding scythes. "I see. Like the Masked Magician."

"I guess so. I hate magic shows, so I have no idea."

She was probably too young to remember those TV specials of the 1990s where illusionist Val Valentino had incurred the wrath of his peers by revealing "Magic's Biggest Secrets" during prime time. Supposedly he'd received several death threats.

"That would breed a lot of hostility from the magic community," Jason agreed. "Even so, you have to know what you're doing to pull off a heist on the scale of this. Someone had to be aware the Khans would both be out that evening and that neighbors would not be unduly interested in a moving van being parked outside for a couple of hours. Also, the unsub would have to know where to fence the articles. You can't just list them on eBay or take them to a local pawn shop. These are valuable items, but the market for them is interest-specific. It's not like unloading a Monet."

That said, a poster featuring Houdini's escape from his Chinese Water Torture Cell had sold for $114,000 in 2017, so it wasn't like the art world was unaware of the value of such items.

Dreyfus said quickly, "Which is where I hope you can help, Agent West. Cheyenne PD is looking for direction, but this is not my field of expertise. I should be out helping my team search for our unknown bank robber." Her tone was slightly aggrieved.

Jason didn't bother to reassure her there would be no shortage of robberies in her career. He was eager to help. The sight of those gorgeous, arcane lithographs stirred him, triggered his boyhood love of both mystery and the mysterious. Absolutely he wanted in on finding and recovering those posters.

"It's possible, but not probable, that your unsub will try to sell the items locally. The most likely scenario is to break up the collection and try to move it through the larger auction houses. Provenance should be more of an issue than it often is. Anyway, I can help you with that. I have the contacts and the resources."

She brightened. "That would be terrific!"

They discussed a few other aspects of the case; then Dreyfus left copies of the insurance photographs and forms, the police report, and the initial interviews with the Khans and their neighbors, prettily thanked Jason in advance for all the help she knew he would be, and departed, ponytail bouncing jauntily as she headed for her unmarked GOV sedan. Jason watched her go. Dreyfus was nearly skipping in delight at having handed off a case she clearly detested.

He shook his head, closed the door, and returned to the dining room to gather up the reports and interviews.

He was already pretty sure one or maybe even possibly both of the Khans—depending on their insurance policies and whether they did really end up getting divorced—were behind the burglary and theft. One of his first lessons on the ACT had been how depressingly common insurance fraud was. Or at least attempted insurance fraud.

If Michael Khan was behind the theft, the entire collection was probably sitting safe and sound in a storage facility somewhere in Laramie county.

If the wife was behind the theft, there was a greater chance the collection would be broken up and sold for parts. That was the way spousal revenge tended to work. He didn't buy the story of the lady magician with such a bad memory that she couldn't remember a couple of security codes. He was also skeptical of the uncompromised front door.

Or were they really supposed to believe another magician had broken in?

That had been Michael Khan's other theory, right? A disgruntled colleague was paying him back for revealing the secrets of the International Brotherhood of Magicians.

Colorful and dramatic, but insurance fraud was a lot more likely, especially when divorce was part of the equation.

Jason settled on the tufted beige sofa with a heating pad for his back and a stack of pillows for his ankle, and began to read through the police report.

Routine stuff except for a little handwritten notation in the margin. *JDLR.* Copspeak for *Just Doesn't Look Right.* Meaning something not quite adding up, in the detective's opinion, nothing the officer could put a finger on, but meriting a second look.

Jason wanted to talk to that investigator. Except…he was consulting on the art angle, not investigating the theft. So unless he could make a case for why he needed to involve himself in the ongoing investigation, he was liable to have Sam breathing down his neck.

Not that Sam breathing down his neck couldn't be a pleasurable thing…

Jason blinked a couple of times and raised his head, realizing he was on the verge of nodding off. Despite a good night's sleep, he was still tired from his recent ordeal. The warmth of the nearby fireplace, the dryness of police reports had a soporific effect.

From down the hall he heard a door close and footsteps coming his way. He sat up, spilling papers onto the wooden floor.

"Hey," he called in greeting.

"Hey," Sam returned. He took the chair in front of the fireplace, dwarfing the fragile arms and spindly legs. He was too big for the chair, for this room with its pseudo Queen Anne furniture—button tufts, wing-backs, and scallop-edges—the mirrors and throw rugs. The décor both here and in the main house was more formal than Jason would have expected, but really, his expectations just exposed his own biases. What had he imagined was Ruby's style? Wagon-wheel tables and deer-antler chandeliers?

"Did I wake you?" Sam regarded him with that all-too-discerning gaze.

"No, no." A yawn caught him off-guard. He admitted, "Maybe."

Sam smiled faintly. "Sleep is exactly what you need. How did your meeting with Dreyfus go?"

"She's a probie for sure. Very disappointed to be stuck pursuing lost art works instead of chasing bank robbers with all the other kids."

"An FBI agent's life is full of disappointments," said the guy with a practically unbroken string of successes to his name.

"I want to do this, though. I want to help her recover this art collection because these pieces are largely irreplaceable."

"And you love magic." The corner of Sam's mouth was tugging toward a smile he seemed determined to suppress.

"Well, I used to. Magic is about uncertainty and possibility, and when you're an adolescent, uncertainty and possibility kind of defines you. So yes, I loved magic. But also, yes, these works are of historical and cultural significance, and they deserve to be protected and preserved. But because they're 'magic posters'"—Jason made air quotes— "there's a good chance they'll fall into the hands of people who won't recognize the value of what they've got."

Sam said, "You don't have to justify your interest to me. The minute I heard about this case, I knew you'd want to be involved." He seemed to consider his words. "I like that you care so much. I admire your dedication."

They had touched on this before, briefly.

Jason said, "I'm not catching killers. Usually. But I think what I do matters."

Sam said seriously, "No question."

It felt like a weight lifted. Why did Sam's praise mean so much to him? Jason had not been conscious of any defensiveness with Sam about what he did. But yeah, maybe. Maybe he did deep down in some unacknowledged corner of his psyche fear that Sam still viewed him as a pretty dilettante. Because certainly at the beginning of their acquaintanceship that was how Sam had regarded him.

Nearly getting nabbed while getting takeout hadn't done wonders for his self-esteem either.

Sam was still watching him in that thoughtful, assessing way. He said, "I have some news."

Jason automatically sat straighter, bracing himself. "Okay."

"From everything we've been able to find out so far, Dr. Jeremy Kyser has been in Canada for the past four days, attending a conference on forensic psychology."

Jason digested that slowly. "Is that for sure?"

"It looks that way on paper."

"What does that mean?"

Sam made a sound that was closer to a growl than a laugh. "It means, he booked the conference and the plane flight months before you were scheduled to return to Quantico for training. It means someone flew to Toronto and attended that conference under his name."

"Someone."

"I'm not convinced either way. I'd like to see some event photos featuring everyone's favorite mad scientist and amateur artist."

"That doesn't seem likely."

"Jonnie's on her way to Canada now."

"The conference must be over."

"Yes. The conference is over, but Kyser is currently MIA. So Jonnie's going to meet with the organizers in an attempt to verify whether he was ever there or not."

Jason thought it over unhappily. "If my attacker wasn't Kyser, who the hell was it? I can't believe Shepherd or Barnaby would come after me in such a crude, mob hit kind of way."

Sam raised his shoulders.

"Where does that leave us?" Jason persisted.

"We're pursuing every avenue."

"Pursuing every avenue? You're kidding, right?"

Sam did not look like he was kidding. He said, "It's not a fast process."

"Okay, I do understand that. But at the same time, I can't remain on sick leave indefinitely."

Sam was unimpressed. "It hasn't been a week. You're still on painkillers."

True. No arguing there.

Jason opened his mouth, but his cell phone rang. He felt around for it, and Sam's phone also began to ring. They looked at each other.

Jason found his phone and clicked Accept. "West."

"Agent West?" The wobbly voice on the other end was vaguely familiar. "It's Abigail Dreyfus."

"Hi," Jason said in surprise. "I'm afraid I've only started reading through the reports and interviews—"

"No, it's not that. I'm not expecting you to have any answers for me yet."

A few feet away Sam said, "It's no problem, Chuck. I owe you one."

Really? Hard to imagine circumstances where Sam owed anybody anything.

Dreyfus said, "Cheyenne PD just informed me that Michael Khan's body was found by campers in Medicine Bow-Routt National Forest a short time ago."

"On my way," Sam said and clicked off. His gaze met Jason's.

Jason knew Sam well enough to interpret the message there. His heart sank. He answered Dreyfus automatically, "Suicide?"

"Undetermined." Dreyfus made an effort to steady her voice. "He was hanging upside down from a tree."

Chapter Nine

Death did not become him.

It did not become anybody, but in particular it did not become Michael Khan. Partly it was due to hanging upside down. The pull of gravity, the pressure of blood rushing to the head...very visual, very disturbing. Jason would try to put the image of Khan's bloodshot, bulging eyes and swollen tongue protruding from that greenish-red face out of his mind, but he knew from experience Michael Khan would be haunting his nightmares for a while.

What the hell must Sam's dreams be like?

Oh, right. Sam barely slept. No wonder.

Jason went back to studying the dead man.

The Hanged Man.

Jason had recognized the staging of the body even before the medical examiner for the Laramie County Coroner's Office discovered the tarot card tucked in the dead man's trouser pocket.

The card was one of the major arcana in the tarot deck. It depicted a man hanging upside down by his right foot from a tree. His left leg was jauntily bent behind him. The figure on the tarot card was smiling serenely, having sacrificed himself of his own free will. Michael Khan... not so much.

Wispy dark hair dangling, hands tied behind his back, one foot tied—wired—to the tree trunk, the other leg bound behind in a terrible parody of insouciance. Khan was not smiling. Jason did not want to remember Khan's expression.

Anyway, it was Jason's own damned fault for insisting on coming when Sam had all but ordered him to stay home.

He found a boulder to sit on safely out of the way of the crime-scene team, while Sam spoke with Special Agent Dreyfus, deputies from the Routt County Sheriff's Office, and the representative from the Forest Supervisor's Office.

The ripple that went through the crime-scene investigators at the discovery of that card made Jason think of people who had just realized they were standing in a mine field.

Serial killer.

No one had said the word, but it was what everyone was thinking.

Everyone but Sam.

It took more than a gruesome crime scene and a single tarot card to excite Sam Kennedy.

It was immediately obvious why Charles Reynolds, SAC of the Cheyenne Resident Agency—busy himself chasing bank robbers on the other side of the county—had called on Sam to pinch-hit in this homicide on federal lands. With the exception of the BAU Chief, murder in the national forest was a new one for everyone present.

Something wet hit the tip of Jason's nose. He stared up at the roiling mess of black and blacker clouds. It looked like Ruby was right about rain before nightfall.

He gazed out across the ancient rock formations. The ever-present wind moaned and whistled eerily around the phallic towers and tumbled piles of red boulders. Ten square miles of granite cliffs and slabs. There was a stark beauty to this landscape. A few scattered trees—winter-bare aspen and Rocky Mountain maples, spiky Ponderosa pine—but mostly it was just fierce rock and empty sky as far as the eye could see. It looked like a setting suitable for the works of Thomas Moran or Charles M. Russell. All that was missing were a few strategically positioned Native Americans in war bonnets.

Better to think in terms of art than what had first occurred to him: great place for a human sacrifice.

The crime-scene technicians were scrambling to gather evidence and do what they could to preserve the site before the sky opened up. Jason huddled down into his coat. That wind slithering around the dramatic rock formations and scrubby trees was sharp as a knife. His ankle was throbbing. He and Sam had already been on site for over two hours, and it did not look like they would be leaving anytime soon.

Across the clearing, the grim process of cutting Khan's body down began. Dreyfus came over to join Jason.

"You okay?" he asked her. She looked very pale. Of course, they all looked pale in the cold and sinister light bouncing off the blood-hued rocks.

She nodded. After a minute or two, she said, "I can't believe it didn't even click that *he* was *that* Sam Kennedy until he started asking questions."

"No one expects the Spanish Inquisition," Jason agreed.

He had answered absently and was surprised when she gave him a sideways glance and a shaky giggle. "You can say that again." She sobered at once. "There's a question of jurisdiction between the Laramie County Sheriff's and the Routt County Sheriff's Office."

"Great."

"He basically told them to get their shit together or get off his crime scene."

"Jesus." *Really, Sam?* Jason rubbed his bearded jaw to cover what would have been an inappropriate laugh.

"I mean, we can't do that, right?" Dreyfus sounded uncertain. "Yes, it's federal land, but we can't—shouldn't—"

"No, *we* can't," Jason said. "But he has his own way of doing things." *Do not attempt this at home!* "They do need to get their shit together. This kind of interterritorial pissing match is how cases end up falling through the cracks."

She nodded as though she ran into interterritorial jousting matches all the time—and maybe she did.

"The coroner won't commit before the autopsy, of course, but she thinks Khan died of strangulation." Dreyfus swallowed. "She thinks he was garroted."

Jason nodded silently.

"*We* don't have to inform Mrs. Khan—"

"No. That will be someone from one of these two sheriff departments." He didn't blame her for not wanting to be part of that. No one enjoyed death duties.

They were silent, watching as the dead man was lowered to a tarp and prepared for transportation. Given the rigidity of the body—barring that ghastly dangling head—Jason surmised death had occurred anywhere from eighteen to twenty-four hours earlier. Sometime late Sunday afternoon or evening.

Dreyfus put a hand to her face. "It's raining."

Yes. It was. Temperature and environment might affect the postmortem changes—and sure as hell would make the trip back to the car all the more fun. He probably should have listened to Sam and waited back at Wild Horse Creek, but instinct—or maybe just impulse—had driven him to ride shotgun. It was hard to see how this homicide tied in with his own case—er, Dreyfus' case—but it obviously did. The coincidence was just too great.

"Why drag him all the way out here?" Dreyfus mused.

Jason shook his head. Why this location? Why that tarot card? Those were just two of a slew of questions that needed to be answered. But not by him.

At this distance, he could not hear Sam, but he could see the effect of his words on the men he was speaking to. They looked varying shades of sheepish and angry.

Having delivered God only knew what verdict, Sam turned and came toward them, his boots grinding the gravel and sandy soil to dust. Dreyfus straightened up as though bracing for impact.

"Ready to go?" Sam asked Jason. His eyes were colder than old ice, but that was not for Jason. It would be for the perceived incompetence of everyone else on this mountaintop.

Jason's hand tightened on the knobby handle of the blackthorn walking stick that had once belonged to Sam's grandfather, and pushed to his feet. "Yep."

Sam turned to Dreyfus. "You've got a briefing scheduled for ten a.m. tomorrow with the coroner, and an eleven a.m. conference call with your SAC and Sheriffs Luna and Corday. Phone me afterward."

Dreyfus said faintly, "Okay."

Sam gave her one of those steely, steady looks, but said nothing else. Dreyfus looked at Jason. He winked at her. She managed a faint grin.

She said to Sam in a firmer voice, "Yes, sir."

"Thank you for not saying I told you so," Jason muttered as they passed another group of deputies.

They were making their way down the increasingly muddy track back to the rental car. Thanks to the lousy weather, it was nearly dark by now, and the poor visibility wasn't helping matters. Lying around Sam's mother's place, Jason had seriously overestimated his strength. Despite the extra support of tape beneath the brace, his ankle was more painful with every step. His back hurt, his hip tingled, and his knee throbbed. He wasn't being as careful as he needed to be about where he stepped, and more than once the only thing that kept him from planting his face on rock was Sam's grip.

Like now, when pebbles skittered out from beneath Jason's boot and Sam's hand tightened on his elbow.

"You're welcome."

The stern tone brought a smile to Jason's mouth, but the march back to the car was way worse than the hike to the crime scene. He could not have made it without Sam's help, and he was mad at himself for insisting on coming along and making Sam's job harder.

To distract himself from the pain of his ankle and other physical woes, he said, "What do you think?"

"I think it's not my case. And it's sure as hell not your case."

"You don't believe the two crimes are connected?"

"I have no idea. Your involvement relates strictly to the missing art."

"I know that. I'm not talking about my involvement." Jason could hear the testiness in his voice. He tried to sound less irritable. "I'm thinking about your involvement. You've agreed to act as an advisor, if—when—needed. So? What do you think about the staging of the body? Could this be—"

Sam cut him off. "It's too soon to think anything. We—they—haven't even received the coroner's report yet."

"Right, but the staging of the body? The tarot card in the dead man's pocket?"

Sam let out a long, weary breath. "I know you know this, but I'm going to remind you anyway that sometimes—in fact, with depressing frequency—a body is staged in an effort to make it look like something it isn't."

"Yes, I do know. But we're talking about more than a few candles or hair clippings or smeared words in blood. It took effort and planning to get that body out here. It takes effort to hang a full-grown man from a tree."

"That's why they call it premeditation. Because it requires planning and effort."

Jason was silent, partly because he needed his breath for this stretch of the trail. As usual, Sam was correct. Trying to stage a body to look like the first in a serial killing was a common trick of murderers hoping to deflect suspicion from themselves and their usually too obvious motives. It was especially popular with kids and spouses—though it had been known to happen in the art world on dreadful occasion.

The logistics involved in a lone woman transporting the dead weight of an adult male up a hillside and then hanging him in a tree would be discouraging, but not impossible given that the suspected woman would be someone whose job would make her familiar with things like leverage and locomotion. Besides, if Minerva Khan was in the process of moving out of her marriage, there was a reasonable chance she had a new romantic interest in her life, and that new romantic interest might very well have ended up as an accomplice in homicide.

On the other hand, if Mrs. Khan was going to knock off her old man anyway, why bother to steal his art collection?

* * * * *

The shadow of your smile

When you are gone...

Engelbert Humperdinck was crooning at ear-shattering decibels as they crossed the yard of Sam's mother's house some time later.

By then it was after eight, and Jason wanted nothing more than a hot shower and his bed. Well, Sam's bed. Possibly without Sam. For the last thirty minutes, he had been listening to Sam reiterating the limitations of his potential involvement in Special Agent Dreyfus' investigation, and he was pretty much done. But it was awkward being aggravated with the person who was holding you upright.

"My sole concern is that missing art collection," Jason had replied. Several times. "I believe I can follow that line of inquiry without getting involved in the homicide investigation. Okay? I'm *more* than happy to leave that angle to Special Agent Dreyfus and the Cheyenne RA."

"That's great," Sam had said. Also several times. "But the first thing Dreyfus did was phone *you*. If that kid was any greener, she'd be a Martian."

"Yeah, but she's not going to run the investigation. Federal lands or not, it doesn't sound like the Bureau will be more than peripherally involved. The minute they're done chasing bank robbers, her SAC is going to hand the file over to an agent with more experience. Dreyfus is only a year into the job, so technically she's still on probationary status."

"That RA is about the size of an outhouse. Dollars to donuts, Dreyfus ends up taking point on the art-crime angle."

"Okay, then all the more reason she needs my help. For God's sake. I'm right *here*. Why the hell wouldn't I help that team out?"

"You're on sick leave."

Abruptly, Jason had lost patience. "I'm on sick leave because *you wanted me on sick leave!* There's no reason I can't be on limited duty. Anybody else would be on limited duty."

Sam's silence confirmed Jason's suspicions.

"I've got a sprained ankle and some bumps and bruises."

"And a missing chunk of time."

Jason was having none of it. "A couple of minutes. At most. My memory's fuzzy regarding the actual assault, but I remember everything else—and according to you, I'll remember the details of the assault too, so..."

"This is not the plan," Sam said.

Jason gave a short laugh. "Plans change, as you'd be the first to tell me, Kennedy."

Sam had not responded. Recalculating, no doubt. Jason did not press his advantage. He knew Sam recognized the weakness of his position. He also knew Sam was not conceding defeat.

So they were not speaking as they walked from the car, but the silence between them was not hostile. Cautious maybe. Careful.

The dogs began to bark, and Sam swore under his breath. They reached the guest house, Sam unlocked the door, and they went inside. It was warm and dry and still smelled reminiscently of the steak they'd had for lunch. Jason could have kissed the oak paneling in relief.

"Are you hungry?" Sam's tone was conciliatory, the expression in his eyes uncharacteristically guarded.

"Probably." He was still too miserable to know for sure.

"Did you want a drink?"

Jason shook his head. "I think maybe I'll take a couple of painkillers."

Sam opened his mouth, caught Jason's eye, and chose to let it go. He proceeded to make himself a whisky sour.

Jason hobbled into the bedroom, found his pain pills, and washed a couple of them down with the stale water in the glass beside the bed. He wiped his eyes, limped into the bathroom to wash his hands and face, and got a good look at himself in the mirror over the sink. He looked as wretched as he felt. White-faced, windburned, eyes watery from pain and fatigue. No wonder Sam was questioning his judgment. Especially since Sam questioned everyone's judgment on an ongoing basis.

When he returned to the kitchen, he found Sam sipping his drink and staring broodingly at whatever he'd thrown into the oven. An empty chili can sat on the counter, the lid of a pot chiming against the rim as the contents bubbled away.

"If our positions were reversed," Jason said, "I'd be doing everything I could to protect you, so I get it."

"Do you?" Sam's mouth curved in a not-quite smile.

"Yes. We don't know who came after me. We don't know if—when—they're planning to come at me again. There are a lot of question marks. And on top of that, I'm not exactly fast on my feet right now."

Sam said nothing.

"So yes, I get it. I also get that my stupidity in leaving my weapon at your place—"

"Wrong." Sam was adamant. "You are not to blame for the actions of your attacker. You are not required to wear your weapon at all times. Nor do we have reason to believe you'd have had a chance to pull your weapon if you had been carrying. No. There you are wrong."

But only there? Jason mentally grimaced.

"Okay, but still. I understand that you're worried about me and that you don't want my photo or name to turn up in the papers or on social media."

"*There* you're correct."

"And I'll do my best to keep out of the limelight. But we both know there's a good chance that at the end of these two weeks we won't have an answer to the question of who's gunning for me. Even if we know who, we may not have them in custody."

He could see by the sudden stark lines of Sam's features he was right.

"I'm not leaving my job. I'm not going into seclusion. At the end of two weeks, ready or not, I'm done with playing hide-and-seek. I'm going back to work." Jason held Sam's gaze with his own. "And if you try to stop me—I don't know how you could, but if you try to call in favors, pull rank, pull strings, whatever, I'll fight you every step of the way. It won't end well. I've had to fight my family every step of the way to keep this job. I don't want to fight you too. This is my decision. If you— There won't be a Happy Ever After is what I'm trying to say."

"I see." Sam did not seem surprised. Nor impressed.

It took the wind out of Jason's sails. He sat down at the table and shut up, watching Sam prepare their quick, impromptu meal: baked potatoes overstuffed with canned chili and topped with melted cheese and sour cream.

Sam set the plate before him. Jason ate his potato. It was probably delicious, but for all he could taste, it could have been stuffed with wood-chips and ashes. He didn't like feeling this distance between himself and Sam. He wanted to bridge it, and he was tired enough not to guard his words.

"To be honest, I'm surprised you didn't think of using me as bait to draw this guy out." That was the truth. Sam was not the most patient personality in the world. It was much more his nature to kick the ball into play than wait on the sidelines for his opponent to make their next move.

A weird expression crossed Sam's face. "I considered it."

The admission gave Jason a funny feeling in the pit of his stomach. He kept his tone neutral. "I believe it. It would be your first instinct, I'd guess."

"Not my first instinct, no."

Jason acknowledged that with a nod. Sam was no liar. Even when it would be the easiest or kindest thing to do. "What changed your mind?"

"I told you. You're too important."

"To you."

"Yes."

Jason said nothing.

Sam was watching him steadily, unflinchingly. "If I could have guaranteed bringing this to a quick resolution, yes, maybe then I'd have opted for that. Time is not our friend."

"I know. You should have run the idea by me. I'd have gone for it."

"I couldn't guarantee your safety."

"Still—"

"No." Sam shook his head with absolute certainty. "No, if I couldn't guarantee your safety, the idea had to be scrapped."

Jason made a sound of disbelief. "Back to Go. It's *my* life."

"Yes."

"You could have at least—"

"No."

Jason sat back, staring. "Jesus. I don't want to get into another argument, especially over something that's over and done, but you do need to understand that, friends or not, I get to make these decisions for myself, Sam."

"Sure." Sam's face remained perfectly, unrelentingly blank. He was saying the right thing, but Jason didn't imagine for one minute that Sam regretted or even second-guessed his decision to keep him out of harm's way.

It was like talking to a wall. Uh, no, it was like hitting your head against a wall.

Jason wanted to understand. Wanted to somehow break through the barrier. Because if Sam felt Jason was too important to take chances with, well, Jason felt Sam was too important not to try to reach some kind of détente with.

"I get that losing Ethan might have—"

Sam said in a hard, flat voice, "This is not about Ethan."

"No? Are you sure about that? Because your attitude is not exactly nor-reasonable."

"You're welcome to your opinion. I've got a lot more experience in this area than you do." His smile was bleak. "Come to think of it, I've got a lot more experience in every area than you do."

Jason hung on to his temper. "Which doesn't change the fact that you don't get to make those decisions for me."

Sam tapped his fingertips on the edge of the table in restless, unconscious tattoo. He caught himself at once. His hand stilled. He said, "It's late. In a minute we're going to be arguing. I think we should both get some sleep."

Going to be arguing? Jason opened his mouth, but Sam was right in that Jason didn't want to fight with him, and he definitely didn't want to fight when they were both tired and already irritated with each other. This was a conversation they needed to have, though, because of course this was partly about Ethan. How could it not be?

"Okay," he said curtly.

Sam hesitated.

Jason rose, and Sam said, "I'll clear up in here."

Whatever. Great. Jason washed up in the master bathroom, too tired after all for a shower, too frustrated to want to be left alone with his thoughts. Sleep was what he needed. A good night's sleep would help him look at things with fresh perspective.

When he left the bathroom, he found Sam stripping down in the bedroom. In the soft lamplight, Sam's bare skin had a warm glow, like living marble. Their eyes met. Neither spoke. How illogical was it that Jason could be feeling resentful, dissatisfied with Sam's highhanded behavior, but the sight of Sam's naked, muscular body left him rock-hard and dry-mouthed with desire?

They undressed in silence and, still not speaking, got into bed.

The disreputable-looking jar of Medicine Man Salve sat on the bed stand next to Jason's side. No comforting backrub or handjob tonight. He picked the jar up, noting the lack of an ingredients label. He set the jar back down.

As though following his thoughts, Sam said, "You should rub that in. It'll help."

Jason nodded, once more picking up the container. He unscrewed the lid. "The way it smells, I'm surprised the jar doesn't explode."

Sam said nothing, gazing at the ceiling, as enigmatic and self-contained as one of those bronze statues of St. George contemplating how to best slay dragons.

Jason slowly, laboriously rubbed in the pungent cream, then made his way back to the bathroom to wash the residue off his hands.

When he returned to the bed, Sam turned his head. "It's not just physical," he said.

"Sorry?"

"You've experienced a traumatic event. You think you're fine, but it takes time to work through it. That's the reason for the sick leave."

Jason opened his mouth to reject this, deny it, but honesty held him silent. He shrugged, then admitted, "Okay. Maybe that's true."

That seemed to be all Sam had to say on the matter.

Jason turned out the lamp, climbed carefully into bed. The afternoon's hike had not done him any favors.

Neither moved. The silence was acute, excruciating. It was so quiet, Jason could hear Sam's wristwatch ticking away on the other nightstand.

Somebody say something, he thought, and then had to smother a nervous laugh. Sam was lying a couple of inches from him, but he had never felt so far apart.

When it became obvious neither of them was going to speak, Jason turned painfully onto his side and closed his eyes.

Maybe he could try counting sheep. Or maybe he should try counting the still-missing art works Fletcher-Durrand was surely responsible for...

He nearly jumped when Sam touched his shoulder. Maybe it was Jason's imagination, but he felt there was something apologetic, almost a longing in that tentative touch.

He was still unhappy, still a little angry with the way that conversation had gone, but he couldn't rebuff Sam's overture. It just wasn't in him.

He rolled onto his back, reaching for Sam. Sam's hot mouth covered his hungrily, and Jason answered that hunger with his own demand.

The sex was fast, almost frantic. There had been too many recent near misses of all kinds. The bed sounded like it was going to come apart under them, frame squeaking, mattress pinging as they rocked and humped. Sam's foot knocked Jason's ankle twice, and even those wrenches of unexpected anguish felt faraway and unimportant in the wake of his driving need for Sam, for whatever Sam could give him. It was never going to be enough. He already knew that. Their rigid, lunging cocks rubbed together, lubricated by the first silky drops of cum.

The creaking bed and their harsh breathing were the only sounds. The silence between them had a deadly earnest quality to it. Well, Sam was always quiet and intense during sex, but Jason... Usually it was a struggle for Jason to swallow everything he was feeling. Not tonight. Tonight, the slick, sliding friction of skin on skin felt like a serious business, a grave endeavor. The naked closeness, the intimacy of the moment was so sweet, it made him sad. He wished he could make it last forever, that the exquisite pleasure of orgasm could be postponed infinitely and they could dangle here on this cusp like the final drop of a toast.

The only magic I still believe in is love?

Sam groaned. Jason buried his head in his neck, breathing in the smell of bare skin and edgy aftershave. He loved the smell of Sam, and he wanted to hang on to this moment and remember that scent and the sounds Sam made because slowly, reluctantly, Jason was starting to suspect they were not ultimately headed in the same direction.

For now Sam was letting him in, sharing a part of his life, but Jason could imagine too clearly a time when the door would shut again and he would be on the outside.

Sam began to come, and Jason could feel tension pouring from balls and brain, the crazy intimacy of shared breath, shared bodily fluids. Jason let go and came too, came in long, blissful surges. Tears stung his eyes, but he closed his lashes against them, gritted his jaw against any outcry.

I love you. It would be better if I didn't.

He knew in his heart that a day would come when this would all be past tense.

Someday he would look back and recognize the last time they had made love. Would he know it was the last time, or would the knowledge only come later?

Chapter Ten

He woke to the warm pressure of Sam's mouth moving on his.

Jason had dreamed of misunderstandings and arguments and good-byes, so it was a relief to wake to sweet and coaxing kisses.

His lips parted, and he smiled beneath Sam's mouth, kissed him back. After all, dreams were not premonitions—unless you turned them into that. Sam drew back, smiling that crooked smile.

"Something's come up."

Jason considered a couple of smartass comments, but he knew what that glint in Sam's eyes meant.

He sat up, and Sam sat back. Jason raked the hair out of his eyes. "There's been a break in the case?"

Sam looked momentarily confused. "No. Not that. Sorry. This is related to my book."

"Your... Oh, right. Good news or bad?" He'd almost forgotten about Sam's book. Maybe because until this moment he hadn't entirely believed the book existed.

"Promising."

Really? Because that was one wintery smile. "Let me guess. Hollywood wants to make a movie? You just got a TV series?"

Sam snorted, and that disdain did sound genuine. "No. I've finally received permission to visit Nelson Bamburg at the high-security federal penitentiary in Florence, Colorado."

After a moment, Jason said mildly, "Fun times." It was the best he could manage. He knew about Nelson Bamburg. Bamburg the Baby

Killer. It was one of the cases that had established Sam's reputation as the Bureau's premier man hunter. The Bamburg chapter in *Shadow on the Glass* was a big part of the training syllabus on serial killers and mass murders at Quantico. In fact, the title *Shadow on the Glass* came from the Bamburg case. "I didn't know you were hoping for a reunion."

"I wouldn't put it quite like that. But I've been trying to reinterview him for about eight years, so I'm hesitant to pass up this opportunity."

"Why should you?" Jason said. "If you're worried about me, don't be. I'm fine right where I am. You need a day or two to interview Bamburg? I say go for it."

"It's about a four-hour flight from Cheyenne to Colorado Springs, so depending on how things go, I probably won't be back until late tomorrow."

"I'll survive."

"Are you sure?" Sam immediately corrected, "I don't mean literally."

Jason laughed. "Sam, come on. Of course I'm sure."

Funny thing. Jason did not think, believe, that he had been relying, either consciously or unconsciously, on Sam to keep him safe, but the knowledge that he would be on his own did leave him feeling instantly more vulnerable.

He must have looked convincingly confident, though, because after a second or two of thoughtful inspection, Sam nodded. "Okay. I won't take any longer than I need to."

"Take the time you need." He was belatedly absorbing that Sam had showered and was dressed for travel, so he was planning to leave right away for the airport.

Well, great. The sooner he left, the sooner he'd be back.

"If anything—and I mean *any*thing—trips your alarm, phone Cheyenne PD and Charles Reynolds at the RA immediately. They're fully briefed on your circumstances. I've already texted you both contact numbers."

"Right."

"Keep your piece at hand at all times." Sam glanced pointedly at Jason's pistol lying in its holster on the nightstand.

"I will." Jason smiled, ignoring the way his nerves tightened in recognition of the possibility of having to use his weapon. Also recognition of the low-key, unobtrusive protection Sam had exerted on his behalf since their arrival.

He drew Kennedy in for another kiss. "You be careful too. You hear me? You're the one keeping company with monsters."

Sam nodded. "I'll call you tonight." He gave Jason a final quick kiss and was gone.

Jason lay back down, listening to the sound of the car engine starting outside. He smiled sardonically.

"Suppose I'd said no?" he said.

After breakfast, which largely consisted of a pot of coffee, Jason spent the morning talking to his contacts at Christie's and Sotheby's.

"We handled the Blackstone collection back in 2002," Inez Parker at Sotheby's told him. "Roughly told, we auctioned off about $350,000 worth of posters, costumes, and props. Mostly to other magicians."

"Other magicians? Is that so?"

"Oh yes. Magicians *are* the market for these items. You must be aware that David Copperfield owns the largest collection of magic memorabilia in the world."

"Yes, that I knew. The International Museum and Library of the Conjuring Arts. It's a private collection."

"Yes. Started in 1991. The only difference between Copperfield and every other magician out there is he has the money to indulge his habit. It's about a very specific clientele wanting to own a very specific piece of history. A number of items in our auction could have been purchased new for a fraction of the price. The spirit cabinet, the prediction chest...some of these things only dated from the 1970s, so they weren't even technically of historical significance, but people paid top dollar. Nowadays they'd probably go for twice that."

"Lack of inventory," Jason said.

"Exactly."

"In the case of a collection like this one—"

"If your thief knows what he—or she—is up to, the sale will either be handled privately or the collection will be held for a couple of years, then broken up and distributed across the major auction houses. If your thief is an amateur, they'll do something like try to immediately disperse the inventory through a site like the Magic Auction. They won't get top dollar, but they also won't have to answer a lot of inconvenient questions."

"The Magic Auction?"

Inez laughed. "You boys and girls on the Art Crime Team need to get out of the museum once in a while. Check out MagicAuction.com. PayPal accepted."

"PayPal?"

Inez said thoughtfully, "Then there's The Magic Auctioneer. Goodman is handling Bill McIlhany's estate. I think he billed it something like McIlhany's Magical Mysteries. But given the scope—and provenance—of the collection you're inquiring about, I suggest you get in contact with Arlo Presley at Potter & Potter. They do an annual Spring Magic Auction. That's coming up in a couple of weeks. This year they're featuring two recently rediscovered Houdini scrapbooks. You know what Houdini items go for."

Not really, but Inez had given him an excellent starting point for his inquiries.

Jason got Arlo Presley's contact info, thanked Inez for her help, and headed over to Ruby's house, wading through the chickens, who tried to take clumsy, aborted flight as he passed.

He found her on her way out the door, bundled in a red and black plaid coat, her purse precariously balanced on the large white banker's box she held in both arms.

"I was just on my way to invite you for supper," Ruby greeted him. "Sam told me you're on your own tonight."

"I am. That would be great. Thank you." He eyed the box. "Are you headed into town, by any chance?"

"Yep. If by 'town' you mean Cheyenne. Got a date with the tax man. Er, tax woman."

"Mind if I tag along?"

"If you're ready to leave now. I'm running late."

"I'm ready when you are."

"Okay, then! Follow me!"

It's not unusual to be loved by anyone

It's not unusual to have fun with anyone

Ruby drove a fireball-red 2018 Lexus IS. When she turned the key in the ignition, Engelbert Humperdinck's—or was that Tom Jones'?—voice blasted out of the stereo speakers and Jason nearly blasted out of his seat.

Which made it three for three because Ruby blasted out of the garage and took off down the dirt road toward the highway like Smoky running from the Bandits.

Jason unobtrusively gripped the door arm and avoided looking at the speedometer.

"Where do you want me to drop you?" Ruby shouted over Engelbert.

"If it's not too far out of your way, the FBI building on Airport Parkway."

"I can do that. How long do you think you'll be?"

"It's hard to say. Don't worry about waiting for me."

"Oh, it'll be you waiting for me," Ruby assured him. "What with the hair salon, the yoga studio, and the Cactus Café, it takes my gal a while to figure everything out."

"You're working three different jobs?" Jason was horrified. Ruby was a lot younger than his parents, but she was no spring chicken.

She guffawed. "No, honey. I'm retired now. My income comes from the businesses I own."

"You own a yoga studio?"

"Sure I do. Yoga is fantastic. Everybody should do yoga. I try to tell Sam he should do yoga. It would do wonders for his nerves."

Jason had no response, momentarily distracted by the unlikely mental vision of Sam in yoga pants.

Ruby chuckled again, apparently at however she interpreted his expression. "I know what you're thinking."

"*I* don't even know what I'm thinking," Jason said. "I had the impression Sam—" Maybe that wasn't very tactful. He didn't finish the thought.

"You're wondering why I let Sam buy me the ranch when I can afford to buy my own ranches?"

"I... Not exactly."

"Sam likes to be the man in the white hat. That's one reason."

The man in the white hat? Meaning the good guy? The guy who always charged to the rescue? Jason wasn't so sure about that. He thought Sam had enough pressure already without the added weight of having to rescue people perfectly able of rescuing themselves.

"Plus, if he can buy me things he thinks I need, he doesn't have to feel so guilty about not spending time with me."

Now Jason really didn't know what to say. Ruby gave another of those chortles and patted his knee. "You're a nice boy. Don't you worry. Sam and I understand each other."

Probably not. Almost certainly not. But if it made her happy to think so, he wasn't about to argue.

* * * * *

It was kind of flattering—also kind of alarming—how very relieved to see him Agent Dreyfus was.

The Cheyenne Resident Agency looked like every other satellite office Jason had been in. Beige walls, blue carpet, cubicles and cubicle-sized offices, plenty of official seals and ceremonious photographs. Or rather, it looked like every other satellite office after-hours, because the building felt like a ghost town. Empty, abandoned. With the exception of Abigail Dreyfus and some support staff, nobody was home.

"I didn't think I'd hear from you so soon," Dreyfus said, showing him into her closet-sized office. A small, homesick cactus drooped atop her bookshelf. There were three framed photos on her desk: a beaming, bespectacled middle-aged couple, a handsome, eager-beaver young guy who looked like every aspiring US Attorney Jason had ever met—he had not noticed until then that Dreyfus wore an engagement ring—and an admittedly cute Pomeranian puppy in a pink party hat. "Agent Kennedy sounded like, well..."

Jason took the chair in front of Dreyfus' spic-and-span desk. "You spoke to Kennedy this morning?"

"I phoned him right after my conference call. He was at the airport. His flight was boarding, so we didn't talk long."

That was clearly a relief. Jason suppressed a smile. "You've had the coroner's report?"

"Yes." She swallowed at some unhappy memory. "Michael Khan died from asphyxiation due to ligature strangulation. The same wire used to tie him to the tree was used to garrote him. Death was approximately at six o'clock on Sunday evening. He did not appear to have had an evening meal."

Unless you were a trained assassin, killing someone using a garrote was a moderately challenging enterprise. Once the blood supply to the brain was cut off, unconsciousness could take anywhere from ten to thirty seconds—worst-case scenario, a full minute—and the victim would presumably be struggling for his life all that time. Even thirty seconds was a long time in a fight. A strong and knowledgeable woman could successfully garrote a man, but it would not be a speedy process and she would probably sustain a few bruises.

"Was there anything unique about the wire used to garrote Khan?"

"No. Just ordinary heavy-duty wire for hanging pictures. They found similar wire at Khan's house."

"And four-to-six weeks before you get the toxicology report?" Jason asked.

"At the soonest."

By which time Jason would be long gone, back to real life and his own job.

"Have the crime-scene technicians come up with anything relating to the tire tracks down below or the footprints at the site where the body was found?"

"They were unable to separate the perp's tire tracks from the tire tracks of the hikers who discovered the body—*and* the tire tracks of park rangers and law-enforcement vehicles."

Jason muttered. "Great."

"I know. As for the boot prints, they think they were able to isolate one pair, size nine at the very base of the tree. Nothing unique about the gait or tread. It could be an athletic woman with large feet or a small but very strong man."

"Just one set of footprints?"

Dreyfus shook her head. "Impossible to know for sure because once again, the hikers and then the forest rangers trampled the surrounding scene before CRT arrived."

Into his silence, Dreyfus said, "Anyway, Routt SO is taking over the homicide investigation. Cheyenne PD is going to continue handling the theft of Khan's art collection."

Jason glanced up. "There's sufficient reason to believe the two crimes are separate?"

"I wouldn't bet money on it. But that's the way Routt wants to handle it."

"It's probably just as well. You've got a shortage of manpower at the moment."

"I'll say," she said bitterly. "There's a reason Wyoming has the lowest rate of bank robberies in the West. They take bank robbery *personally* here. Every SO in the state is out looking for these yahoos."

"Where are you from originally?" Jason asked.

"Arizona. I was hoping I might get posted there, but nope."

First-office postings were almost never in the agent's own backyard, and there were good reasons for that.

She made a face. "Anyway, I've been informed Routt doesn't require our assistance."

"Okay, well, you've got plenty to keep you busy working the theft angle—assuming Cheyenne PD still wants help?"

Another expression of disgust from Dreyfus. "Oh sure, Cheyenne wants our help. They're only too happy to hand an art theft off to us."

Jason grinned sympathetically. "Makes sense," he said. "We've got the resources. They don't."

"I guess. But if the two crimes are connected, I don't see how we can investigate the one and not the other."

He ignored that. "I did some calling around this morning." He brought Dreyfus up to speed on what he'd learned from his contact at Sotheby's.

"You believe the collection is going to be broken up and auctioned off?"

"Unfortunately, unless the thieves have already arranged for the private sale of the entire collection to a specific customer, that's the most likely scenario. They can't put the collection as a whole on the open market because it's bound to be recognized. Things like an original copy of a rare poster or that mind-reading machine? There aren't that many of them floating around, so collectors keep an eye on who's holding what."

"Is it possible a private collector could have hired the thieves?"

Jason smiled approvingly. *Now* she was getting into it, showing a little ingenuity.

"It's possible, but I think unlikely because of the type of collection it is. Khan owned a lot of unique and valuable pieces, but as a whole they aren't thematically cohesive."

"How are they not thematically cohesive? They're all things to do with magic."

"True, and I'm not arguing that the collection as a whole isn't extremely valuable. But it's not like Khan was collecting all Houdini's show and personal effects. Or the show and personal effects of any one magician. If that were the case, the idea of a fanatical collector would be more plausible. Obsession is focus."

"Obsession is focus," she repeated obediently and made a note on a legal pad.

"But here we have a number of items of unknown provenance, which is always tricky, not least for insurance purposes."

"One person we can rule out is Michael Khan," Dreyfus said.

"No. Unfortunately. We can't. Especially if the prevailing theory is correct and the crimes are unconnected."

"But surely he had to be killed by the same person who stole his collection?"

"Forty-eight hours later? Why?"

"Well..." Dreyfus looked confused. "Because it's too much of a coincidence. Isn't it?"

"Coincidences happen. Even if Khan *was* killed by the same person behind the theft, it doesn't mean that person wasn't Khan's confederate."

"But if they were confederates, why kill him? How does that make sense?"

"What's the saying about when thieves fall out?" He shrugged. But yes, the question remained, why had Khan been killed? Why then? Why there? Why— But he had pretty much promised Sam to stick to investigating the art theft as a separate crime, and that's what he intended to do.

"Why would anyone *else* kill him?" Dreyfus persisted. "And why stage the murder scene so elaborately?"

"The crime scene could have been deliberately staged to raise those very questions. As to why turn on Khan? There could be any number of reasons. It's way too soon to draw conclusions. I know it's difficult, but you can't be distracted by any of that. You have to follow the art."

She sighed. "Okay. Where do I start, then? Mrs. Khan?"

Jason pointed at her. "Exactly. You start from the inside and work your way out."

Dreyfus bit her lip. She threw him a doubtful look. "Would you want to—"

Jason picked up his coat and rose. "I would," he said.

Chapter Eleven

A shapely blonde woman in a silver bodysuit and sequined heels stood at one end of the brightly lit stage. She was speaking as she faced the sea of empty tables and chairs. "I want you to watch that marked bullet very, very carefully," she instructed the imaginary audience. "At no time will that bullet leave The Maestro's hand until the moment he loads it into the pistol."

On the opposite end of the stage, an African-American dwarf in navy silk trousers, red smoking jacket, and a cravat, held up a small and shiny object for everyone to see before turning away to tap the bullet against a glass target set up in the center of the stage.

Minerva Khan, the grieving widow, was trying out her act in preparation for Top Hat White Rabbit club's Friday grand opening.

"Wyoming is not LA," Arturo the bartender was saying to Jason and Dreyfus as they watched The Maestro and Minerva prepare for their bullet-catch trick. "If this convention is a success, it could completely change Cheyenne's status in the world of magic. This convention could put us on the map."

"It is impossible for that bullet to penetrate the glass target without breaking it," Minerva said from the stage.

"What is she doing?" Dreyfus asked as The Maestro loaded the bullet into a Luger. "Is that a real gun?"

"Bullet Catch," the bartender said. "It's what she's famous for. She doesn't perform it much anymore, which is why management is letting her rehearse it here for Thursday's performance. You don't want to make a mistake with that trick."

"I thought the club opened on Friday?" Jason asked.

"Officially. Thursday night is a special Magicians Only night."

"I see. Who owns the club?" Jason asked.

"Doug Devant. He's a local magician."

They watched Minerva and The Maestro for another moment.

Dreyfus said uneasily, "They're not using real bullets, are they?"

"The bullets are usually real," Jason said. "It *is* a trick, though. The most dangerous trick in magic."

According to legend—and Ben Robinson's book—at least twelve magicians had died while performing the bullet catch.

"Don't tell her!" Arturo objected.

Dreyfus rolled her eyes. "Please. I know it's not magic."

"It's still a great trick, and it ruins it if you know how it's done."

Silently, they watched The Maestro mount a small blue ladder and aim at Minerva, who had taken her place at the opposite end of the stage. Minerva tossed her hair back and lifted her chin. She raised her left arm.

Despite knowing the different ways the trick could be worked—or maybe *because* he knew—Jason felt queasy.

Minerva's arm dropped; The Maestro fired. The glass target shattered. Dreyfus gasped as Minerva staggered back. Minerva steadied herself as The Maestro jumped from his ladder and ran to her. He held up a small silver plate, and Minerva spat the bullet onto the plate. The Maestro picked up the bullet and held it up for the invisible audience to *ooh* and *ahh* over.

"How the heck did she do that?" Dreyfus murmured.

"Minerva!" Arturo yelled. "You got company."

Minerva's head jerked up. She raised her hand in acknowledgment, then spoke a few words to The Maestro before exiting the stage. A few moments later she joined them at the bar. Her skin was shiny, the hair at her temples damp. She smelled of cigarettes, a lot of perfume, and just a hint of perspiration. Maybe she *was* old-school when it came to her illusions.

"*More* police?" she said.

Her husband's body had only been found the day before. If she was tired of cops now, she was in for a rough few weeks.

"FBI." Dreyfus held up her identification. "I'm Special Agent Dreyfus, and this is Special Agent West with the Art Crime Team."

"Art Crime Team? So you're not here about Mike?"

"Only as far as your husband's death may be related to the theft of his collection."

"Of course it's related to the theft of the collection. And it's *our* collection," Minerva added. "I paid for at least half that collection. Mike hasn't—hadn't—had a steady gig in four years. Not once word got out that he was the one going around spoiling everyone's acts. I warned him he would ruin his own career, but as usual he knew best." She lit a cigarette. "Look where it got him."

"You can't smoke in here, Minerva," the bartender said. "You know that."

In reply, Minerva blew a stream of smoke in his direction.

The bartender shook his head as if at a naughty five-year-old sticking her tongue out. "It's bad for your health."

"Really, Arturo? Have you seen my act? You think I'm worried about my social security going to waste?"

Arturo shrugged. "It's bad for my health too, you know."

Jason couldn't help asking Minerva, "Have you ever been shot?"

"Once. When I was first starting out." She pushed her platinum hair back, and he saw the faded white line of a bullet scar along her jaw. "It was just a graze."

Not really. Not judging by that scar.

He had to hand it to her. She'd nearly had her head blown off, but here she was years later, still pretending to catch bullets between her teeth. Jason had been shot once—well, four times on one occasion—and he still got night sweats dreaming about it. Not as bad as it had been right after Miami, but bad enough.

Jason asked, "What makes you think your husband's death is connected to the theft of your art collection?"

"Are you kidding?" She exhaled thoughtfully. "It's too much of a coincidence otherwise. Right? I know damned well Mike was behind the robbery. And, as usual, he got greedy. Obviously, his partner or partners decided to knock him off."

"How do you know he was behind the robbery?"

She gave him a deliberate look from beneath her false eyelashes. "Believe me, I spent ten years watching that man perform lousy magic. He didn't have many secrets from me."

"I understand. Do you have actual evidence?"

"Evidence." She shook her head at the idea, took another drag off her cigarette.

Jason cocked his head. "Forgive me for saying so, but for someone who spent ten years of her life with the guy, you don't seem overly grief-stricken."

Her lip curled. "Oh please. I'm sure you know perfectly well that Mike and I were in the middle of an ugly divorce."

"Why was it ugly?"

She glared at him. "What are you? Some kind of idiot savant? *Because* Mike's the kind of guy who would rather go to the trouble of fake-stealing his junk collection than fairly splitting our assets down the middle. That's why. He had no honor. As demonstrated by the fact he went around spoiling people's magic acts."

"Can you take us through the events of Friday evening?" Dreyfus inquired.

"Sure, although I've already given my statement to the police."

"Sometimes people remember things they forgot to mention the first time around."

"Not me. I have total recall."

"Is that so?" Jason asked politely.

"Yes. That's so." She glanced at Dreyfus. "I left the house at five thirty to do a show at Miller Insulation. One of the biggest companies in Wyoming, for your information."

"Were you performing the bullet catch?" Dreyfus asked.

"No. I only perform the bullet catch on special occasions now. At one thirty in the morning I got a call at—from Michael saying we'd been robbed. He pretended to accuse me of being behind it all."

Pretended?

Jason said, "So, your theory is your husband hired someone to come in and steal the collection after you left on Friday night?"

"Exactly. It's not a theory. That is exactly what happened."

"What do you think the plan for the collection is?"

She narrowed her eyes at some thought, studying the red tip of her cigarette. She shook her head.

"Do you believe your husband intended to sell the collection?"

"I don't know. He definitely didn't want to sell, but if it came down to selling or letting me have my half of it, yeah, he'd sell first."

"He'd still have to split the insurance money with you."

Her smile was tight. "He'd prefer that to me getting my hands on his precious floating light bulb."

"I'm sorry?" Dreyfus said.

Minerva's gaze dismissed her and returned to Jason. "It was personal with him. All the way."

"Do you have any idea who this accomplice of your husband's might be?"

Her gaze was approving. "Yes. I sure do. I'll bet you money, Mike got Ian Boz to help him."

Jason asked, "And Ian Boz is—"

She looked taken aback. "You're kidding."

"Nope."

Minerva looked from Jason to Dreyfus. "You really don't know who Ian Boz is?"

Dreyfus looked at Jason, but Jason was drawing a blank on that one.

"Don't tell me you don't watch TV? Boz was on that show *America's Most Talented*. He's a magician. Was. Not bad either. He got all the way up to Judges' Pick Round, but then some reporter found out he'd been in prison for identity theft—among other things—and that he was on the run after violating probation. Anyway, he was recaptured by the authorities and put back in prison. When he got out, Michael helped him open Boz's Brew."

Jason vaguely remembered something about the tabloid-dubbed Indictable Illusionist. "Which is what?"

"A magic shop. The biggest magic shop in Wyoming."

"Why would your husband do that?" Jason asked. "Aid an ex-con like Boz. Were they previously acquainted? Were they friends? Had they worked together?"

"You must be joking. Michael didn't do anything out of the goodness of his heart. No doubt he figured Boz would eventually make himself useful—which I believe he did Friday evening."

"Again, do you have any actual evidence that your husband and Ian Boz conspired to commit theft and possible insurance fraud?"

"See, this is why I pay taxes," Minerva said. "That's *your* job."

Chapter Twelve

The pale, slender youth behind the counter at Boz's Brew was too young to be Ian Boz.

As Jason and Dreyfus pushed through the glass doors of the shop—to the accompaniment of pixie dust door chimes—the youth glanced up from a hardcover copy of *Mandrake the Magician,* smiled, and recited, "Hi! Welcome to the largest selection of supplies for sorcery, spells, and shticks in the Western United States. How can I help you?"

Dreyfus showed her badge. "Mr. Boz?"

"FBI?" The kid's smile faltered.

"Agents Dreyfus and West. Are you Ian Boz?"

Jason sighed inwardly. Dreyfus was *so* young—practically as young as the kid behind the counter.

"N-No. I'm Terry. Terry Van der Beck."

Dreyfus said in her most official voice, "Is Mr. Boz in, Terry?"

Terry's green eyes rounded in dismay. "Sure. I-I'll get him."

He left the counter and vanished into the back room.

"Are you really not going to tell me how she caught that bullet in her teeth?" Dreyfus said.

"It's against the magicians' code to reveal a secret."

"It's not against the FBI's code!"

Jason laughed. He moved away to examine a row of framed posters.

He whistled softly.

"What is it?" Dreyfus came to join him. "Did you find something?"

Jason nodded at the row of posters featuring such notables as Marshall the Mystic and His Hats, Ionia, L'enchanteresse, and Prince Ali Raji Oriental Magic—with the confusing tag: African Magician. Magic had changed a lot through the years, but one thing that had not changed was its diversity.

"I think these are legit."

She said skeptically, "*Legit?*"

"The real thing. Not repros."

"Oh." She leaned in to study the price tag on the 20 x 30" half-sheet lithograph of a young woman in a red gown, reaching out to a tuxedoed man standing amidst a crowd of gentlemen. The bold typeface heading read: *CAN YOU LIFT HER?* And below: *Twenty men try it every night— & fail.*

"$4500! They're priced like they're the real thing. That's for sure."

Jason moved on to a 1925 poster of a winged devil cranking the handle of a small box from which ghostly figures and tiny turbaned people spilled out. The giant floating head of a magician frowned disapprovingly on the whole operation. The header read: CHEFALO – MAGICIAN & ILLUSIONIST. Typeface at the bottom of the poster proclaimed: ASSISTED BY THE MAGDA-PALERMO MIDGETS!

A bargain at $3500. He took out his cell phone and snapped a photo. He moved down the row of posters, taking photographs of each one.

Here was an obvious potential fence for the Khan collection. Too obvious? Maybe.

There were advertisements for Jansen, Chung Ling Soo—incidentally, a victim of the bullet catch—Mrs. Eva Fay, oh, and who could forget that "Jolly Prince of Funmakers," Mr. Herbert L. Flint.

"Why so many devils and demons?" Dreyfus whispered—as though fearing the devils and demons might hear her.

"It's code. The magicians have learned the arcane secrets of the spiritual world."

"Why not angels and saints, then?"

"Angels and saints wouldn't be nearly so interesting. *This* knowledge is forbidden knowledge."

"And what about the flames?"

"A lot of early illusions revolved around fire. Fire breathing, fire swallowing, fire bathing, walking through fire, flames shooting from the magician's head—"

"Now you're joking."

"No. Not at all. The idea was that magicians could control the elements—as well as the spirit world. Plus, fire is symbolic. It represents all kinds of things: purification, knowledge, rebirth, divinity, inspiration, hell... It's subliminal advertising."

Dreyfus made a sound of disapproval. "Okay. Never mind. I get it. In that case, I won't ask about the turbans, harem girls, snakes, buzzards, lizards, and sinister Asian men. Do you recognize anything from the Khan collection?"

He shook his head. "No. But I don't remember every piece of the collection off the top of my head."

"If these are the real thing, how would someone like Ian Boz get his hands on them?"

Jason turned as Terry called from the doorway to the office, "He's not here."

"You said he *was* here," Dreyfus said.

"I know, but he's not in his office. I thought he was in the bathroom, but he must have stepped out for a coffee or something. He uses the back door sometimes."

"Then he's coming back?"

Terry shrugged. "I guess."

"How long have you been working for Boz?" Jason asked.

"About two years." Terry looked defensive, as though he feared he was about to be arrested for working for Boz.

Jason smiled. "Do you like it?"

"Sure. Yeah." Still wary.

"Are you a magician too?"

The kid—okay, not really a kid, because he was probably in his late twenties, now that Jason had a closer look at him—relaxed a little. "Yes. Well, I'm training to be."

"Are you Boz's apprentice?"

Terry wrinkled his nose in distaste. "Not him, no. I was training with Mateo Santos." A shadow crossed his face.

"Do you know Michael Khan?" Dreyfus asked. "Was he a regular visitor to the store?"

Terry's expression grew wary once more. "I know he's dead. Everyone knows. They found his body at Vedauwoo."

"*Vedauwoo?*" Jason repeated.

Both Dreyfus and Terry looked at him in surprise. After all, it was a National Park and a popular destination by all accounts. It was just he'd only ever heard of it in connection with Ethan's death.

"Everyone's talking about it," Terry said. "What it means that he would be found there."

"What does it mean?" Jason asked.

"It's a sacred place. Sacred to the Arapaho anyway. It's where the young men went for their vision quests. Where the medicine men went to make their medicine pouches."

Dreyfus said in the tone of one who does not want to encourage superstitious nonsense, "It's a campground as well as being very popular with climbers and photographers."

The sound of pixie dust sprinkled over them, and the glass door to the store swung open. The man who entered was about forty, medium height, and built like a classic cartoon henchman. He held a bag of fast food. The tips of what appeared to be some pretty impressive ink tickled his jawline and covered his massive hands. The impressiveness of the tats and his array of piercings was sort of undercut by a skimpy hairdo that more than anything called to mind Tintin.

"Ian Boz?" Jason inquired.

Boz's beady eyes moved from Jason to Dreyfus, who was reaching for her badge like it was a magic amulet. "Who wants to know?"

Terry wavered. "It's the FBI!"

Boz reared back, feeling for the door handle behind him.

"Don't run," Jason warned him.

Boz turned and ran.

The door swung shut behind him with another twinkling of pixie dust.

Jason swore. Dreyfus yelled, "FBI, halt!"

"Dreyfus, we don't have just ca—"

Dreyfus bolted after Boz, the musical sound of fairies floating down as the door opened and closed again. Two seconds later she raced past the rain-streaked plate glass front windows, shouting, "FBI! I said *halt*."

"Are. You. Fucking. *Kidding*. Me?" Jason said.

Terry met his eyes and spread his arms in a Don't Look at Me, Man.

Jason pulled out his phone. "Where's he live?" he asked Terry.

"You think he's going home?" Terry was doubtful.

"Yep. I think he's running straight home the way he's been doing since he was five years old. Because that's what they *all* do."

"He lives down the street. Over the old fun house."

Well, yeah, of course, because this was an alternate universe called Wyoming. "Where the hell is the fun house?" Jason questioned.

"Down the street to your left. It's the big yellow and blue building with an evil clown over the doorway and a neon sign that says Fun House. You can't miss it. It's right on the corner."

Plus...evil clown. Kind of a giveaway. Jason pressed Dreyfus' contact info. The number began to ring as he reached the door.

Dreyfus did not answer her phone.

Jason pushed through the door, closing off the silvery sprinkle sounds, and found himself on an empty sidewalk. He listened tensely but did not hear gunshots, so that was the good news. In fact, he did not hear anything but the rush and splash of cars speeding past. He started walk-running in pursuit, trying to avoid the rain puddles, ignoring the pain of his ankle, which was not healed enough for running or even cautious jogging.

"Dreyfus, I'm going to ground you for the rest of your life." He tried her again.

No reply.

No sign of her up ahead either.

He hop-skipped on, wishing he'd thought to bring dear old Grandad Kennedy's shillelagh on this jaunt. At least he was carrying his Glock. That would make Sam happy. Although hopefully Sam would never hear about this.

His cell rang. "Where the hell are you?" he barked.

"Just getting into my car, honey," Ruby said after a surprised instant. "Where would you like me to pick you up?"

Someday this would be funny.

Unless Dreyfus got hurt. Or worse.

"Um, why don't you head on back to the ranch. I'll find my own way back."

"It's no problem. I can wait for you."

Jason, still clumping along as fast as he could, panted, "No, really. Thank you…but I'm in the…f-ouch…middle of something…I don't know how long…I'll be."

Ruby said reluctantly, "If you're sure? We're still on for dinner?"

"…yep!…still on…what time?"

"How about six?"

"…see you then…" Jason gasped, and disconnected.

He covered two long slippery blocks of city sidewalk, and finally came to a painful halt at a large intersection. There was no sign of Dreyfus or Boz, but he could see the fun house on the opposite corner. Terry was right. You couldn't miss it.

Jason hop-hitched across the street, managing not to get hit—or drowned—by the passing cars. Out of breath and pissed off, he reached the double doorway beneath the giant leering head of the evil clown.

It was an old structure. Probably early 1900s. A large, long building with a plain brick façade and plenty of industrial-style windows. It had probably begun life as a factory of some kind.

The weather-beaten wooden sign on the door said CLOSED.

Which was false advertising given that the door stood open about a foot. On the other side of the entrance was a spilled bag of fast food.

"Dreyfus?" he yelled.

To his relief, he heard her yell back, "West! In here! I can't find the darned door!"

Fan-fucking-tastic.

Did he call for backup or continue on? Technically, legally, Boz was within his rights to refuse to answer their questions. They did not have a warrant. Boz had not been placed under arrest. Running away was strange and highly suspicious, and they could probably charge him with some variation of fleeing, eluding, and obstructing, but no way was that ever going to trial—unless he did turn out to be involved in the theft of Michael Khan's art collection.

No. The best thing to do was find and retrieve Dreyfus and persuade Cheyenne PD to execute a search warrant on that shop, Boz's home, this place—and whatever additional storage facility Boz owned.

What he did not want to do—could not afford to do—was turn up in any police report or newspaper story. If that happened, Sam would have a fit—and rightfully so.

He slipped through the open door, avoiding the spilled soda and slimy contents of several scattered burgers, and found himself in a dark corridor about the size of a large walk-in closet. It smelled old and unstable: an unhealthy blend of deteriorating wood, rotting cloth, and fried electrical circuits.

The only light was afforded by the daylight from the outside entrance. He did not see an interior door, but he walked up a gradual incline to the wall in front of him, pushed, and the wall turned out to be a giant swinging door. Jason walked through the door and found himself in another longer, slanted corridor. By the illumination of the yellowed emergency lights, he could see the peeling walls were painted with clowns chasing balloons and rabbits and each other. The style looked maybe mid-20th century. The faces of the clowns seemed oddly malevolent, but their pastime looked harmless enough.

There were several identical doors in a row. Jason tried one, and it led to another corridor which led to another corridor which led to another corridor which led back to the room with the clowns.

Square one. Literally.

The second and third doors opened onto closets as black as night and painted with glittering stars and planets. The floor of one closet was a few inches lower, so when he stepped inside it felt for a crazy second like he was falling through space. Which, given the swollen and soggy condition of the wood, was probably a real possibility.

The fourth door led down a corridor which led to a mirror maze. So...progress? Jason glimpsed disorienting views of himself stretched ten feet tall and then ten feet wide and then upside down. Sometimes his head was enormous and his body tiny. Some of the mirrors were broken. One of the mirrors was not a mirror but a silvered painting on glass, so that it looked like a hooded figure was staring at him. That one made Jason grab for his weapon, even though he knew better, and did not improve his mood.

Dust. Cobwebs. Mold. All present. In fact, the only thing missing was booming, maniacal laughter coming from everywhere and nowhere. Happily, no way would the sound system in this place still work. Even turning on the lights was liable to set the structure on fire, and he hoped to God Dreyfus did not press any buttons or throw any levers.

"Dreyfus?" he yelled.

This time she did not answer.

"Shit." But she could easily be a couple of corridors ahead and not hear him.

He had to hand it to Boz. Leading them in here had been smart. He had basically invited them to get lost—and they had accepted the invitation. By now, their quarry was probably halfway across the county.

To Jason's relief, the maze of mirrors led onto a deck with a huge skylight. Despite the years of grime, gray daylight poured down, illuminating macabrely cheerful wall paintings of more demented clowns and anthropomorphic animals wearing sailor suits and ballerina tutus. The artwork here was more modern, maybe late forties, early fifties? Jason could finally see where he was—and that seemed to be the heart of the fun house.

Several rickety staircases led off in different directions, he glimpsed the middle section of a giant slide disappearing into what was probably the bowels of hell, and four distinct clown-head entrances led to rooms that almost certainly meant more delays and sidetracking. No thank you.

A sunken floor in the center of the deck offered a view of dingy stuffing spilling out of ripped padded walls surrounding some kind of giant disk. Presumably, in days of yore, fun seekers had piled onto the disk so they could be hurled against the wall for laughs. What would liability in a place like this be now days?

Anyway, down was not the direction to head. Boz's clerk had said he lived over the fun house, which meant they needed to go *up.*

They needed out of this deathtrap, and they needed to go upstairs and see if by some miracle Boz had not yet left the building.

"Dreyfus?" Jason called again—and again, she didn't answer.

He had never been in a fun house before, but he had a vague understanding of how they worked. Some of the attractions, like that monstrous seven-foot automaton juggler in the corner, were mechanical. But some of the attractions would require human attendants to reset props or jump out at people (thereby setting them up for years of therapy).

That meant there would be service panels and control booths.

There would be interior walkways behind these flimsy plywood walls to reach those control booths.

There would be entrances and exits.

Exits.

He left the railing and went to examine the walls. In several places the wood was buckling, panels popping out. He grabbed hold of one panel and yanked. There was a horrendous tearing away sound, and a section of wall came down, sending up a cloud of dirt, splinters, and mold spores.

Jason tried to cover his nose and mouth with his arm, squinting through the dust and flying particles at the gaping hole in the wall.

Yep, behind the wall was a service passage.

Chapter Thirteen

He had not gone too far when he heard voices.

"You're just making it worse for yourself," Dreyfus said. She sounded very young.

"I'm about to make it worse for you, if you don't shut up."

They sounded like they were on the other side of the wall. Jason pressed against the studs of the flimsy wooden barrier, putting his eye to a crack through the panel. Dreyfus stood a few feet away, her back to him. There were cobwebs in her ponytail. She had her hands up.

Ian Boz was pointing what appeared to be a Smith & Wesson .357 at her.

From his vantage point, Jason could see Dreyfus' hands flex, her muscles bunch, preparatory to her jumping for the gun.

No. No. God no.

He took a step back, bumped against the other side of the makeshift passage, and charged forward, launching a kick with all his strength at the fragile plywood. Rusted nails screeched as a section of wall toppled forward like a falling stage set. Jason saw Boz's astonished face and he saw Dreyfus leap forward.

It seemed to happen in slow motion. Boz realized what was happening and turned back to Dreyfus, but instead of shooting her, he smashed the fist holding the revolver in her face.

Dreyfus cried out and crashed down on the floor at Boz's feet. Boz turned the gun on Jason.

"Freeze."

Jason froze.

Boz vented his feelings in a long stream of swearwords. "Get up," he said finally to Dreyfus. His chest rose and fell in agitation.

She clambered to her feet, holding her hand to her face. Her nose was bleeding. Her eyes met Jason's, and he could see the apology and misery there.

Jason tried to give her a look of reassurance, and God knew what that looked like because he was scared for her and furious with himself.

He said to Boz, "Listen to me, Boz. Don't do anything more stupid than you've already done."

He couldn't tear his gaze from the pistol weaving between him and Dreyfus. He could see Boz's lips moving, but could barely hear the words over the blood rushing in his ears.

Don't shoot. Please don't shoot...

Boz's words filtered through. "I'm warning you. I won't go back to prison."

Talking was good. The longer Boz talked, the less likely he would shoot.

"Okay," Jason said. "If that's what you want. Go."

Boz's jaw dropped.

"We can't stop you," Jason said. "But you need to understand. If you run, it'll be interpreted as an admission of guilt."

Boz steadied the pistol, pointing it straight between Jason's eyes. Dreyfus made a pleading sound, sharply cut off.

"*Or* you could tell us your side of the story." Jason was astonished to hear his own voice sounding relatively calm, even reasonable. "Since that's all we were looking for."

Boz's eyes flicked back and forth between Jason and Dreyfus. "Bullshit. Why would the fucking feebs be involved? You don't fool me. There's something else going on here."

Like what? What the hell else was this nut involved in that he imagined the federal government was likely to show up on his doorstep?

"We're not— Listen to me. We're with the Art Crime Team. The items stolen from Michael Khan's collection are considered to be of historical and cultural significance."

Boz gave a hysterical laugh. "You're bullshitting. *Stop lying to me!*"

"No. I'm not lying. We just wanted to ask you a few questions about Friday night and Michael Khan—"

"I had nothing to do with that. *Nothing.* He wanted me to help him, I said no. I turned him down."

Wait a minute. Hit Rewind.

Jason said, "Michael Khan wanted you to help him do what?"

"Hide the collection from Minerva. Help him pretend it was stolen."

"You're saying Khan faked the theft of his own collection?"

"Are you deaf? *Yes.* But I did not help him. Did not. Did not. Did not."

Dreyfus, her voice squished by the hand clamped to her nose, said, "He couldn't have done it on his own."

"Did not. Did not. Did not. Did—"

"Okay, stop," Jason said. "If you didn't help Khan, who did?"

Boz waved the revolver wildly. "How would I know? Maybe he hired someone."

"A name," Jason pressed. "Your best guess."

"Zatanna Zatara. How the fuck should I know? It wasn't me."

"Where would Khan store the collection?"

"Why are you asking me? I'm telling you, *I wasn't involved.* Maybe he hired a moving company. Maybe the collection is on its way across country. I don't know. I don't want to know."

"Did you kill Michael Khan?" Dreyfus asked.

Boz made a sound like a bull about to charge and turned the pistol her way. Jason instinctively put his arm out—because, yeah, that was going to protect her. Clearly, he had seen too many magician posters.

"No. I did not," Boz said from between his teeth. "Plenty of people had motive to want Mike out of the way, but I wasn't one of them. We were kind of even friends. Until he asked me to risk going back to prison for him."

"Then why in God's name did you flee just now?" Jason demanded. "Why not explain what happened?"

"Like you're going to believe an ex-con?"

"I believe you so far." Well, he didn't *dis*believe Boz. He would *prefer* to believe him. He hadn't made his mind up either way.

Boz hesitated. "Because…because…then Mike accused *me* of stealing his collection."

"Wait a minute…"

"I don't know what he was trying to pull, but whoever he was working with must have known he was going to double-cross them. That's why they killed him."

Khan had tried to recruit Boz to help "steal" his collection. Boz had refused. Khan had then accused him of really stealing the collection in order to cover his own tracks. That was the story?

Maybe Boz believed it. Maybe he was blowing smoke up their asses. He wasn't telling them everything, that was clear, and what he was telling them was so convoluted…

But the fact that he was talking and not killing them—that was a big point in his favor.

"Okay, let's call this a misunderstanding," Jason said. "Why don't we sit down and talk about it? Because this is not helping you. And it's not helping us."

Boz laughed. "Right. The minute we leave here I'll be thrown in prison and you'll swallow the fucking key."

Swallow the key? Wyoming must have one interesting prison system.

"I really won't. The only thing I care about is getting that missing art back."

Boz ignored him, looking around with frantic jerks of his head.

"Boz, listen," Jason said. "You need to make smart choices now. You don't want to do anything that—"

"Got it," Boz interrupted. "I got it. Both of you. Head for the clown on your left. The one with the blue hair. There's a slide inside his mouth. Go down the slide. Hurry up!"

Jason and Dreyfus picked their way across the debris-strewn room to the large clown-shaped entrance. Sure enough, the mouth of the clown led to a small platform at the head of a very tall hardwood slide.

"Go down the slide!" Boz called.

Jason stared into the gloom. He could see about eighty feet down. Was the whole slide even there? He couldn't tell.

"Where does that lead?" Dreyfus whispered.

Jason shook his head. "I don't know."

"Get your asses down the fucking slide!" Boz screamed, losing patience.

"Age before beauty," Jason muttered. He took his jacket off, gingerly sat down on it, and awkwardly pushed off. He'd hoped there might be some possibility of slowing his descent or at least controlling it. No. It was like flying. He shot down the chute like a rocket—he could hear Dreyfus shrieking as she followed a few seconds behind.

He landed hard on what felt like rotted cushions on crumbling hay bales, and rolled out of the way in time to avoid getting hit by Dreyfus.

"Are you okay?" Jason scrambled over to where he could hear Dreyfus panting. "Dreyfus?"

She moaned. "I'm okay. Where the heck are we?"

"I'm guessing the basement." He helped her up. "I bet there's an exit around here somewhere."

More valuable time was lost stumbling around in the dark. There was some natural light provided by a bank of high windows, but not enough to keep them from crashing into the old concession stands and falling over broken planks in the floor.

At last they found the exit, pushing open the door. The gray daylight seemed dazzling, and the smells of car exhaust and rain were sweet compared to the smells inside the building.

Jason and Dreyfus splashed through puddles on their way around to the front of the building.

Boz was long gone. No surprise there. The surprise was that he'd left his pistol lying on the inside of the doorway. Had he dropped it and not realized?

Jason stared at the silver gun. His scalp prickled.

He bent to pick up the weapon.

Shit. Shit. *Shit.*

That's what fear did to you. Colored your vision so that you thought you were looking down the barrel of a Smith & Wesson .357 Magnum when in fact you were staring at an 11" Abbott's New Bang Gun, circa late forties, probably.

He swore quietly.

"What's the matter?" Dreyfus asked.

He showed her the pistol. Her eyes widened.

"Yeah. Exactly." He pulled the trigger, and four tiny arms sprang into view above the barrel. Red and yellow discs spelled out the word B-A-N-G.

One of the unexpected perks of unofficially consulting on another agency's case was Jason was not required to wait around for the cops with Dreyfus or help her fill out reports. In fact, he was strongly encouraged by SAC Reynolds to get his ass out of there.

Jason interpreted that to mean his "unofficial" assistance really *was* unofficial—something cooked up by Sam and Reynolds all on their own—and would probably be defined by the Bureau brass as unauthorized and unwarranted.

He told Dreyfus he would meet her back at the office when she was finished talking to Cheyenne PD, and headed over to Boz's Brew.

Terry looked up as the pixie dust door chimes announced Jason's return.

"Hi! Welcome to the largest selection of *oh*." His face fell. "It's you."

"Yep. It's me."

Jason limped down the aisle to the sales counter where Terry had been screwing D-rings into the back of a heavy-framed photograph of a mustached man in a tuxedo. The man sprawled on the floor, gazed up in wonder at an angel—or more likely a ghost. The ghost was surrounded by floating magical instruments, and intriguingly, a disembodied hand.

The caption at the bottom of the photo read: *Spirit photograph of the Dutch magician E. Chambly, ca. 1890.*

The rivalry between mediums and magicians had been fierce in the early days of Spiritualism. Some magicians incorporated elements of the occult and supernatural into their acts, but others, like Houdini, believed they had a mission to expose the frauds and tricksters.

Jason said, "I'd like to ask you a few questions."

"You kind of already did."

"A few more questions."

Terry said reluctantly, "I guess."

"Where do you store extra stock?"

"The storeroom."

"What about off-site?"

Terry looked confused. "We don't have an off-site storage facility. We don't keep that much extra stock. Everything is pretty much out on the floor."

"What about large items?"

"How large? Boz is refurbishing a Chinese Water Torture Cell in the back. That's about the biggest item we've handled."

Jason thought it over. "What about other magic stores? Who are your competitors around town?"

"What other magic stores?" Terry scoffed. "Mostly everything is sold online these days. From props to tricks. There aren't many places left like Boz's Brew. Not in Wyoming, that's for sure."

"Hm. Good point." Jason considered Terry's indignant expression. "Why do you think your boss ran like that?"

"He doesn't like cops."

"We're not the cops. We're the feds."

Terry said with an unexpected flash of humor, "*Nobody* likes the feds."

"Ouch." Jason smiled. "I know he's got a record. And I know he and Michael Khan were pals."

"Maybe."

"No?"

Terry said, "Michael Khan only cared about Michael Khan."

"What makes you think so?"

"Do you know he's the Kubla Khanjurer?"

"No," Jason lied. "What's a Kubla Khanjurer?"

"It's not a what. It's a who. Khan was a hack. He couldn't cut it as a real magician, so he tried to build a career out of revealing the secrets of magic."

"The secrets of magic? And that made people angry?"

Terry said hotly, "Of course it made people angry. Khan tried to claim that it was because he loved magic so much that he wanted to force magicians to abandon old and tired tricks and reinvent the art so that it would be able to compete in the modern world. It was total self-serving bullshit. He didn't care if the art was able to compete. He didn't care if he ruined peoples' acts and spoiled everything for the audience. He didn't care about magic—real magic—he just wanted to make a fast buck, and that was the only way he could."

"Is that how most people feel? People within the community, I mean."

"That's how everyone feels. His own wife can't stand him."

"But he and Boz managed to stay friends? He helped Boz open this store?"

Terry said grudgingly, "Yes."

Jason gazed around the room appreciatively. "It really is a great store. It probably functions as a center for the magic community?"

"Yes. But it's all changed now even from when I was little."

"Those posters are amazing. They're the real thing?"

Terry's smile was genuine. "Oh yeah. Absolutely."

"Where do you find stuff like that?"

"Auctions. Estate sales. The Internet. Yard sales. People bring in stuff. They don't always know what they've got." He studied Jason curiously. "Are you interested in magic?"

"Not like I was when I was a kid, but I appreciate a good magic show."

Terry said wisely, "Magic is performance art, but it's also a way of life."

"I'm beginning to see that. Who do you think killed Michael Khan?"

Terry stared at him as though the question did not compute. He said finally, tentatively, "Whoever stole his collection?"

"Your boss suggested Khan stole his own collection."

Terry blinked that over for a moment. "You mean the whole thing was sleight-of-hand?"

"That's an interesting way to put it." Jason glanced down at the framed sepia photo. "When people bring things in—people off the street, I mean—what's your policy for handling items that aren't accompanied by original bills of sale?"

Terry looked taken aback. "Almost nothing that comes in like that is accompanied by bills of sale. We don't...don't check for provenance, if that's what you mean. We're not an art gallery or a museum. We're more like a thrift store."

Not with posters going for three to five grand, they weren't, but Jason just nodded. "I see. Just out of curiosity, where were you Friday night?"

Terry licked his lips. "Me?"

Jason nodded.

"At a memorial service for a friend."

"Where was the service held?"

"At a pub. Hocus Pocus. It's on East 17th Street."

A memorial service at a pub? A magic-themed pub at that. Jason made a mental note. "Was Boz there?"

"Maybe for a little while. I don't recall. If he was, he didn't stay."

"Do you have any idea where Boz might go now?"

Terry looked confused. "You didn't catch him?"

"No. We didn't catch him."

"I don't know."

"Does he have family here? Friends?"

"I don't—I don't think so. He's from Florida, not Cheyenne. He's only been here a few years."

Jason held Terry's gaze. "Do you think he might get in contact with you?"

Terry looked terrified. "*Me?* No. I just work for him."

After a moment, Jason handed Terry his card. "If he does get in contact with you, give me a call. He assaulted a federal officer, so *now* he's in trouble."

Terry took the card gingerly. "Okay. Is she—the other agent—okay?"

"Yes. She is. She's not happy, though, so you definitely don't want to get between her and Boz."

"No, no. Of course not. He wouldn't come to me anyway. He'd—" He stopped, his expression stricken.

Jason smiled. "So there *is* someone you think he might turn to?"

If Terry had looked uncomfortable before, he looked agonized now. "No, not really. I mean… Not really."

"Terry, do yourself a favor. Don't lie to a federal agent."

"Elle Diamond."

"And Elle is…?"

"They used to be together. I think maybe Boz still— It wouldn't be Elle's fault or anything. But she's got such a big heart. I don't think she could turn anyone away. She has a ranch out near Lake Hattie. Really, it's an animal preserve. She runs a rescue for mistreated circus and magic-show animals."

"What's the name of this ranch?"

"China Creek."

"Okay. Thank you. Can you think of anything else that might be helpful?"

Terry slowly shook his head. "He was trying to rebuild his act, you know."

"Who? Boz? As a magician, you mean?"

"Yes. He wrangled it so he was going to be one of the opening acts this weekend. There's a new magic club opening up."

"Top Hat White Rabbit?" Jason asked.

Terry looked as amazed as if Jason had pulled his own white rabbit out of a top hat. "Yes. That's right. He hadn't performed in front of a big crowd for years, so he was kind of nervous."

Was that supposed to explain Boz's guilty behavior?

"Thank you," Jason said. "Don't forget you've got my number if Boz contacts you—or if you think of anything that might be helpful."

"I won't forget," Terry said.

As Jason was on his way out, he passed a shelf of vintage magic kits. A 1960s Zenith Magic, a 1970s Remco Magic Kit, and a 1990s Pressman Magic Act Kit… There were plenty of new kits too. He pointed to the 1940s 102 E-Z Magic Starter Kit for Kids & Adult Magicians. "I had one of these. It was used. Half the booklet got soaked and was unreadable, but I still loved it."

Terry said, "Yeah? It would be worth something now."

Jason smiled. "It was worth something then."

Chapter Fourteen

"I can't believe I walked right into that punch." Dreyfus moaned.

She was sitting behind her desk, holding a plastic bag of ice against her swollen face. They had been going over their case, such as it was, for the last ten minutes.

"I still don't understand why you went after him," Jason said. "We didn't have anything on him. He was within his rights to refuse to answer our questions."

She raised her head and glared. "Why did he run, then?"

"Sometimes people do."

"Why'd he punch me, then?"

"I don't know. I'd say he really, really doesn't want to go back to prison." They'd already had it out over her leaving her partner in the dust and failing to wait for backup. No need to belabor the point. He liked the fact that she had taken the reprimand without getting angry or defensive. He liked that she took a black eye with a sturdy sort of resignation. He liked *her*. She was green, but she had guts and grit.

She shook her head. "Did we get *anywhere* today?"

"Sure we did. We learned that almost everyone believes Michael Khan was behind the theft of his own collection—and that there's no shortage of suspects in Khan's murder." He added hastily, "Not that the last is relevant, because we're not investigating Khan's murder."

Dreyfus muttered her discontent and shifted the ice pack.

"We learned that Minerva Khan looks to have an airtight alibi on the night of the theft. Although we also learned she claims to have total recall, yet told investigators she has trouble remembering the security codes to her own home."

"Hey, that's right."

"She's strong and she's got nerve, but judging by her skimpy stage costume, she doesn't appear to have sustained any injuries or bruising, which she probably would have if she had garroted her husband."

"She could have hired someone."

"True. And it sounds like there was no love lost there, but most people settle for slaughtering each other in court. Anyway." Jason once again remembered that they were not investigating the murder of Michael Khan. He said briskly, "If Ian Boz is to be believed, we learned that although Khan planned to steal his collection, someone else got there first. Unless Khan accused Boz in an attempt to cover his own tracks."

"But is the word of a con man and trickster to be believed?"

"Probably not. Boz certainly has the knowledge and resources to traffic the Khan collection. Khan obviously thought Boz would make the ideal fence. And we know Boz does not have an alibi for the night the Khan collection vanished or he'd have offered that up."

"True. And the same of Sunday night."

"Maybe. Although he might not realize Khan was killed Sunday night. I don't think the Sheriff's Office has made a statement to the press yet."

They fell silent. The rain spattered soundlessly against the bullet-proof window, blurring the view of the parking lot.

"Why do you think there are so few female magicians?" Dreyfus asked suddenly.

"Not sure. It probably wasn't considered respectable? Women weren't supposed to go on the stage."

"But I mean even now, it seems like there are relatively few female magicians."

"Yeah, I don't know."

Dreyfus said, "I looked up the meaning of that tarot card they found in Khan's pocket. The Fool. It means the start of a new journey. New beginnings. Everything is still possible."

Jason looked up from his phone. He kept hoping for a text from Sam, but nope. Nada. Out of sight, out of mind, apparently. No messages from anyone. It was like he'd fallen into another dimension. "Doesn't the meaning change depending on whether the card is upright or reversed?"

"Yes, but I think we have to assume the intended meaning would be the upright because Khan's killer would have to know there's no guarantee in what position the card would be found."

"You don't want to make assumptions about an unsub's thought process." He stopped. "Wait. Wasn't the card found at the scene The Hanged Man?"

Dreyfus looked confused. Her eyes widened. She laughed. "Oh my gosh. You're right. Where did I come up with The Fool?"

"Not sure."

"I was looking at a bunch of different cards and their meanings. I guess I got distracted."

She picked up her phone as though preparing to re-google. Jason said, "Honestly, it doesn't matter. For all we know, Khan carried that card as a talisman or good luck charm. Or the card was added to the crime scene simply to throw investigators off the trail."

She gave him an exasperated look. He shared her frustration. At the minimum, being barred from including Khan's homicide in their investigation reduced their access to potentially helpful information gleaned at the murder scene. He'd have to wait for Sam's return to know what, if anything discovered at Vedauwoo, related to their case.

Sam.

His heart warmed in anticipation of that eventual homecoming. To distract himself, Jason said, "I wonder why Boz panicked the instant he saw we were federal agents."

"That should be obvious!"

"Maybe. But we didn't have anything on him. According to him, there's nothing to have. At least as far as the Khan investigation is concerned."

Dreyfus said, "That reminds me. I spoke to George Cohen, Khan's agent, and Khan did show up for their dinner Friday night. He didn't leave until around nine thirty."

"Then regardless of whether Khan set up the burglary, we know he wasn't actually on the premises when it occurred. What about the security footage from the neighbors? We want to keep on top of that. It's our best bet for getting a look at who showed up in the moving van."

"I'll check with Detective Ward at Cheyenne PD."

Jason nodded. "I've got a few calls in to people. I heard back from Arlo Presley at Potter & Potter, and he says no one has contacted them about the collection."

"That makes sense if Khan stole his own collection. He wasn't planning to sell anything. He was just going to sit on it until the divorce was over and he thought it was safe."

"Maybe. The thing is, I don't think it's a coincidence the Khan collection disappeared right before this magic convention."

"What do you mean?"

"Everyone I've spoken to seems to agree the magic community is the obvious and best customer for those stolen items. This convention means a bunch of potential consumers are about to arrive on the scene."

"Uh-oh."

"Uh-oh is right."

Dreyfus sighed. "It's almost five. Too late to tackle Elle Diamond tonight. You want to try to interview her tomorrow?" She gazed at Jason hopefully with her one good eye.

"Sure. Okay." After today's performance he was not leaving Dreyfus on her own to sort this thing out. His heart had nearly stopped when he'd seen that pistol turn her way. Not on his watch. He'd rather be shot himself.

"We could grab some dinner and keep talking over the case?"

Jason sat up straight. "Oh, *hell*," he exclaimed. "I've already got a dinner date—and I'm going to be late."

* * * * *

"I was beginning to think you weren't going to make it." Ruby pushed wide the back door to the kitchen, and Jason waded through the flock of poodles.

"Sorry I'm late. I needed to shower." He felt a little off-balance. He couldn't help wanting to make a good impression with Sam's mom. Not only was he late, he should have picked up flowers or a bottle of wine, but Dreyfus had been kind enough to give him a ride, and he hadn't wanted to ask her to make an extra stop.

"Don't you worry about it. You're here now."

"It smells wonderful in here."

It did. The smell of roasting meat and simmering vegetables filled the warm, cheerfully lit room.

One of the poodles suddenly screeched, and Jason jumped, afraid he had stepped on it.

"Adele! You stop biting Remy. You bad girl. They get overexcited," Ruby informed Jason. "What would you like to drink?"

"Anything." Wait. He didn't want to sound like a raving alcoholic. "Beer?"

"Sure. Or I've got Canadian Club, if you like it. It's what Sam drinks. Same as his Uncle Jim."

"That's fine too." In fact, the idea of Canadian Club was kind of comforting—or maybe that was just the thought of Sam. Jason asked, "Do you have a lot of family in Wyoming?"

"Not a lot. Jim's living in Florida now. Our folks are gone. I've got a bunch of cousins, nieces, and nephews, but we've never been that close."

"Right." He remembered that she'd been an unwed mother at sixteen. What had that been like nearly fifty years ago in rural Wyoming? Probably not a whole lot of fun.

"I hope you're hungry. We're having leg of lamb for dinner. That used to be one of Sam's favorites when he was a boy."

"I'm starving," Jason said, which was true. He hadn't had much for breakfast, and there had been no time for lunch.

One of the poodles nipped his ankle, and he jumped again. "*Ow!*"

Ruby spun away from the counter. "Esme, what have I told you about that?" She handed Jason his drink and shoveled up the dogs in one scoop. They were already howling protest before she closed the laundry room door on them.

"Usually dogs like me." He was chagrined her dogs regarded him with such suspicion.

"Don't take it personal. Those hooligans don't like anyone. I guess they're spoiled, but then they're the only grandkids I'm going to get, I guess."

Jason sipped his drink and said nothing. He wasn't about to touch that one.

"Mashed potatoes and gravy okay?"

"Sounds great," Jason answered honestly. He squatted down to inspect the framed photos on the corner shelf of the island. He smiled faintly at the towheaded second-grader Sam. "What did Sam want to grow up to be when he was this age?"

Ruby threw the photo an indulgent look. "Not a policeman. He wanted to be a very rich rancher."

Jason laughed.

"It's the truth. Not just a rich rancher. A *very* rich rancher." Ruby snorted at that long-ago memory.

"He doesn't seem like the ranching type."

"Not anymore." Ruby began to whisk the gravy using juice from the meat, honey, and a lot of whisky. She said after a moment, "I wasn't like the other moms in the PTA." Her chuckle was derisive. "It used to make him mad that people thought they were better than us. Better than me." She smiled. "Back then he thought being rich would change that."

It got to Jason in a funny way. The idea of that little, long-ago Sam feeling humiliated and scorned by a bunch of small-minded hicks, wanting to defend and protect his young mother by getting rich and... well, however the rest of that childhood fantasy played out.

"It seems like you've done okay for yourself."

"Oh yeah," Ruby said, still smiling. "You're damned right I did. And Sam did too."

They chatted briefly about Jason's day—Jason leaving out the more interesting parts—while Ruby finished preparing the meal, then moved to the dining room and the nicely set table.

Fine china and crystal stemware. Jason was flattered. Plus, the food was very good. He saw where Sam got his knack for cooking.

Jason listened to Ruby talk about her involvement in various community projects and participation in clubs and committees. Clearly, she was a wealth of information, but it was innocuous stuff. He realized she was not as indiscreet as he'd originally thought.

"Sam likes me to stay involved," she said a little sardonically—yet again reminding Jason of Sam. "He thinks I need to stay busy so I won't get lonely."

"Well..."

"Like I don't have enough to keep me busy." She shook her head.

Ruby drank quite a bit. She wasn't drunk, but she was always talkative, and the alcohol made her more so. Sam liked to drink too, but drunk or sober, he had not inherited Ruby's loquacious streak.

Although Ethan's name was mentioned in passing, there were no revelations over dinner, and Jason relaxed. Nothing was said that Sam would care about, and Jason was now sure that Ruby had not been trying to make some point when she had first spoke to him about Ethan.

Jason was drinking too, though, because when they finally reached the stage of freshly baked cowboy cookies and coffee (spiked, naturally, with still more booze), he heard himself asking, "When did Sam and Ethan meet?"

It was as though she'd been waiting for him to bring up the topic. Ruby said at once, "Second to last year of high school."

He immediately regretted opening that line of conversation. He sincerely believed it would be a mistake to know too much about Ethan. He wanted to understand how losing Ethan had affected Sam, but he did not want to become preoccupied with Ethan himself—and that would be all too easy to do.

"They were the original odd couple."

"Ah." Jason tried to think of a way to change the subject.

"Sam always knew where he was going and what he wanted. Ethan was a dreamer. He tended to let things drift. It used to drive Sam crazy."

"I bet."

"Maybe it's the artistic temperament."

"Maybe."

"He just always figured everything would work out. And things did mostly work out for him. Until that last summer."

No, he really did not want to hear this. Did not want to know. "Does Sam have other friends still living in Cheyenne?"

"One or two, I guess. Charlie Reynolds. They go back a ways. Sawyer Hunt. Sam was always, well, choosy about his buddies."

Was that a nice way of saying Sam had always been a loner? But then, he hadn't been a loner. He'd had Ethan. And one or two friends who still lived locally.

When they finished dinner it was nearly ten. Ruby insisted on leaving the dishes, and Jason tactfully avoided yet another final drink, and walked back to the guest house.

The floodlit stretch of yard between the main and guest house seemed a long, windy walk. The shadows were deep, the silence profound. Common sense told him he was a lot safer in the middle of nowhere than his own high-crime neighborhood, but he still had a creepy-crawly feeling down his spine as he let himself into the guest house.

He'd left the lamps on in his hurry to shower and change, and the bright light and warmth were welcome. He slipped off his jacket and went into the kitchen for a drink of water. The stars outside the window over the sink were dazzlingly large and bright. Beyond the stars there didn't seem to be another light for as far as he could see.

He drank his water, set the glass in the sink.

He felt homesick—and he missed Sam. Ruby's reminiscences of Sam's boyhood had dissolved some of Jason's doubts, made him feel affectionate toward and protective of that long-ago Sam.

He checked his phone. Ten thirty and still no message. He was disappointed, but not worried. It would have been nice to hear Sam's voice before he turned in for the night, but okay. Knowing Sam, he was still working.

As he turned to go down the hall to the bedroom, he noticed the closed door of Sam's office.

Something about the way Sam always kept that door so firmly shut suddenly struck him. Maybe it wasn't odd, but...well, yes. It was odd.

Why? Why was that door always closed tight? Even when Sam stepped out to use the john, he closed the door completely behind him.

Maybe it was second nature. His job required him to routinely deal with a lot of sensitive information and disturbing materials, and it was natural that he would be careful about keeping his office locked. Restricting access to his office was probably automatic. But this wasn't Quantico. Jason wasn't support staff or a civilian. They were sharing a house. They were sort of a couple now.

In fact, before they'd been living together, Jason would have answered confidently that they *were* a couple now.

There was no reason for that closed door to raise his suspicions, and yet...

He walked down the hall to Sam's office and tried the handle. He half expected it to be locked, but the knob turned. He opened the door.

The room smelled of toner, paper, and faintly, comfortingly of Sam's aftershave. Jason felt for the wall switch. The overhead lamp came on.

There were several mostly empty bookshelves, a credenza filing cabinet upon which sat a fax machine/printer—its tray spilling over with printouts—a matching desk covered with papers and files.

It looked like Sam's desk at Quantico. It did not look like the desk of someone writing a book. Not that Jason knew what that would look like. He was exasperated though unsurprised to see Sam had brought his caseload with him.

He did not intend to snoop or spy. He would not have left the doorway at all except he happened to glance across and spotted his name scrawled on the whiteboard hanging opposite Sam's desk.

WEST circled in black with numerous spider legs leading to other names, also circled, which lead to smaller notes in green and red. The note leading from the name MARTIN PINK, for example, read: *lifer, solitary, restricted.* The note next to ERIC GREENLEAF read: *awaiting trial, monitored.* SHEPHERD DURRAND had the notation *unknown.*

His heart dropped. In fact, he felt like he was falling down a black and bottomless distance. Dropping like a stone into the abyss. Jason did not move. He barely breathed. He could not tear his gaze from that whiteboard with that spiderweb of arrows and notes and circles surrounding his name. He knew what it meant, but he couldn't seem to think past it.

Finally, he moved from the doorway and walked to Sam's desk. He picked up the file lying on top. In some faraway corner of his brain he wondered if these were the originals or if Sam kept copies of all his cases. He read the name on the file.

BIRD, CARL.

He opened the file.

As grisly as the photos were, he barely noticed them. Barely noticed anything but the word POSSIBLE scrawled across the top of the file in red marker. He blinked. Read some of the notes that had been highlighted.

In 2002, Carl Bird, already serving a life sentence, had been found guilty of trying to put a hit on then Special Agent Sam Kennedy. At his sentencing—which was surely as ho-hum as it got, given his existing stretch—Bird had vowed to wipe out Kennedy's entire family, including pets and "fucking house plants."

Jason set the file aside. Opened the next one. GILYEARD, MULLIN.

Another red-handed POSSIBLE. In 2010, convicted serial killer Gilyeard had escaped from Arizona State Prison and started across country on a quest to kill Special Agent Sam Kennedy. He murdered a gas-station attendant in Arkansas and a waitress in Tennessee before being recaptured. Gilyeard also vowed to slay everyone and everything that mattered to Kennedy.

Jason realized he was shaking. He sat down in Sam's chair. He was not afraid. He was sick. Not at the knowledge that his relationship with Sam made him a target in the eyes of some very disturbed people. He already knew that. What shook him to the core was the realization that Sam had lied to him.

"Is it possible someone you're investigating might try to distract you by getting rid of me?"

"It's not impossible."

"You'd considered that?"

"Yes. I'm considering all possibilities."

"Is it likely?"

"Very few people outside the Bureau are aware of our relationship. No, I don't think it's likely. But like I said, every avenue is being explored."

No. In fairness, Sam hadn't lied. He had admitted this was a possibility. But he had totally downplayed it, made it sound like the longest of long shots. When in fact, he believed it was a very real possibility. These files, these notes… This entire office was set up like an incident room. Worse. The scrawled notes and arrows, the highlighter and Post-it notes…it looked manic. It looked like the room of a conspiracy theorist. All that was missing was the cat's cradle of colored yarn and thumbtacks.

He was deeply shocked that Sam had kept all this hidden. He had a right to know. He had a right to be able to trust what Sam told him. This…rocked the foundation of their relationship, certainly his understanding of that relationship.

First there had been Ethan. Now this. What the hell else was Sam hiding?

His cell rang, and Jason sprang to his feet, on edge as if someone had thumped on the window. *Shadow on the Glass* indeed. His heart pounded as he checked the caller ID, and he was not reassured when he recognized the photo of Dirty Harry. In fact, he felt a little nauseated.

He almost let it go to message. But no, if he didn't answer, Sam would keep calling.

"West." His mouth was gummy, the word sounded thick.

"Hey." Sam's voice was warm. He sounded pleased, as though reaching Jason was a happy surprise and not the inevitable result of calling his cell phone.

Jason literally could think of nothing to say. He managed a stiff, "Hi."

"How's it going?"

Jason's gaze traveled to the scrawl-covered whiteboard. WEST circled in frantic thick strokes. "Okay."

"How's the ankle?"

He experienced a sudden and completely weird urge to cry. A very short time ago he had been desperate for any crumbs of concern and caring Sam thought to cast his way. Now...he didn't even know who Sam was.

"Better," he said.

"Any luck tracking that missing art collection?" There was a note of teasing in Sam's voice, and once again Jason's eyes stung.

"No." He made an effort. "How was your... Were you able to interview Bamburg?"

Sam answered. Jason had no idea what he said. Sam continued to talk, and Jason continued to think in that roaring silence.

Sam said suddenly, "Are you all right? You sound like you're catching cold."

"Yes," Jason said. "Tired."

"You're sure?"

"Yes. Of course."

"You sound... You don't sound..." Funny to hear that uncertainty in Sam's voice.

Jason tried to pull himself together. He had to give Sam a chance to explain. However strange and unreasonable Sam's behavior seemed, he was clearly trying to protect Jason. He deserved to be able to offer his side.

But it wasn't even that clear-cut. It wasn't that Sam had a different version of events. What different version could there be? It was more like Jason had been granted a peek into Sam's brain, and what he had discovered seething there appalled him.

He said automatically, "Sorry. Nothing's happened. I'm just beat. And this situation is... wearing on me."

"Jason—"

"I'd like to...want to...talk it over with you when you get back."

"Yeah, of course." Sam's tone took on that odd, almost tender timbre. "We'll talk it all out when I'm back. Meantime, try not to worry."

Jason gave a half laugh. "Sure."

"If you do feel unsafe, the sheriff—"

"I don't feel unsafe."

"Okay." Sam hesitated.

"Are you still coming back tomorrow?"

Sam gave a funny laugh. "Didn't we just discuss this?"

Had they? Jason had no recollection. "Right."

"I'll see you tomorrow evening."

Jason said mechanically, "See you."

After another hesitation, Sam disconnected.

Jason sat motionless, watching the screen of his cell go dark.

Chapter Fifteen

It took him a long time to fall asleep.

It was not easy to scrub the memories of the photos he had seen—which was surprising because at the time he hadn't thought they even registered. All those blood-drenched Rorschach spatters and sprays.

When he did finally manage to put them out of his mind, it was only because he started thinking about Jeremy Kyser. Now there was a guy to keep you up all night—and not in a good way.

"I am curious about your secrets. I sensed a natural affinity at our first meeting. I will contact you soon to explain how we may work together. With admiration and affection."

Etcetera. Etcetera. Etcetera.

He knew perfectly well, from numerous academy courses, that stalking was always about the stalker and not the victim. Yet he still couldn't help feeling that somehow, he'd done something to bring this about. That somehow this was his fault. His failure.

But mostly what kept his brain running for hours through its painful, endlessly winding and rewinding loop was the thought of Sam. Sam whose unexpected thoughtfulness in picking up a bag of potato chips or a pair of warm socks could melt Jason's heart—or freeze same heart by interrogating Jason as if he was a suspect at a crime scene. Sam, who acted—*acted*—as bland and offhand as if they were on some tropical vacation, all the while covertly running a one-man protection task force.

Jesus Christ. Those notes and jottings had looked *frenzied*.

Yet Sam had pretended to be as blank and businesslike as if…as if…

We can't go on like this.

His heart ached at the logical conclusion, but he could not envision any scenario where Sam even really listened to him, let alone conceded. Because Sam did not think Jason got a say in this. Any of this.

"Come to think of it, I've got a lot more experience in every area than you do."

In Sam's view they were not equals. Never had been. Never would be.

Where did that leave them?

Nowhere.

Around three a.m. he dozed off—and a couple of minutes later the poodles began to bark.

Jason's eyes flew open. He rolled over, grabbed his pistol, and got out of bed, wincing at the pain flashing through his unbound ankle.

Seriously. Of all the dumbest movie-of-the-week clichés: *a sprained ankle*? Like some goddamned romantic-suspense movie heroine.

He hobbled over to the front window, peered through the blind. Ruby had turned the floodlights on—or maybe they were attached to motion sensors? Anyway, a battery of lights brightly illuminated the yard between the main house and guest house.

Damp fog had rolled in during the last few hours, shrouding the trees, the coils of chicken wire, and old oil drums. Nothing moved.

The dogs continued to raise the alarm.

Unease slithered down his spine.

Maybe they did this all the time.

Maybe not.

His heart was beating hard and fast against his collarbone. His Glock felt weirdly heavy. Were his hands *shaking*? For God's sake. Because a pack of four-footed throw pillows were yapping?

Pull yourself together, West.

No wonder Kennedy thought he couldn't take care of himself.

He continued to listen, his ears sifting night sounds: the dogs, the metal squeak of the blinds, the scratch of brush against the house siding.

Stop. Go back.

There was no brush against the house. No shrubs. No trees. Nothing that should be scraping against the outside—and no wind to shake the branches anyway.

There it was again. Traveling beneath the side windows, moving around to...where? The back door?

Jason's heart stopped. Had he locked that door?

He let out a breath. Yes. Both the front and back doors had secondary locks. Single-sided deadbolts. The back door had been locked when he turned in. He remembered checking.

Now that he was sure there really was something out there, Jason steadied. His training kicked in. There was protocol for this.

It could be an animal, of course. He needed to verify he wasn't dealing with a raccoon before he summoned the sheriffs. That would be...embarrassing. At the least.

He listened, tracking the movement down the side of the house, very slight, very quiet. It very likely *was* an animal. Hopefully not a bear. Could a 9mm stop a bear? No, it wasn't a bear. A bear would not be subtle. Whatever—whoever—was moving around out there, they were making an effort to conceal their activity.

Jason moved quietly to the front door, easing it open. He slipped outside, so keyed up he barely felt the cold through his sweatshirt or the frozen ground beneath his bare feet. He tiptoed down the length of the building, the pain of his ankle a far off, unimportant thing, his senses attuned to every sound in the fuzzy gloom.

The lights were on at the main house. The dogs were still going nuts as he picked his silent, careful way around the front and side of the guest house, and then risked a quick look around the corner.

First peek, he didn't see anything. He ducked back.

Second time, his eyes searched the darkness, and his heart stopped as he made out a motionless form standing beside the back door.

He looked harder, focusing on that out-of-place figure. Were his eyes playing tricks? Was that really... Yes. A slight shadow among the other shadows. As he stared, he began to pick out the pattern of a flannel shirt, the glint of fair hair, the gleam of eyes.

Whoever this was, it was not Jeremy Kyser.

He brought his weapon up and stepped out, ready to use the corner of the house to shield himself if he had to. He said loudly, "Nice way to get your head blown off."

There was an audible gasp. The shadow jumped and whirled his way, hands rising up defensively.

"Don't shoot. Please. Don't." The shaking voice was barely above a whisper. "It's me. Terry."

"Terry?"

For a second, he couldn't remember a Terry. Then it clicked. The kid at the magic store. Boz's clerk. Terry Van der Beck.

"What the hell are you doing sneaking around here?"

"I-I have to tell you something."

Jason snapped, "Try knocking on the door first. I could have shot you!"

"I can't—I'm afraid he's watching me."

This was very weird. How had the kid known where to find him? Jason did not lower his weapon. He did not like this one little bit. "Who? What are you talking about?"

"Boz."

"What about Boz?"

"I think he..." Terry swallowed the words, managed, "Might come after me."

"Why would he come after you?"

No answer. He saw motion as the kid shook his head.

"You're not making a lot of sense," Jason said. "If you're afraid of Boz, why wouldn't you tell me that this afternoon?" He threw a quick, uneasy look over his shoulder. The dogs had fallen silent. The floodlights had gone out again. The fuzzy darkness seemed to swirl around them.

"I have to go." Terry began to sidle away.

Jason hesitated. Should he hold him for the cops? This whole situation was definitely hinky. But an arrest for trespassing? A little severe. And what if he was telling the truth?

"Wait. What is it you came out here to tell me?"

Terry stopped. "Michael Khan came to the shop Sunday evening."

"Khan did? You're sure?"

"We were closed. I came back to get my jacket. They didn't hear me. Khan and Boz were in the back arguing. I snuck out again."

"Did you see Boz attack Khan? Did you see him kill Khan?"

"No."

"Why didn't you report this to the police?"

"Nobody came to interview me but you."

"Nobody's interviewed you? At all?"

"Only you. I thought—it doesn't matter. I think maybe Boz did something bad. I don't know for sure. But if he did, he might start wondering if I noticed anything."

"*Did* you notice anything?" Jason asked. "Beyond seeing Khan there that night?"

There was no answer.

He took a step forward, peering into the darkness.

Terry was gone.

*　*　*　*　*

A small, shaggy black and white goat was riding a chunky palomino pony around and around a large corral.

In the center of the ring stood a tall woman with long black hair. She wore jeans, a sheepskin coat, and a cowboy hat. Every so often she whistled commands to the animals.

When she spotted Jason and Dreyfus, she put her fingers to her mouth, gave a final sharp whistle. The pony slowed to a trot before a small red staircase. The goat dismounted as the woman climbed over the fence to meet them.

"That's not magic." Dreyfus' tone was critical. "That's animal abuse."

"It's supposed to be an animal rescue," Jason said. "Maybe this is occupational training."

The pony was now chasing the goat around the corral. Jason wasn't sure if they were playing or not.

Dreyfus restricted herself to a sound of disgust. Diamond was now in earshot.

Maybe Ian Boz had been serious when he had thrown out the name Zatanna Zatara, because this woman looked uncannily like the DC Comics magician and superhero. Her eyes, a brilliant blue, studied Dreyfus' black eye and Jason's healing bruises. "IRS, I presume?" she drawled.

"Ha. Funny," Jason said. "Elle Diamond, I presume?"

"That's right."

"FBI." Dreyfus showed her badge. "Agents Dreyfus and West. We're investigating the theft of a valuable art and antique collection at the home of Michael and Minerva Khan."

Diamond said, "Really? I heard you were hunting Ian Boz."

Given her lack of surprise, Jason was confident Terry Van der Beck had already warned her the feds would soon be on her doorstep. By now, Terry had probably warned everyone in the magic community—maybe that's what he'd been up to last night. A creepy take on Paul Revere making his rounds. Jason still didn't know what to make of Terry's visit.

Dreyfus continued, "In connection with the theft at the Khan home."

"Don't look for him here."

Jason glanced toward the surrounding barns and pens. "Not a bad place to hide."

Dreyfus said, "Where *do* you suggest we look?"

"How should I know? If you've got a warrant, you can look where you want."

A warrant. Now that was interesting.

Jason said, "We're just here to ask a few questions, ma'am. We understand that you and Boz are friends. Maybe more than friends."

She was not exactly beautiful. Her eyes were oddly slanted and her high Slavic cheekbones were a little too sharp, but she was striking. Put her in a top hat and black sequins, and she'd be mesmerizing. Way out of Boz's class, goats and ponies notwithstanding.

Diamond said, "We know each other."

Jason smiled. "It's a little more than that, isn't it?" He felt Dreyfus' look of surprise.

Diamond's eyes narrowed. "Says who?"

You just did. But Jason only smiled again.

Diamond's hair was severely straight and reached all the way to her waist. It reminded him of a horse's tail, and when she tossed her head, the equine resemblance was even greater. "Well, what of it? That was over a long time ago."

"Maybe so," Jason said. "But you're in the business of rescue and rehabilitation, so we have to ask."

Diamond laughed. She mimicked, "Maybe so, but I draw the line at big, dumb animals that forge checks."

"That'll put a strain on a friendship."

"Yes."

"What else can you tell us about Boz?" Dreyfus asked.

Diamond regarded Dreyfus for a moment. "Do I know you?"

"No." Dreyfus threw Jason a quick, uneasy look. "I don't think so."

"Funny. You look like a girl I used to know. Andy Alexander. She was part of a brother and sister act."

"I was never part of any magic act." Dreyfus sounded mildly out-raged. "Can you please just answer the question?"

Diamond shrugged. "Anyway, I can tell you this. The forged checks were a long time ago. Boz isn't— He didn't have anything to do with the theft of Mike Khan's collection."

Jason said, "What makes you say that?"

"Minerva Khan. She's the one you want to look at."

"Minerva? She seems to have a pretty solid alibi. Performing her act in front of almost five hundred people at a private company function."

"Things are not always what they seem."

"Now there speaks a magician."

Diamond said, "I don't blame Minerva. Khan was a piece of work."

Dreyfus said, "You believe Minerva Khan is behind the death of her husband?"

Diamond looked startled. "I didn't mean that. No. Minerva isn't a murderess. I meant I don't blame her for orchestrating the theft of that collection. From one perspective, the collection was half hers. She's the one who really supported them for the past ten years. But Wyoming isn't a community-property state. Also, the legal ownership of a number of items in the collection is in question. The one area where Khan really *was* a magician was in finagling the books. There's a reason he was known as the Kubla Con."

"You're speaking from experience?" Jason asked.

"Yes. I am. Not mine, though. Boz's. Among others within the community."

"It's interesting you say this," Jason said. "Everyone else, including Boz, has suggested Khan orchestrated the theft of his collection."

Her brows rose, but it was polite inquiry, not surprise. She was not at all surprised.

"Maybe Boz already told you that," Jason said. "When was the last time you saw him?"

"Who? Khan or Boz?"

Jason said, "Both."

"It's a long time since I've seen Michael Khan. Months at least." She squinted thoughtfully. "Boz? I'm not sure. Last week, I think."

"At the memorial Friday night?" Jason suggested.

He could tell by her eyes he'd scored, but he was unclear how or why.

"I don't remember if he was there for the entire service. People came and went."

"But he was there for part of the service?"

"I don't remember. It was a difficult night for me. Mateo was not young, but...even so."

The name rang a bell, though Jason couldn't quite place it. "Mateo?"

She combed her hair out of her face. "Mateo Santos. He is—was— the most highly regarded close-up magician in the entire Western United States." Her voice was cool, but Jason didn't think he had imagined the flash of pain when she'd first mentioned Mateo's name.

"Close-up magician?" Dreyfus questioned.

Jason said, "Table magic. Magic performed right there with the audience standing around you. Sleight-of-hand, misdirection, cardistry."

"He was so much more than that," Diamond said impatiently. "Mateo's thoughts on the art were so...significant. So far beyond the rest of us. Not since the Professor, has anyone so profoundly understood the mysteries of both psyche and...spirit." She turned away to wipe her eyes.

"I'm sorry for your loss," Jason said.

Diamond said in a suffocated voice, "Mateo's death is everyone's loss. Everyone in this community."

Dreyfus had an odd expression on her face.

"Who else attended the memorial service on Friday?" Jason asked.

"Everyone."

Patently not. She couldn't recall if Boz had been there. Khan had been meeting with his agent. Minerva was performing at her corporate event.

"Was Terry Van der Beck there?"

"I'm sure he was."

He believed her grief was genuine, but that she was perhaps playing up the extent of her distress. Diamond was a cool customer. She probably had a more accurate idea of who had attended the memorial service—and for how long—than she was letting on.

"Did either of the Khans stop by at any point during the evening?"

"No."

"You said that you believe Minerva Khan is behind the theft of her husband's art collection. Putting aside hocus-pocus for the moment, how do you think she could have managed that?"

Diamond's expression was impassive. After a moment, she said, "I would imagine she hired someone. Or, more likely, she asked Ted Fields to hire someone. Ted is Minerva's longtime manager—and current boyfriend."

"Interesting." Jason handed her his card. "If you can think of anything else that might be of help..."

She tucked the card away without comment.

Dreyfus said suddenly, "Why do you think there are so few female magicians?"

Diamond considered her for a thoughtful moment. "Men don't like to be tricked by women."

"Do they like to be tricked by other men?" Jason asked.

"They consider the risk to be part of their normal competitive dynamic." She shrugged. "Just an opinion, of course."

"One last thing," Jason said. "If Ian Boz is not involved in Michael Khan's death or the theft of the Khan collection, can you think of any reason he'd panic at the sight of federal agents on his doorstep?"

She made a sound that was disarmingly close to a groan. "God. Poor Boz."

"Not following," said Jason.

"Did you ever hear the story of a T-Rex named Sue and the Federal Government's insane persecution of the paleontologists who uncovered the fossil?"

Jason winced. "Yes."

"*That's* why. Not everything in Boz's shop is going to pass government inspection, if you get my drift. We're not talking serious violations, but Boz is, I think understandably, paranoid."

She turned at the sound of tires on dirt. A battered green pickup bounced down the pothole-riddled road and pulled into the nearby lot already occupied by horse trailers, a small moving van, and two old-fashioned red and gold circus train stock cars.

A slender, fair-haired man got out.

Jason shaded his eyes. "Is that Terry Van der Beck?"

Diamond's expression softened. "Yes. Terry helps out with the animals. He has a wonderful energy. They love him."

"Speaking of help, thank you for yours," Dreyfus said.

Diamond didn't reply.

"That was a waste of time," Dreyfus said as they walked back to her Dodge sedan G-ride.

"Do you think so?" Jason was surprised.

"She tap-danced around every question. You'll notice she blamed the theft on the one person who has a rock-solid alibi."

"I did notice that."

Terry stood beside his truck, watching them as they approached. When Jason's eyes met his, Terry scowled.

"What's his problem?" Dreyfus muttered when they were in the car and buckling up.

"Not sure." He almost added, *he seemed okay skulking around my house last night*, but it wasn't actually funny—plus he hadn't mentioned his moonlight encounter with Terry to Dreyfus, though he wasn't quite sure why.

Terry was still unmoving, still scowling as they got in their car and drove slowly past.

Chapter Sixteen

Ted Fields was with a client, but his secretary—a leggy nineteen-year-old who looked like her night job was Magician's Assistant—insisted on ushering them into Fields' office anyway.

"Ted, it's the FBI!" she announced.

There were two men in the office. A blandly handsome, middle-aged blond sat in front of the desk, shuffling a deck of cards like some people unconsciously caressed rosaries. At the receptionist's announcement the cards went flying up in a paper fountain—but then landed neatly back in his right hand. The man behind the desk—Ted Fields—was older, darker, and more dangerous-looking. He reminded Jason of Vegas crooners circa 1960s—the mob connected ones.

Fields sat back in his chair. "How can I help you, gentle— Oh." His dark eyes popped. "Baby, what happened to *you*?"

Dreyfus did *not* like being called *baby*. She made like Wonder Woman with her badge. "Special Agent Dreyfus. This is Special Agent West. May we have a word, sir?"

Fields put up his hands, grinning. "Say no more, Officer. I have an alibi. You can talk freely in front of this gentleman."

"An alibi for what?" Jason asked with interest.

"For anything you want to hang on me." He put his hands down. "No, seriously. For Michael's murder. Minerva and I were dining out Sunday night. We had reservations for eight o'clock at L'Osteria Mondello. We arrived early. After dinner we ran into friends and ended up staying until ten; then we went back to my place where we spent the rest of the night."

That was nice and pat—as well as peculiarly light-hearted. He'd obviously been practicing.

Which didn't change the fact that Khan had died around six o'clock on Sunday evening, so dinner at eight was not an alibi.

"Routt Sheriff's Office is handling the investigation into Mr. Khan's murder," Dreyfus said. "At the behest of Cheyenne PD, Agent West and I are looking into the theft of Mr. Khan's art collection on Friday evening."

"I have an alibi for Friday too," Fields said promptly. "I was watching Minerva perform at a corporate event held at Miller Insulation. Over five hundred people watched her show that night."

Dreyfus opened her mouth, but Fields wasn't done. "Anyway, that collection was—is—half Minerva's."

"We understand that ownership of the collection was a point of contention in the divorce."

Fields made a sound of disgust. "Everything was a point of contention in that divorce. That was all due to Michael. He couldn't stand the thought of losing his meal ticket. If Minerva had been killed, there would be no question of who was behind it. But Minerva had no reason to want Michael dead."

Again, practice made perfect.

"Can you think of anyone who might have wanted to harm Michael Khan?" Jason asked.

"Who didn't?" the blond man with the deck of cards suddenly spoke up. "Anybody who knew him."

"Sorry," Jason said. "You are—"

"Douglas Devant. You may know me as Dyfan Disgleirio: Master Illusionist." Devant did another of those quick waterfall cascades with the cards.

"Uh-huh," Jason said. "Do you include yourself among people who wanted Khan dead?"

"I didn't mean *literally* everyone wanted Khan dead. I didn't like him, but I didn't have anything to gain by his death—or to lose by his continuing to breathe."

"What about Ian Boz?" Jason asked.

Devant and Fields looked at each other in alarm. Devant demanded, "What about him? Did something happen to Boz?"

"No. Would you include Ian Boz among those who wanted Michael Khan dead?"

"*Oh*. No. Of course not. Hell, Boz was pretty much Khan's only friend. Boz is no killer."

"Okay, well, that's three down. Next best guess as to who in the magic community might want Khan out of the way?"

Devant looked thoughtful, but Fields said, "What kind of question is that?"

One that usually produced interesting answers. Not this time, though, and as much as Jason wanted to follow this line of inquiry, he was supposed to be investigating the art theft.

"Minerva seems to believe Boz may have colluded with Michael to fake the theft of the collection."

Once more Fields and Devant exchanged looks. "I can't see that," Fields said. "I don't want to contradict Minerva, but..."

Devant pulled a pocket watch out and exclaimed at the time. "Sorry, Ted. Officers. I have to run. I'm late for my audition."

"Don't be late for your audition," Fields agreed quickly.

"One last question," Jason asked. "Where were you Friday night?"

Devant stared at him, laughed, and walked out of the office.

"Seriously?" Dreyfus said.

"You'll have to excuse Doug," Fields said. "He gets nervous before an audition."

Devant had not presented like a guy with a nervous bone in his entire body, but Jason let it go. He thought Devant's reactions had been interesting throughout the short interview. "What's his act?"

"Doug's an old-school illusionist. Did you ever hear of Harry Blackstone—Senior, I mean."

"Sure."

"Really?" Fields looked surprised.

Jason nodded. "The Great Blackstone. Yes."

"Well, Doug modeled himself on Blackstone. He does the whole white tie and tails bit, and he even performs a lot of Blackstone's routines. The Kellar Levitation, sawing a lady in half, that kind of thing. And then stuff for the kiddies too. Pulling rabbits out of hats and bouquets from under tables. Very classy. Very traditional. He does a terrific version of the Floating Light Bulb."

Dreyfus murmured, "The Floating Light Bulb?"

"Right. It's the trick that made Blackstone famous. He invented it. In the trick, the magician takes a glowing light bulb from a lamp and makes it float around the stage and through a hoop. Then the lamp itself floats out over the heads of the audience. It's still a terrific gag, even after all this time."

"How does it work?" Dreyfus asked.

Fields gave an exaggerated shrug. "Magic."

Jason sighed. "Any idea of where Devant was on Friday?"

"He'd have been at the memorial for Santos. Doug was a huge admirer of Santos."

Fields had plenty more to say, mostly about what a wonderful thing the magic convention was going to be for Cheyenne magicians and the magic community, and mostly not useful. He did offer Dreyfus and Jason tickets to the sold-out Friday night opening of Top Hat White Rabbit.

"No thank you," Dreyfus said firmly.

Fields handed the tickets to Jason. "Bring a date."

"You know he just bribed you," Dreyfus said as they left Fields' office.

"I really do want to go to that opening," Jason said.

"That makes it worse."

"No, I mean, I want to attend that show in an official capacity. I said before, I don't think the timing of the convention and the murder of Michael Khan—and theft of his collection—are coincidental."

They walked around the building to the parking lot in the back and found Doug Devant leaning against Dreyfus' car. He was still shuffling his cards, but he snapped them together and dropped them into his pocket as Jason and Dreyfus approached.

"Aren't you going to miss your audition?" Jason asked.

Devant nodded as though awarding Jason a point. "They'll wait for me. It's a formality anyway. She's got the job. I wanted a word with you two."

The penny dropped. Jason had thought the name Doug Devant sounded familiar. "You *own* the club where Friday's magic show is taking place. Top Hat White Rabbit."

"That's right."

"What is it you want to tell us?"

"I have no idea who killed Michael Khan. Khan was no loss to the magic community—or any other community. Most of his collection was built by screwing other people over. He bought posters and props from other collectors and never paid for them. He outright *stole* my Floating Light Bulb—stole it from my dressing room! I wouldn't sell, so he stole it. It was one of Blackstone's original bulbs, and Khan used it in that god-damned show of his where he ruins magic for everyone by showing the audience how the trick is done."

"That would be pretty upsetting," Jason said.

"How is it done?" Dreyfus asked.

Devant threw her a distracted look. "Magic." He said to Jason, "You have *no* idea. And that trick was *licensed*, by the way. Competition plays a big role in the magic community. Frankly, thievery is rife, but stealing a guy's magic light bulb, that's a whole new level of scumbag. So as far as Khan is concerned, good riddance to bad magic. But."

Devant seemed to need a moment to compose himself. "But," he repeated, "Khan may not be the only one."

"The only one what?" Dreyfus inquired.

"The only dead magician."

After a moment, Jason said, "Go on."

"The magic community is so damned secretive, so unless someone was paying close attention... That memorial for Mateo Santos?"

"Yes?"

"I just wonder if anyone has bothered to actually look into Santos' death."

"Was there something strange about it?"

"You mean other than the fact that he would never have committed suicide in a million years?"

"Was Santos' death officially ruled a suicide?"

"Yes. That's the story. Nobody who knew him believes it. But the cops didn't know him. The coroner didn't know him. They'll believe anything. Up to and including that Santos would decide to poison himself in the middle of rehearsing his act for the opening of a new magic club. I mean, that's ridiculous. On every level. To start with, if he was going to kill himself, he'd do it in the privacy of his own home."

Not necessarily. Daryl Easton had hanged himself at the Magic Castle in Los Angeles. Or no—come to think of it, Easton's death had ultimately been ruled accidental. In the 1940s Theodore Annemann had gassed himself at home. Larry Grey had shot himself in the 1950s outside his house. Maybe the real point was magicians committing suicide was a quite a rarity.

Dreyfus said, "If your friend's death has been ruled a suicide, there's not a lot we can do. The only reason we were brought into the Khan case is his body was found on public land—and we were already assisting Cheyenne PD with the missing art collection."

"You investigate serial killings, don't you?"

"Whoa," Jason said. "No."

"He's with the Art Crime Team," Dreyfus explained as though in apology.

Jason said, "Not unless we've got a very good reason—like we're brought in by local law enforcement. And even then, we mostly just advise and support as requested. We don't—can't—reopen cases based on—"

"You don't have to reopen. You could look into Khan's death in the larger context. That's what I'm saying." He turned away. "Fine. Ignore a suspicious death. Don't say you weren't warned."

They watched him climb into a midnight-blue Volkswagen Beetle. The door of the Beetle was adorned with a painted magic wand. Splashes of pink, white, and blue flashed from the wand's tip. Stars and sparkles decorated the hood and trunk of the car.

They watched the Beetle trundle down the alley and disappear around the corner.

Dreyfus met Jason's eyes. "What do you think?"

"I think we go talk to Cheyenne PD."

* * * * *

"Come on, seriously," Dreyfus was saying as they walked through the entrance of Cheyenne Police Department.

Jason sighed. "Lighting, thread, mirrors. It's actually a series of tricks strung together."

"Hm."

He glanced at her. "See? Now the trick is spoiled."

"It's not spoiled because I don't believe in magic. I *hate* magic. The biggest bores at parties are the guys who want to show you magic tricks. Oh, and the guys who think they do great impersonations."

"You hate magic because you've only been exposed to bad magic. A great magic show is…magical."

"Oh brother." They had reached the front desk. Dreyfus requested Detective Ward. A minute later they were shown into Ward's office, where they were offered bad coffee and good information.

"You know, it's funny," Ward said. She was a petite blonde with a short wispy haircut and wide gray eyes. "I was thinking about that case when I was brushing my teeth this morning." She smiled, offering a glimpse of her perfectly straight, white teeth. "Had the victim been anyone other than Mateo Santos, we'd have labeled it a suspicious death.

But there was virtually no motive for getting Mateo out of the way, you'd have trouble finding a more beloved figure in this town."

"Nobody is universally loved," Jason said. Gee, he was starting to sound like Sam.

Sam.

He felt a pang, like someone twisting a knife in his guts. Tonight, he would talk to Sam, and he was not looking forward to it. Dreaded it, in fact.

"Ordinarily, I'd agree with you," Ward said. "But Mateo was held in such esteem, such *affection* by so many people. Within the magic community and without. He was just a genuinely good person. I don't know how else to describe it. I never heard him say a harsh or ugly word about anyone. He not only taught magic to disadvantaged children and at-risk teens for free, he shared all his knowledge with his peers—his competitors. If you know anything about the magic community, you know how rare that is, but I think he really cared about this next generation of magicians, sincerely wanted them to be great. Certainly, within the magic community, he was regarded as an icon."

Law enforcement jaded you. That was a fact. You didn't often hear cops extolling the virtues of other humans, so Jason gave weight to Ward's assessment.

"What is it about his death that, in other circumstances, would have raised flags for you?" he asked.

"For starters, drinking poison backstage in an empty nightclub. It's a weird way for anyone to kill himself; it's especially weird for someone like Mateo. It was so dramatic, so theatrical. That really wasn't his style. Not in his professional life and not in his personal life."

"But he was a performer," Jason observed. "And magic shows are, by definition, dramatic and theatrical."

"Yes. Exactly. While on one hand suicide seemed out of character, it was not completely out of character."

"The suicide took place at Top Hat White Rabbit?"

"Yes. He was supposed to be rehearsing his act for this Friday when the club officially opens."

"How did he do it?" Dreyfus asked.

"He mixed the sedative Carfentanil into a glass of Licor 43. Carfentanil is a very powerful animal tranquilizer, and Mateo was in his late seventies, so death was pretty much instantaneous. Once he ingested it, there would have been no way to save him."

Dreyfus said to Jason, "We just received a bulletin on the rising epidemic of Carfentanil overdoses. It's increasingly being used to cut heroin, but it's almost always deadly."

Nice way to reduce your customer base. But drug dealers were not geniuses.

"And almost undetectable," Ward said. "Except, by some stroke of luck, the first officer on the scene had just completed training on the safe handling of it. He saw a few specks of powder on the table and leaped to the conclusion of Carfentanil—and he was right."

"Why would someone bother rehearsing if they were just going to kill themselves?" Jason asked.

"Rehearsing wouldn't be a bother to Mateo. In fact, it would probably be a pleasure, a comfort. Maybe a way of saying farewell."

Maybe.

"Where would Santos get something like Carfentanil?"

"We know where he got it. There's no mystery there. He got it from his girlfriend. Ex-girlfriend. She runs the China Creek animal preserve. She's got an elephant out there and a couple of tigers, so she's licensed to keep the drug on hand."

"That's Elle Diamond?" Talk about a small world. But then magic *was* a small world.

"Correct. As far as we could ascertain, Diamond took reasonable precautions, but Mateo had access to her files, her keys, her everything. She was able to confirm that a couple of grains—which is more than enough—of the drug were missing. Enough to kill but not enough to notice unless she was looking for it."

"Was Santos rehearsing on his own?" Jason asked.

"Yes. According to Arturo Sanchez, the bartender, he was alone in the back. He did not have visitors. The only fingerprints on the bottle or glass were Mateo's."

"And what would be his motive in taking his life?"

She shook her head. "That's the part that sticks in my craw. He had some health problems. Nothing immediately life threatening, but at his age, decline is inevitable. I wouldn't have thought that in itself would be enough to drive him to take his life. But following the health scare, he broke off the relationship with Diamond. According to her, he had decided she was wasting herself on an old man. He wanted her to find someone younger and more..." Ward turned her hands over in a silent *voilà*.

Jason suggested, "Virile?"

"Exactly."

"Did Diamond believe Santos killed himself?"

"I don't think anyone wants to believe it, but it couldn't be an accident. He could not have accidentally procured Carfentanil."

"Who gains by his death?" Dreyfus asked.

"No one. He had no family. He did not own property, he had no money, no worldly possessions to speak of. He shared his magic tricks with anyone who asked. He did not leave a will. If there was a motive, it's not apparent."

"People are sometimes killed for no apparent reason," Jason pointed out.

"Not often. Not in my experience."

Not in Jason's experience either. Spending time with the BAU had widened his perspective—most murderers had their reasons, even if their reasons did not make sense to anyone else.

Ward said, "There's nothing I can put my finger on, but it just doesn't feel right. Which is why, although the case is officially closed, it...haunts me."

JDLR. That had been the notation on the police report after the Khan burglary. Just Doesn't Look Right. There seemed to be a lot of that going around the Magic City of the Plains these days.

The three of them were silent for a moment.

"Was there anything out of the ordinary about that crime scene?" Jason asked finally.

Ward shook her head. "Nothing—beyond the fact that there *was* a crime scene."

"What kind of magic was he rehearsing?"

"Cardistry."

Dreyfus looked up from her phone. "Was there an extra card at the scene? Like a tarot card maybe?"

Ward stared at her. "It's weird you mention it. Yes. There was a tarot card. It was in Mateo's pocket."

"What was the card?" Jason asked.

"The Magician."

Chapter Seventeen

At three, Sam phoned to say his flight had been delayed and he would not be arriving until around eleven that evening. For the first time ever, Jason was relieved to hear Sam would be late, relieved that he would have more time to put off the inevitable confrontation.

Dreyfus had been frankly disappointed when Jason had instructed Detective Ward to contact Routt Sheriff's Office to tell them about the tarot card found at the Santos suicide, and then he'd shepherded Dreyfus out. He tried not to notice, but she was still brooding about it when they finally stopped for a very late lunch.

"It's not our case," he reminded her over tacos at Guadalajara Mexican Restaurant.

"We're the ones who made the connection of the tarot cards."

"Yes. But in fairness, that's because there are two different law-enforcement agencies in two different jurisdictions, handling what appeared to be two different crimes."

"Which turned out to be connected."

"Maybe."

She gave him a chiding look. "West, do you really believe the Santos supposed suicide and the Khan murder aren't connected?"

No. He did not believe that. Not for one minute. He said, "I'm reserving judgment," and reached for a tortilla chip.

She scowled. "No, you're not. You just don't want to get involved."

Not true. Well, partly true. He needed to keep a low profile, for sure. He had already stretched way, way beyond the boundaries of merely consulting on this case. He was actively pursuing the theft of the Khan collection with Dreyfus, and Sam would not be happy to hear it.

But then Sam would probably not be happy to hear anything Jason had to say that evening. He dipped another tortilla chip in salsa and morosely crunched away.

"You got me thinking," Dreyfus said. "I googled the meaning of The Hanged Man when the card is reversed." She held up her phone and read softly, "'In a reading, The Hanged Man reversed serves as a warning. Opportunities have been lost or wasted. The inability to change will lead to downfall. Egotism and selfishness will lead the seeker in a dangerous direction.'"

"We have no idea which way the card was intended to be read." She opened her mouth to argue, and Jason added, "Also, that's a very generic reading. You could probably apply that warning to anyone."

"It sure sounds like Michael Khan to me. Okay, well, listen to the reading for The Magician." Dreyfus scrolled with her thumb. She quoted, "'With the power of the elements and all suits at his disposal, The Magician takes the potential innate in The Fool and manifests it into being with the power of desire. The Magician provides the bridge between heaven and earth, for he understands the meaning behind the words 'as above so below.' Create the inner world and the outer world will follow.'"

"I have no idea what that means."

Dreyfus smiled. "I bet Sam Kennedy does."

Come to think of it, he could *really* use a margarita right about now. Jason said, "I bet Sam Kennedy would have a word or two about us sitting here reading tarot-card interpretations when we're supposed to be tracking down a missing art collection."

Dreyfus made a pouty face and dropped her phone in her purse. "Fine. No guts, no glory."

He grinned at her. After a moment, she reluctantly grinned back.

While Jason was working, it was easy—well, possible—to push aside all—okay, most—thoughts of Sam and the confrontation—no, *conversation*—they would have to have that evening.

Having had time to reflect, he could see that his own reaction to the discovery of what Sam was really working on had been emotional and perhaps extreme. He realized that Sam was correct, and that his own recent brush with violence was bothering him more than he wanted to admit. His desire to put the attack behind him and move on, to get "back to normal," was typical of people dealing with trauma, typical of people trying to avoid dealing head-on with fear and loss. The loss of his sense of safety, his certainty that he could take care of himself in any situation. The fear that he might be attacked again.

He knew that Sam's history, and particularly Ethan's tragic fate, had to color Sam's reactions in circumstances like these. How could it be otherwise? Jason had only to remember the ferocious scrawls on that whiteboard to understand that in his own taciturn and imperious way, Sam was freaked out too. Losing one boyfriend to murder was bad. Having a second imperiled boyfriend probably felt like he was being careless—or cursed.

Jason also knew Sam was unused to being questioned, second-guessed, or having to account for his decisions to anyone, let alone someone he clearly regarded as the junior partner in a relationship.

Theirs was not a relationship of equals; that was painfully obvious—and kind of a deal breaker. More than anything, he wanted to believe that they would talk everything through like reasonable, rational adults and reach some sort of agreement on boundaries and autonomy, but the conversation the other night hadn't gone well. He had no reason to think tonight's would go better.

Jason thought through half a dozen different scenarios and even tried rehearsing a couple of openings on the theme of honesty and openness in a healthy relationship. Even so, he couldn't envision any outcome that did not end with him and Sam acknowledging they did not have a future together.

It tore him up. He loved Sam. He had believed they were really, truly working things out, and then this goddamned stint in hell had begun. Which, again for the record, was not Sam's fault.

But regardless of whether it was fault or fate, the end result was Jason's belief that he did not really know Sam. At all. And that Sam didn't really know or understand him.

Which Sam, he was quite sure, would dismiss as proof of Jason being overly imaginative, overly dramatic, and getting bored with the script. Or something. Something that Sam need not take seriously, let alone act on.

Or worse, that Sam would see Jason's demands as an indication that Jason needed to go the way all Sam's liaisons—at least post Ethan— went. Namely, Sam would erase Jason from his iPhone's starred contacts, as well as from his emotional memory bank, and move on.

It was probably inevitable anyway. If not tonight, eventually.

In between these depressing thoughts, Jason's natural optimism would flicker into brief life. He was not by nature insecure. He believed in fighting for what was important to him. And, embarrassing as it was, he did believe in the power of love.

But from the first, something about his relationship with Sam had knocked him off-balance. He just couldn't seem to keep his footing. And every time the path seemed to smooth out, they were hit with an asteroid or something else from out of left field. Maybe it was just a matter of right guy, wrong time. Was there really such a thing?

Probably not. If it was the wrong time, it was the wrong guy.

A relationship with Sam Kennedy was always going to be challenging.

And, in fairness, a relationship with Jason probably wasn't a cake-walk either. Jason was just as obsessed with work and career, just as busy, just as used to having things his way, just as unused at having to accommodate and compromise.

At seven Dreyfus phoned.

"You're not going to believe this," she said. "We got the security footage from the neighbors who live across the street from the Khan house."

"I believe it," Jason said.

"Not that," Dreyfus said exasperatedly. "Wait till you see the footage. I'm emailing it to you now."

Jason clicked in to his email. "You want me to call you back?"

"No, I'll wait."

They waited for the email to arrive. "You want to give me a hint?" Jason asked.

"No."

His email pinged. "Got it." Jason clicked on the email, downloaded the attached file, and studied it.

"Well?" Dreyfus demanded. "What are we looking at?"

Jason was silent, watching the indistinct, faraway figures running back and forth through the shadows.

"Burglary. Grand theft. Grand larceny. Impersonating a wizard without a license."

Dreyfus said tartly, "Are you *sure* they don't have a license? It looks like Halloween out there."

Yes, it did. All those top hats and capes and cloaks and masks. It did look like Halloween. There was a lot of trick and self-treating for sure. A lot of coming and a whole lot of going. Michael Khan's entire collection had gone, in fact. But this was April, not October, and that was not a gang of larcenous trick-or-treaters. It was a gang of magicians—or whatever a group of magicians was called. An illusion of magicians?

Unfortunately, this was no illusion. More like a conviction of cops— and an imprisonment of thieves.

He had dinner at his laptop and worked steadily until about ten thirty when he turned off his computer, made himself a Kamikaze, and sat down to wait by the fire. At eleven, Sam had still not shown up. Jason had another drink.

The red and yellow dance of flames in the fireplace, the mournful howl of the wind beneath the eaves, and the lack of sleep from the night before caught up with him. He closed his eyes. The next thing he knew he was coming awake to the sound of Sam's key in the lock.

The front door swung open in a gust of cold night air. Jason sat up. Sam stepped inside the house.

Caught off-guard, still half-asleep, Jason felt like he was seeing Sam almost as a stranger would. He saw that Sam was tired, that the lines around his eyes and nose were more pronounced, that there were shadows beneath his glittery eyes. He looked thinner too. Sharper. All cutting edges and lethal points. He looked hard and cold and dangerous.

Then Sam looked across the room and saw him, and something changed in his face. It wasn't so much that his expression softened, more that it warmed. Like a light came on behind his eyes.

He said, "Hey, you didn't have to wait up."

It was the note of surprised pleasure that got to Jason. Undermined him. The idea that Sam was surprised he wanted to stay up to see him... People said he was arrogant and overbearing, but there was this side of Sam too.

Jason rose and went to him, and Sam dropped his carryall, hooked an arm around Jason's waist, and drew him in for a long, deep kiss. Jason wrapped his arms around Sam's neck, kissing him back hard. He thought, *If this is that last night, let it be a good one.*

"Christ, I missed you," Sam muttered when their lips parted enough for words, for breath.

"Same," Jason said. "Always."

Probably a strategic mistake, but the simple truth. He did miss Sam all the time they weren't together. Something to keep in mind before lines were drawn in the sand.

Sam scanned his face as though looking for signs of wear and tear. "You okay?"

"Yes. How was your trip?"

"Unnecessary," Sam said wearily. "The flight was a bitch. I think we bounced the whole way from Colorado Springs to Cheyenne."

"Are you hungry? Thirsty?"

"I could use a drink."

"I'll fix it for you."

Jason thought Sam might head for the bathroom to wash up, but he followed Jason into the kitchen and leaned against the counter as Jason prepared his drink. Jason squeezed lemon juice into the ice and whisky mixture, and nearly jumped as Sam reached out and gently traced one of the healing cuts near the corner of his eye. Sam smiled ruefully at Jason's flinch, but it was such an uncharacteristic gesture from Sam. He was tender in the bedroom, but he was not one for intimate gestures where the rest of the floorplan was concerned.

"You look a lot better. You're not limping as much."

"I told you I'm a fast healer."

"You did, yeah." He took the glass Jason handed him. "You're not drinking?"

"I'll have a drink." Jason hastily slopped together his own drink.

"Cheers." Sam touched his glass against Jason's.

Jason knocked his drink back in two gulps. Sam made a sound of amusement. "Feeling a little stressed?"

"It's been a long two days."

"It has that."

They drifted back to the fireplace and sat down on the sofa. Sam stretched his arm along the back, and Jason moved closer. More than anything, he'd have liked to rest his head on Sam's shoulder, close his eyes, and put off until tomorrow any conversation that was liable to ruin the quiet contentment of the moment.

But if he put it off tonight, it would be harder, maybe impossible, to challenge Sam tomorrow. He would keep putting it off, keep stalling, until it all blew up again.

Sam's fingertips lightly tickled the back of his neck. Jason shivered. Sam made a soft, knowing sound. Indulgent, intimate. Jason's heart ached. He did not want to lose this. Couldn't bear to lose this.

He tried for a neutral approach. "Were you able to interview Bamburg again?"

Sam's fingers stilled. He sighed. "Yes."

"How did it go?"

Sam moved his head in negation. Which meant?

When he didn't continue, Jason asked, "Why did you want to talk to him again?"

"Partly because I'm older and a lot more experienced now. The first time around I just wanted to catch him. Convict him. Not just convict him. Put him away forever. My perspective on a lot of things has changed through the years." He absently shook the ice in the dregs of his drink. "Though not on putting psychopaths like Bamburg away forever."

Jason looked down at his hand resting on Sam's muscular thigh. It was not easy to get the words out. His voice was very quiet. "It wasn't because you think he might be soliciting someone to kill you—or people close to you?"

He counted two heartbeats before Sam said carefully, "Where did you hear that?"

Jason met his gaze. "I didn't hear it. I read it in the files in your office." Jesus. Despite all that mental rehearsing, it was still coming out badly, baldly.

Sam's brows lifted in inquiry. He said nothing. His eyes were watchful.

"I wasn't going through your things," Jason said. "I want you to understand that. I did not have any intention of looking through your files."

Sam made an unamused sound. "Okay."

"I'm not even sure why I opened the door to your office. Honestly, I think I was missing you." Sam's eyes flickered. He didn't speak. "But when I opened the door, I saw the whiteboard with my name on it."

"I see."

"And I realized that you *do* believe that someone from your past could be the one who came after me."

"I told you it was a possibility."

Jason's smile was twisted. "Yes. You did. But you made it sound like a long shot. Whereas in fact, you think it's a very real possibility. Maybe the most likely possibility."

It was another second or two before Sam said, "You feel that I lied to you." That detached observation was Sam the Psychologist. The guy who had a master's in criminal psychology, but who wasn't always so great with normal personal relationships.

"That's how it feels. I know that it was—at most—a lie of omission, but it still feels like you deliberately kept me in the dark."

Sam leaned forward to put his empty glass on the coffee table—which meant taking his arm from around Jason's shoulders. Jason felt the loss of that comfortable weight like the reverberation of a slammed door. Sam was not looking at him as he said, still even-voiced, unemotional, "Let me ask you this. Do you think it would have helped you immediately after the accident to know that there were multiple suspects—people you refer to as monsters—who might wish you harm?"

Jason closed his eyes. He tried to keep his voice level. "Could you… please not use that analyst's couch voice on me?"

Sam said, "Sorry." And then, "You haven't answered the question."

Jason's eyes snapped open. "I don't know, Sam. Maybe it wouldn't have been the thing to say when I first regained consciousness, but once we were here, once I asked you about it? Then I think the correct course would have been candor. I have a right to know where the danger might be coming from."

"I don't know where the danger might be coming from. That's the problem." Sam's voice was flat.

Jason moved so they could face each other. "It's a problem that at the very least, we should share. Look, I know that what happened to Ethan has some bearing. That maybe because of that you feel you have to—"

Sam's expression grew closed, shuttered. "You don't know anything about it," he cut across Jason's words, but he did not sound angry. His face and voice were cold. No. Worse. *Bored.* "You have no idea what you're talking about."

It was effective. It made Jason feel he was being dramatic and emotional—as well as prying into things that were none of his business.

This is how he fights people he dislikes.

But as the thought formed, Jason realized he was wrong. The adult Sam simply annihilated his opponents. This was how the boy Sam had fought. Hiding his own insecurities, his vulnerabilities, behind dismissiveness, derision.

"Not just a rich rancher. A very rich rancher."

Why should that memory close his throat? Bring that sting to the back of his eyes? It did.

Jason said in a low voice, "You're right. I have no idea because you've barely said a word about Ethan since that night at the Buccaneer's Cove two months ago."

Sam's eyes were dark with anger. "Why would I? Ethan has nothing to do with us."

"Really? Because his photos and paintings still hang in your mother's house." He could hear the hurt in the huskiness of his voice, and that was the very thing he had not wanted to do—not say those words, not show that pain. But the words came anyway. "Because we broke up over him once already."

Such a mistake, because Sam's expression tightened. He said in a cold, clipped voice, "What do you want to know?"

"Jesus, Sam." Jason struggled to put it into words. He felt he had one shot at this and was already blowing it. "It's not— I don't have a list of questions. It just feels strange to me, wrong to me, that we talked about him that one night and he's never been mentioned since. No, I take it back. He was mentioned the night we arrived and your mother said I looked like a ghost."

There was no softening in Sam. If anything, he was getting angrier. He bit out, "What do you imagine is left to say?"

Not pleasant being on the receiving end of that hostility. Maybe annihilation wasn't so far behind after all.

"Nothing you don't want to tell me. But…" Jason tried to keep any more accusation or hurt from his tone. "Can you not see— I can't help feeling like some of your attitudes, behaviors, whatever, stem from what happened to Ethan. Are you seriously telling me you don't think Ethan's death has any influence on our interactions?"

"I don't think it has as much influence as you imagine."

"You told me you became an FBI agent because you didn't want Ethan to have died for nothing."

"And?"

There was no relenting, no leniency—not even understanding. This was private property all right. Posted and protected. Walking out onto that minefield had been one of the biggest mistakes Jason could have made, because there was no going back from this. No possible retreat to safe ground. He was on his own now.

Something flickered and then died inside him. Hope? After a moment, he shrugged. "Okay. None of my business. Fair enough."

Sam's face turned toward the fire.

Jason stared at him.

The firelight wavered across Sam's stony profile.

Jason waited, giving it time, hoping Sam would say something.

Nothing.

Finally, Sam glanced down at his glass as though only then noticing it was empty. He rose and went into the kitchen.

Jason listened to the sounds of ice clinking, spoon against sugar bowl, liquid being poured. Unhurried. Deliberate.

He got up from the sofa and left the living room.

Chapter Eighteen

When he reached the bedroom, Jason stopped, staring at the bed, at their partially unpacked suitcases, unsure of what his next move was.

He could not imagine lying in bed—the three of them—that night. But the idea of sleeping on the sofa seemed overly... What was the word Sam had used in the hospital? Operatic? Anyway, there was a good chance Sam would sit up drinking all night.

He was suddenly exhausted. He sat down on the edge of the mattress and stared out the window at the enormous full moon. Then he remembered Terry Van der Beck sneaking around the house the night before. He rose and snapped shut the blinds. When he turned from the window, Sam stood in the doorway.

Sam did not speak.

Jason met his look steadily. He couldn't read Sam's expression, but he thought maybe he looked a little less arctic and a lot more tired.

"Jason."

Jason shook his head. Because what could he say? Sorry? He was sorry. He was sorry to do anything that gave Sam pain. He was sorry to wreck things between them. Maybe his timing could have been better, but he did not believe he had been wrong. He did not believe he really had a choice.

"It's not easy for me to talk about...any of this."

"I know." It wasn't easy for him either. The difference was, he cared enough about Sam to try—and keep trying.

"Were you like this with Ethan? Were you..." They had fought to reach a somewhat precarious balance. He didn't want to tip them back into another argument.

"Withdrawn?" Sam asked drily. "Uncommunicative? Secretive?"

"I was going to say guarded, but okay."

Sam was silent, seeming to think it over. His blue gaze lifted to Jason's. "Yes," he said at last. "I was. Which is why I don't want to make the same mistakes with you."

That helped. A lot.

"I've never been good at this part of relationships." Sam's mouth twisted. "If Ethan were here, he would say the same."

That...was less helpful.

When Jason didn't reply, Sam said, "What is it you want to know?"

"Sam, I don't have a list. There's a part of me that doesn't *want* to know. Any of it. Anything to do with Ethan. But the fact that you can't talk about it. About him. Won't talk about him. Worries me. And it's not just Ethan. In fact, Ethan is probably the least of it. Walking into that room last night and seeing that whiteboard and those files... It makes me feel like I don't know you."

"I don't talk about Ethan because it was a long time ago. Not because it's too painful to think about or because he was too important to share my feelings about him."

"You went into the FBI because of Ethan."

"Yes. Ethan's death changed my life. But that happened twenty years ago. We were very young. My life was going to change anyway." He observed Jason for a second or two, then continued reluctantly, "To some extent, I've used Ethan as an excuse not to get too involved, not to care too much for anyone. Until you. I was a man on a mission. Emotionally, that's a safe place to be."

That was unexpectedly honest. It surprised Jason.

Watching Jason's face, Sam said, "I know you don't believe this, but what happened to Ethan is not a factor in our relationship."

Jason opened his mouth, and Sam amended, "It was a factor in my decision as to whether there would *be* a relationship. We're past that now. From my perspective, we're past it."

"Okay." He wanted to believe it.

Sam must have read his uncertainty because he gave another of those pained grimaces, and said, "If it does factor in, it's only in that Ethan's death taught me how quickly everything can change. People are…fragile."

"Yes." Jason understood. He worried about Sam. Worried about some psycho coming after him. Worried about the emotional and mental toll of working the cases Sam specialized in.

"Which is why it is…" Unexpectedly, Sam's voice shook. "…unbearable…to think…" He stopped. Jason looked closer, saw the impossible too-bright shimmer of Sam's eyes.

His heart stopped, speared in place like an unlucky fish, and he left the window and went to Sam.

He didn't know what to say, but words were not needed. Sam's arms locked around him. Jason held him tight. Sam said into his hair and collar, "If I opened that door… If I made you a target…"

It was the last thing Jason had expected to hear. That Sam felt responsible? Guilty?

"Jesus, Sam. This isn't your fault."

"If you're— If something happens—through me—"

Jason pulled back, trying to see Sam's face. "Don't. What happened to me is not your fault. You can't think like that. You can't take that on yourself. We don't even know who came after me." He remembered who he was talking to and added doubtfully, "Do we?"

The softness of Sam's mouth straightened into its usual hard line. "Not yet. We don't. Jonnie has photos of Kyser in Toronto."

"Kyser was at his conference in Toronto?"

"It looks that way."

"It was *not* Kyser who came after me?" It was a jolt. Jason had been almost convinced Kyser was his assailant.

"It doesn't appear so."

For a moment Jason was lost in his own thoughts.

Sam used the edge of his hands to irritably wipe the wet from his eyes. He said brusquely, "Jason, whatever you think—whether you think it's enough—I love you."

Jason believed him. He knew that Sam loved him. Love wasn't always enough, but it was surely three quarters of the equation.

"I love you too. Maybe I'm just out of my depth." For sure, he couldn't ever remember needing reassurance from a boyfriend before.

"I am who I am. I can't promise that I'm going to change for you."

Jason's smile was crooked. "I'm not asking for a personality transplant."

No answering smile from Sam. He was as grim as someone swearing to uphold the laws of the land. "But I will try. It's worth it—you're worth it—to try."

Jason said, "Just don't shut me out. At least, don't shut me out of the things that concern me. That's all I'm asking. And if you can't trust me to make the right decisions, at least accept that it's my right to make the wrong ones."

Sam nodded bleakly. Not happy, but willing to acknowledge it was a fair request.

Jason bumped his face against Sam's, seeking his mouth, and Sam kissed him back. His lips were so soft. There was something heartbreakingly sweet about that kiss, as though Sam was apologizing—not simply for past hurts, past misunderstandings, but for the future ones. The inevitable wounds ahead.

Jason kissed his way to the curve of Sam's neck, resting his face against Sam, absorbing the warmth of his skin, the tickle of his hair, the scent of his aftershave, the quiet, steady fall of his inhalations-exhalations.

Sam hugged him, not speaking, and there was something comforting in just this, holding each other, listening closely to what the other was not saying, maybe couldn't say.

Jason whispered, "Do you think everything happens for a reason?"

"No."

"Me neither."

Sam nudged his face, found his mouth, kissed him. He said gently, "That doesn't mean good things can't come out of bad things."

* * * * *

Sam did not need a lot of sleep.

Four or five hours a night was his average. His morning routine was to run, shower, and read the newspaper while having his first cup of coffee. So for Jason to wake the next morning and find Sam still lying beside him, still sleeping soundly, felt special, like a rare treat.

Just to have the freedom to study Sam's face to his heart's content…

It worried him too, though. Even after a night's sleep, the lines of weariness and tension were not entirely erased from Sam's face. There seemed to be more threads of silver in his thick, fair hair.

It hadn't occurred to Jason that Sam might be feeling responsible, even guilty for the attack on him. He had assumed Sam was just being his usual obsessive, control-freak self. Now Sam's behavior made more sense. Not that his instinct to protect Jason by keeping him in the dark was correct or a good one, but it was more understandable in this context.

It had been a close call last night. Jason still felt a little shaken by how close they had come to snapping apart, but every time they weathered one of these conflicts, he felt like they were that much stronger, understood each other that much better. Given how little time they actually spent together, there were bound to be some serious disconnects.

And no end in sight on that. They lived on opposite sides of the country and, despite working for the same agency, their jobs rarely brought them into contact. They never spoke about a possible future. Their relationship existed strictly in the here and now.

Sometimes that was enough. Most of the time it was not nearly enough. Not from Jason's perspective. He did not know how Sam felt. It was not something he was about to push. Not now. One close call per visit.

He closed his eyes, willing himself to go back to sleep. It was still early. He could hear the restless, unceasing Wyoming wind whispering outside the window, the *cluck-cluck-clucking* of the chickens in the yard, the plaintive braying of the blind donkey in his corral.

He started thinking again about Jeremy Kyser. If Kyser really had been at his conference in Toronto—and it sure sounded that way—he couldn't have come after Jason, and they really were back to square one. One of the takeaways of looking over Sam's notes had been the worrying realization that Sam truly had no idea who had attacked Jason.

That was what was making Sam crazy. It wasn't doing a lot for Jason's mental health either. The attack in the China King parking lot had happened one week to the day, and they were no closer to an answer as to the key questions of who had come after Jason and why.

"That's a mighty ferocious-looking frown," Sam murmured.

Jason opened his eyes, turned his head to find Sam studying him with a faint, rueful smile. Sam's eyes looked so blue, so bright, and, oddly, now that he was awake, he looked more relaxed, at ease.

Jason smiled, shook his head a little, opened his mouth to say— something, who knows what—but Sam slid his arm beneath his shoulders and rolled him over against him.

"Come here, you." Sam planted a warm, moist kiss on Jason's startled mouth. Jason smiled, bumped his nose against Sam's. Fluttered his eyelashes against Sam's eyelids.

"Mmm...morning..."

"Morning." Sam's big hand moved between Jason's legs to cup his balls, and Jason pushed into his touch with an encouraging murmur. His cock stirred, and he closed his eyes, savoring the leisurely caress. Sam's mouth brushed his again, nuzzling, his tongue pushing against Jason's lips, and Jason opened to the deeper kiss.

One of the things that had initially surprised him about Sam was the fact that Sam took nothing for granted in bed, equally at ease giving or receiving, but this morning Sam was all sexy aggression and classic male dominance, and it felt good. It felt great.

Sam lightly tickled Jason between his balls, chuckling when Jason squirmed and gasped. He trailed his fingertips to the opening between Jason's ass cheeks and ran a teasing finger across the sensitive opening of Jason's anus. Jason gulped. No matter how many times they did this, it still felt extremely…personal.

Sam reclaimed Jason's mouth. Jason could taste the words. "You like that?"

Jason swallowed, nodded, because yes, of course. Invasion of space or not, it felt so good. Physical sensation, for sure, but also the emotional satisfaction of knowing every inch of him was appreciated, attention-worthy.

"Hmm?" Sam queried, gentle, teasing.

"Touch me there," Jason whispered, closing his eyes, concentrating solely on the shivery sensations Sam's contact aroused. So delicate, so discerning… He could feel the tiny scratch of Sam's fingernail. Hell, he could almost feel Sam's fingerprint. His cock hardened, shifted to nudge Sam's own full and fleshy erection.

"Where?" Sam teased. His fingertip pressed against the resistance of quivering muscle, pressed a little harder. "Here? Or what about here?" As Jason shuddered and gasped, Sam's voice deepened. "Yeah? Oh, you like that… How about here…" A lot of talking from Sam, who was usually so silent, so grave during sex.

A bird was singing outside the window. The bed smelled of flannel sheets and the musky scent of precome. How lovely to know there was no rush. No hurry. They could take all the time they needed.

Jason moaned and whimpered and whispered in response to the delicious, naughty things Sam was doing to him. "Oh God, that. Do that again. Feels so good. Don't stop. Oh, God, *Sam.*"

He knew his lack of inhibition amused Sam a little, but it turned him on too—what wasn't to like about having your efforts acknowledged and appreciated?—and that turned Jason on as well. As if Jason wasn't already turned on enough.

"You want me to fuck you?" Sam muttered through another of those rough, wet kisses, and Jason moaned and nodded frantically.

"Yes. God. Yes. Do it. Fuck me."

Sam gave a funny, breathless laugh. "Christ, West, you're— I love you."

And then he got up and went into the bathroom.

"Uh, was it something I said?" Jason asked after a moment. He raised his head from the pillow.

Sam returned wearing a big grin and a bigger erection. He held up a tube.

Jason's gaze moved from Sam's engorged cock to the tube. "*Oh, right. Yes—*"

Sam pounced and turned necessary preparation into pleasurable foreplay that left Jason hot and breathless and pleading with his body in small, restless arches and humps.

"Go on, tell me what you want," Sam urged hoarsely. "I like to hear it. I like it when you say it."

"Jesus, Kennedy. Are we going to actually *do* this because I think I'm gonna come—" His breath caught raggedly as Sam grabbed him beneath the waist, sweeping him up and over—Jesus Christ, he was *strong*—so that Jason was straddling Sam's hips, astonishingly, exquisitely impaled on that massive cock.

Jason whimpered, panted, gazing into Sam's eyes as Sam watched him, waiting for him to catch up. "You're beautiful," Sam told him. "You really are…beautiful."

Jason's muscles relaxed, his body accepting the challenge as it always did. He took a couple of deep breaths, steadied, even gave a little impatient wriggle. Sam smiled up at him. There was humor in that smile, and something else. Something harder to read. Satisfaction? Possessiveness? A little of both?

"Up-and-coming Special Agent Jason West," Sam teased softly.

Jason gave a shaky laugh. He didn't mind the teasing. Not when Sam said it in that voice. Not when Sam looked at him with that expression. He closed his eyes and began to move, rocking his hips, silently urging Sam to take him, and Sam obliged, thrusting into Jason with strong, steady surges. Jason rolled into that rhythm, losing himself in shattering, overwhelming sensation as the head of Sam's cock grazed across the swollen gland of his prostate.

He cried out. "Good. So Good. Fuck me, Sam. Fuck me." He leaned back, shifting angle so he could be more deeply, satisfyingly penetrated.

"So hot... So tight..." Sam growled. "So sweet..."

Sam's fingers sank into his buttocks, leaving bruises for sure, and he pumped his hips fiercely into Jason, taking him now with short, powerful thrusts, driving him on as they performed their own frantic, ferocious bullet catch.

Jason's orgasm had been lurking in the wings since Sam's hand had closed caressingly about his balls. It needed nothing more than a few waves of that most intimate of wands to bring about detonation. His cock felt ready to burst, his balls clenched tight. Colored stars danced behind his eyes. Sparks seemed to dance at the root of his cock, tingle at the base of his spine.

Sim Sala Bim and abra-fucking-cadabra.

He began to come. Come so hard he would not have been surprised to see actual fireworks.

That spray of hot, wet release seemed to send Sam toppling over the edge. He yelled and bucked and came too in stringy, silvery jets of semen like silly strings. Sam reached out, and Jason collapsed in his arms. Sam folded him close, and they lay together, hearts pounding in time, breath rising and falling, still one.

So good. Maybe the best yet.

Magic.

Chapter Nineteen

"We could have breakfast in bed," Jason said dreamily sometime later.

Sam had been gazing at the ceiling. He turned to look at Jason. "Is that what you'd like?"

"You're on vacation. I'm technically on sick leave. I could phone Dreyfus and tell her not to worry about picking me up. I'll come in later."

"You don't have to go in at all. That's actually the point of sick leave."

Jason wrinkled his nose. "True."

"But?"

"Why don't I tell you while we fix breakfast?"

Cooking breakfast together. That was a first. It felt sort of luxurious just to be together doing simple couple-type things like arguing over scrambled vs. fried and hunting for the Tabasco sauce.

And while Sam did say, "This kitchen isn't big enough for both of us," when Jason bumped into him a second time, he was smiling and there was a teasing warmth in his eyes.

"We make a good team," Jason said when they carried their piled plates of scrambled eggs and turkey bacon and hash-brown potatoes back to the bedroom.

"Not too bad," Sam acknowledged. "The bacon could be crisper."

Jason joked, "Is that supposed to be a double entendre?"

Sam's smile was twisted. "No. I think my bacon is probably crisp enough already."

Jason laughed, but he sobered. He ate a few bites of egg and potato, then put his plate aside and said, "About my consulting gig with the Cheyenne RA."

Sam swallowed a mouthful of coffee and raised his brows in inquiry.

"I may have expanded, or say, slightly pushed the boundaries of my purview."

Sam said, "I'm not going to like this, am I." It was not a question.

"No," Jason admitted. "For the record, I did strenuously resist getting pulled into the murder investigation."

Sam put his coffee cup down. He set his breakfast plate aside. "Okay. Let's hear it."

Jason filled him in on everything that had happened since Sam had left for Colorado on Tuesday morning.

At the end of his recital, Sam said, "Let me see if I can summarize. You believe the theft of Michael Khan's art collection is unconnected to his murder? You believe the Khan homicide is connected to the earlier death—possibly suicide, possibly homicide—of a man named Mateo Santos?"

"Correct." Jason couldn't help adding, "I think."

Sam cocked an eyebrow but let that go. "You believe it will be impossible to recover the Khan art collection because—and this is where I get confused—you suspect a band of local magicians stole the collection in order to redistribute pieces to people within the magic community, who have arrived in Cheyenne for a magic convention. These would be people Michael Khan injured by ruining their acts, stealing from them, or just generally doing them wrong."

Jason cleared his throat. "When you put it like that, it sounds a little...unlikely."

"I wouldn't say that," Sam said. "I would say it sounds a *lot* unlikely."

Jason scowled. "Maybe it does, but the thieves were definitely dressed like magicians. And it would explain how they got in through the front door without having to break anything."

"Magical powers?" Sam suggested.

"No, wise guy. A lot of magicians carry picklocks."

"I see. Okay." Sam picked up his coffee mug and took a thoughtful swallow. "Lock-picking magicians aside, that's a lot of supposition."

"I know."

"Your only evidence seems to be the security footage, and yet you said the unsubs on the video were unrecognizable."

"That doesn't mean no one will be able to recognize them. Just that I can't. Plus, the security footage is unenhanced. It's possible that the images could be cleaned up and enlarged."

"True. Do you have a theory as to who these magical unsubs might be?"

"Yes." Jason took a deep breath. "Again, this is liable to sound a little…fantastic."

"It's never stopped you before, West."

Jason gave a reluctant laugh. "Well, first we have to start with the victim, Michael Khan. He seems to have been universally loathed within the Cheyenne magic community. I mean, we didn't speak to anyone who seemed upset at the news he'd been murdered. Or even surprised. The common refrain was that he lied, cheated, and stole from his peers whether through ruining their acts by revealing the secrets of magic or out-and-out theft and fraud of art and memorabilia."

"Not a nice guy. Got it."

"His collection was a particular sore spot with a lot of people, and to understand why that's significant, you have to understand the role that tradition and history play in the magic community. It's a little different than the rest of the art world because magic itself is an art."

"You're starting to lose me." Sam pointed to Jason's mug. "You want a top-up?"

Jason shook his head.

"I'm still listening." Sam rose and went into the kitchen. Jason followed, still talking.

"The main market for art and props and costumes like those in Khan's collection is other magicians, who tend to think of themselves as custodians of…"

"Don't say magical artifacts." Sam refilled his coffee cup, dosed it with cream and sugar, and leaned against the kitchen counter, regarding Jason.

"Obviously not magical artifacts, but valuable heirlooms. Items of cultural and historical significance to a small and close-knit community. So when word got out that the Khans were divorcing and that Minerva Khan wanted her share of the collection, I think there was widespread concern for the fate of these items. Especially given that a lot of people still felt they had a claim to things that Khan had not paid for or had obtained through unfair or even illegal means."

Sam said, "You're making a convincing case for robbing Michael Khan. What have you got beyond that? I'm guessing you think you know who was behind the theft."

"Yes. I think the raiding party was organized by a woman named Elle Diamond. One of her coconspirators subconsciously called her out when he mentioned the name Zatanna Zatara."

Sam opened his mouth, and Jason hurried on, "Never mind. In the back lot of her ranch, there's a moving van that fits the description of the one parked outside the Khan house. She's got several barns and sheds and storage units that would be ideal for hiding the more than one thousand bits and pieces that make up that collection, *and* she was the first and only suspect to bring up the topic of search warrants."

Sam grunted.

"There was a memorial held for Mateo Santos on the night of the robbery. I believe that Santos' peers took that opportunity to celebrate a master magician's life and work by pulling the ultimate sleight-of-hand—and in doing so, settle a score and liberate that collection. It was the perfect time because a lot of Khan's victims will be in town this weekend for the convention."

Sam took a thoughtful swallow of coffee. "You're going to need a lot more than that in order to get a search warrant."

"I know."

Sam tilted his head, as though considering Jason from another angle. "Am I missing something here? You don't want to get a search warrant?"

"I'm…not sure."

"I'm definitely missing something."

Jason said, "Sam, there are some really valuable items in that collection. Rare. Irreplaceable. A couple of the lithographs are as valuable as any number of paintings in museums. They go for a lot more than, say, Granville Redmond's work."

"'Items of cultural and historical significance,'" Sam quoted. "You mentioned that a couple of times. So?"

"So let's say Dreyfus and I are successful in obtaining a warrant and we do find the collection on Diamond's ranch. There are several possible scenarios, and almost none of them have to do with the preservation of—"

"Okay, stop," Sam said, and he meant it. "You don't get to make that kind of call. The fate of that collection is not up to you. Your job is not to decide who's the best custodian for that art. Your job is to find the art and initiate the return to its legal owner. And if you can't do that—"

"It might not even go to its legal owner. Given the number of claims people had against Khan… The entire collection could be held as evidence for years while the courts try to sort it all out, and you know what evidence lockers are like. Things get lost, damaged. There's no question of climate control or—"

"Jason, stop."

Jason stopped.

"You're a sworn officer of the law."

"Yes."

"*I'm* a sworn officer of the law."

"I know." He realized abruptly that he had just placed Sam in a very difficult position. "I'm sorry."

"This isn't— You're not your grandfather saving the world's cultural heritage from the Nazis. These are a bunch of stage props and costumes and posters—and yes, I understand that some of those lithographs are extremely valuable—but this is a matter for the courts."

Jason met Sam's gaze and nodded.

"At *best* it's vigilantism."

Jason did not answer.

"You learned that one in fucking nursery school. Two wrongs don't make a right."

Ouch. Jason nodded.

Sam shook his head, turned away to put his mug in the sink. He turned the taps on, rinsed the cup. Turned the taps off. He glanced at Jason. "You're not even officially on this case, so if you're... I don't know. Ethically conflicted? Ethically compromised? The thing to do is step away. Do you understand what I'm saying?"

"Yes."

"If you cannot do the job, you need to step away."

Jason said tersely, "I heard you. I understand."

"Have you shared your theory with Dreyfus?"

"Not yet. No."

Sam said nothing, but Jason could feel his gaze.

Sam said finally, "You could be wrong. Basically, this is instinct and guesswork. You don't have any evidence yet."

Jason nodded. "True."

Sam was silent again. Then he said in normal tones, "I'm going to have a shower."

"Okay."

Sam hesitated. Said lightly, "Want to join me?"

Jason appreciated the message behind the invitation. He smiled faintly. "Rain check. I think I should give Dreyfus a call."

"Right." Sam smiled too. There was a hint of sympathy in his eyes, but for Sam this situation was black and white, no shades of gray possible. "When I come out, you can explain to me why you think there's a serial killer stalking the magic community of Cheyenne."

Jason's lip curled. "Don't tell me you haven't already heard from SAC Reynolds about that possibility."

"I want to hear it from you."

"It's instinct and guesswork there too."

"But see, I trust your instincts," Sam said.

Yeah. Well.

Sam disappeared into the bathroom. Jason sat on the bed and turned on his laptop, listening absently to the sound of the running shower as he checked his email.

There was a brief message from Shane Donovan in NorCal saying that he had spoken to Ursula Martin and she had informed him she had reached an out-of-court settlement with Fletcher-Durrand.

"Goddamn it," Jason muttered. Not that it was really a surprise. It was a disappointment, though. With Martin's defection, their case was now officially dead and buried.

On the bright side, this eliminated any motive anyone associated with Fletcher-Durrand had to get rid of him.

Speaking of which, he spotted an email from Jonnie with an attachment.

Jason opened the email.

Hi Jason,

Hope you're feeling better. Sam asked me to forward these photos of Dr. Jeremy Kyser attending the Toronto conference on forensic psychology.

Not the best quality, but the man in the photos does resemble the man on Kyser's book jackets and photo ID. Let me know what you think.

J.

Jason clicked on the first attachment, which turned out to be a photo of people attending some kind of banquet. They looked as thrilled as people always did when facing an evening of long-winded speeches and hotel conference food.

At first, he couldn't even find Kyser in the mass of scholarly faces. Finally, he located him at a table in the back. Not a great photo, as Jonnie had said, but at that distance the man did appear to be Jeremy Kyser. It had been nearly a year since Jason had seen Kyser—and he'd only seen him the one time and for no more than a few minutes—so yeah, he *thought* that was Kyser.

He wouldn't want to stake his life on it.

He clicked on the next photo. This shot was a formal group picture, and everyone's head was about the size of the hole left by a paper punch. There were at least three wild-haired, fever-eyed, intense-looking mad scientist guys in that photograph that could have been Kyser. Jason couldn't have sworn to any of them.

Nor could he swear they *weren't* Kyser.

He heard the taps squeak in the bathroom, the sound of running water turning off. He heard the *pop* of the glass door.

He clicked on the third and final attachment.

This was a candid shot taken in a hallway. The photo had been snapped at a much closer range. There were several people wearing name badges, milling aimlessly around a hallway as people were prone to do between conference sessions. They carried cups of coffee, pastries, laptops, business-card cases, notepads, and chargers—and all wore the vaguely uncomfortable look of people silently practicing their "elevator pitches"—all but one.

Kyser was nearest the conference-room door, and he was greeting two colleagues with a smile that was best described as frantic. Jason frowned at that manic grin and popping eyes.

Overall...the guy looked right, looked as Jason remembered. Tall and rawboned, a frizzy mass of salt-and-pepper hair framing a bony, gaunt face. He couldn't see the subject's eye color, but his eyes seemed to be dark, so that was right. It all seemed right, seemed to line up with what he recalled of that one brief encounter.

And yet…something about the man in the photograph struck Jason as off. False. A ringer.

The problem was, his memory of Kyser had faded over time, and looking at these images of Kyser-like guys wasn't helping.

The bathroom door opened, and a gust of warm, soap-scented air wafted out.

"It's all yours," Sam said.

"Mm-hm."

What was it that wasn't right? Or was he imagining it? He went back to studying that too-big smile and those frightened eyes.

Frightened eyes…

"Something wrong?" Sam asked.

"Hm?"

What was the guy—Kyser?—so frightened of?

Jason looked closer, inspecting the people greeting Kyser. It was like examining all the figures in one of those crowded Italian Renaissance paintings. Like in Botticelli's *Spring* or Raphael's *The School of Athens,* sometimes you learned more about what was really going on by scrutinizing the supporting cast rather than the major players.

And those two unknown scientists greeting their colleague, Dr. Jeremy Kyser? One looked surprised. One looked confused.

They thought they knew you, but they don't.

Jason went back to poring over Kyser's expression.

And you know they don't.

He jumped as Sam rested a hand on his bare shoulder. "You okay, West?"

Jason stared up at him.

Sam's brows drew together. "Jason, what's wrong?"

"It's not him," Jason said. "He wasn't at the conference. That isn't Jeremy Kyser."

Chapter Twenty

Sam was still on the phone when Jason stepped out of the shower.

He nodded silently at Jason as Jason stood in the doorway, toweling his hair. "Okay, thanks, Jonnie." He listened for a moment. "I'll have to get back to you on that."

Sam clicked off. "According to Kyser's PA—"

"Kyser has a personal assistant?"

"Yes. Kevin Anderson. According to Anderson, Kyser most certainly did attend the conference in Toronto. He claims his boss is currently on vacation and out of the country."

"Out of the country where?"

"Still traveling in Canada."

"Then he should be able to be reached by phone, right? He should be able to answer a few questions?"

"You would think, but according to Anderson, the purpose of vacation is to not answer phones."

Jason said sardonically, "He's obviously never met you."

There was a warning glint in Sam's gaze. "Or you."

"Point."

"Anyway, we're looking for him. That's all we can do at this juncture."

"I know."

Sam said grimly, "Put some clothes on. I want to show you something."

Jason dressed quickly, wondering what was up. Sam was waiting for him in the kitchen. He nodded at the back door.

"I know it's locked. I checked it last night," Jason said.

"It's locked." Sam unlocked the door and stepped outside. Jason followed.

Sam walked over to the large picture window and pointed to the square screen leaning against the house.

Jason stared at the screen. He felt slightly sick.

"Look at this." Sam indicated gouges in the wood siding where someone had attempted to pry the inexpensive metal window frame from the wall. Sam's eyes met Jason's. "He was coming in. That was his plan." And in case Jason didn't get it, "Van der Beck didn't come to talk."

Jason could feel blood draining from his face. It had not even occurred to him to check for an attempted break-in. He had been suspicious of Terry's middle-of-the-night visit but had imagined he'd intercepted him almost immediately. He hadn't realized how fast and determined Terry had been.

Sam said, "He couldn't get through the doors because of the single-sided deadbolts. So he went for the window. If the dogs hadn't woken you, he'd have been inside in a matter of minutes."

Jason swallowed. "Yes. I don't know how he— He must have followed Dreyfus when she drove me home."

Sam said, "We need to have a word with Mr. Van der Beck. Let's get over to the Cheyenne RA, and you can bring Chuck Reynolds up to speed on your magician murders."

An occasional tumbleweed bounced and rolled along the side of the road as Sam drove toward Cheyenne. Jason stared out the car window at the endless sweep of blue sky and tall green-gold grass rippling in the wind. In the distance he could see blue snow-dusted mountains.

Sam had not had much to say since they had left Ruby's. The sexy, playful morning seemed like a long-ago interlude, but Jason was used to that. He had been reassured by their conversation the night before. Sam's honesty had been unexpected, but really, why? If anything, Sam erred on the side of too honest.

He did still wonder about a couple of things, and since Sam had seemed to indicate the topic of Ethan was not off-limits, he decided to take a leaf from Sam's book and just ask.

"Did you—they—ever catch Ethan's killer?"

He thought he knew the answer, so he was astonished when Sam replied, "I think so. I believe we got him when we got the Roadside Ripper." Sam's gaze never left the long, empty road ahead. "I'll never know for sure, but that's my best guess."

Jason stared. "You think Ethan died twenty years ago at the hands of the Roadside Ripper?"

"Yes. I believe so."

"Do you have corroboration, a confession from the Ripper?"

"No." Sam was still not looking at him. He sounded detached, analytical. "The timing is right. The MO is right. I think there's a lot of indicators that the Ripper is—was—our guy."

Jason felt another of those unpleasant jolts. Why wouldn't Sam have said anything about this? He hadn't given even a hint that he believed Ethan's murderer had finally been brought to justice. It was just…weird. Right? Not that Sam was typically communicative about a lot of his work, but this wasn't the usual case. Even for a personality as stoic as Sam's, this had to be a big deal.

Uneasily, Jason kept picking at it, despite his sense that Sam already regretted giving him permission to ask these questions. "But I thought the Ripper's hunting ground was Interstate 5?"

"It was. For the last fifteen years. But we don't have a clear picture of where he was during the five years before he returned to the West Coast. We know he spent some time driving trucks in Montana and Colorado. My theory is he was in Wyoming as well."

"That's…kind of news."

Sam said nothing.

"Are you going to tell Ethan's father?"

"I did tell him. The last time I was here. I told him we did not have conclusive proof, would not be able to get conclusive proof, but it's my belief Ethan's killer is dead."

Jason had no response. If anything, he felt more confused than at the start of their conversation.

Sam glanced at him. "If you're thinking about Ethan because of the threat against you—"

"It's not that." But actually, yeah, maybe it was partly that. Jason was afraid. Not so afraid that he couldn't function. Not so afraid that he couldn't put his fear out of his thoughts. But yes, knowing someone wished him harm, was actively out there trying to do him harm, did weigh on him.

To distract himself—and Sam—he said, "When you retire, do you think you'll move back to Wyoming?"

"Retire?" Sam repeated it like he'd never heard the word.

"Yeah. Eventually."

Sam seemed to think it over. "No. Wyoming is a nice place to visit, but..."

Poor Ruby.

"I wouldn't mind visiting again," Jason agreed. "I still haven't seen a buffalo."

"I like Virginia," Sam said. "I wouldn't mind staying in Virginia."

Virginia was nice. Jason liked Virginia. But it would be difficult to leave California for a lot of reasons. Of course, it wasn't like Sam had ever asked him to leave California. Or ever would.

Into his silence, Sam said casually, "I like California too."

Jason looked at him, and Sam's mouth quirked. "You have a very nice smile, West," he said and turned his attention back to the road ahead.

* * * * *

"So you're the art expert?" SAC Reynolds greeted Jason when Sam introduced them.

"Next best thing," Jason answered, shaking hands.

The minute Jason saw Sam with SAC Charles Reynolds he knew Reynolds was one of the old friends Ruby had referred to when they'd talked about Sam's boyhood. He should have made the connection sooner, of course, but for some reason he just didn't think of Sam as having friends within the Bureau.

The change in Sam wasn't dramatic, exactly, but it was obvious from the relaxed set of his shoulders to the warmth of his gaze that he knew Reynolds well and liked him a lot.

And it was obvious from the easy, no-bullshit way Reynolds talked to the legendary Sam Kennedy, that Reynolds felt the same. In fact, it turned out that Reynolds was the one who had originally talked Sam into joining the Bureau all those years ago. He was probably a wealth of information on the topic of Sam Kennedy, but there was no time for reminiscences.

The bank robbers had been successfully captured. The Cheyenne RA was fully staffed again and a bustling hive of activity. In fact, the only person missing was Abigail Dreyfus, who had phoned in sick that morning.

Jason had received a brief call from her before they'd left for the drive to Cheyenne.

"I'm so sorry about this," she'd apologized. "I had grocery-store sushi for dinner last night, and it turns out to have been a *huge* mistake."

Sushi in Wyoming? And grocery-store sushi at that? That did sound like a mistake.

"I'm sorry to hear it. I hope you feel better," Jason replied.

"I'm sure I'll be fine tomorrow. I'll see you then."

Yeah. Maybe not.

In the meantime, Sam was waiting for Jason to make his case to his old pal.

Reynolds was as tall as Sam, but rail-thin. What Jason's grandfather had called "a tall drink of water." Reynolds had to be Sam's age, but he looked older. Iron-gray hair and mustache. Pale gray eyes that appraised Jason with a shrewd but not unfriendly directness.

Reynolds led the way to his office. "Take a chair, son. Either of you want coffee?"

Jason and Sam declined coffee.

Reynolds gave Jason another of those keen-eyed looks. "Sam tells me you think we've got a serial killer running around Cheyenne, knocking off magicians?"

Jason winced because yeah, that just sounded really...ridiculous.

Sam closed the door to Reynolds' office and took the chair next to Jason's. "I've only heard half the story, but I think it's worth listening to. West has an eye for details."

"Well, the devil's in the details," Reynolds said. He nodded at Jason. "So far I haven't heard from Cheyenne PD, but okay. Let's hear it. What have you got?"

Not a lot. Jason would have been the first to admit. He told them about Mateo Santos—a man nobody could possibly wish harm to—and Michael Khan—a man everyone wished harm to. He told them about the tarot cards, which were not items used in either man's magic act, but historically had been used for divination purposes—and were still regarded by some to hold mystical and spiritual significance.

Reynolds heard him out, only once stopping Jason in order to buzz his assistant over the intercom. He requested background checks on Ian Boz and Terry Van der Beck. "Okay, go on," Reynolds told Jason.

When Jason was finished, Reynolds was silent for a moment. "That's pretty thin, Sam." He glanced at Jason. "No offense, West."

"It's thin," Sam agreed. "And the MOs don't line up. If the kid at the magic store hadn't come after West, I'd be inclined to wait and see what turns up during the course of the Khan homicide investigation."

"The Van der Beck kid's behavior is concerning," Reynolds agreed. "It's not like he didn't know West was FBI. That wasn't just bold, it was downright defiant. We don't know what action he would have taken had he gained access to the house, but that's probably just as well."

Jason said, "Van der Beck is a member of the magic community. He was acquainted with both victims. He has access to picture-hanging wire like that used to strangle Khan, and I'm assuming he has access to Carfentanil. He works at the animal preserve where the drug used to kill Santos was taken from."

Reynolds said, "Noted. But the same could be said of the magic-shop owner, Ian Boz. He doesn't work at the animal preserve, but in all likelihood, he would know how to gain access to those drugs."

"True," Jason admitted.

"Also, we don't know for a fact Santos was murdered. His death was ruled a suicide."

"I'd like to see the coroner's report," Sam said.

"Of course you would," Reynolds said drily. "Well, I'll make sure you get to see whatever you want. And I'll have Cheyenne PD put a BOLO out on Boz. Meanwhile, I think paying Terry Van der Beck a visit might be a good idea." He gave Sam a droll look. "That is, I'm assuming you'd like to have a word with him?"

Sam smiled. His eyes were like ice chips.

"Oh, I'd like a word," he said.

* * * * *

Detective Ward of Cheyenne PD met Jason and Sam outside Boz's Brew with a search warrant, but the warrant turned out to be unnecessary.

Although the lights were off and the CLOSED sign hung on the front entrance, when Ward tried the door, it opened, and the sound of pixie dust sprinkled down.

Ward called, "Ian Boz? Terry Van der Beck? Cheyenne PD. Show yourself."

No answer. Nothing moved within the aisles of books and CDs, DVDs, silk bouquets, velvet doves, stuffed rabbits, colored handkerchiefs, cards, posters, stacks of top hats… The rows of magic miscellany seemed to stretch on and on into the gloom. On either side of the door, two automatons in satin tunics and goofy, jeweled turbans silently tried to stare each other down.

Ward looked back at Jason and Sam. She raised her brows in inquiry.

Cars whizzed past on the street behind them. The silence from within the shop was absolute and unsettling.

Sam nodded. Ward drew her pistol. Jason had resisted the urge to pull his weapon until Sam had pulled his, but his nerves were jangling like a seven-bell fire alarm.

Not good. Definitely not good. Something is not right.

Ward pushed the door the rest of the way open, and they followed her inside.

"Is anyone in here?" Ward called. "Cheyenne PD. Show yourself."

One of them must have brushed against the tall wire racks because something tumbled from above and landed in the aisle. A blue and white stuffed rabbit in a black top hat, holding a magic wand, gazed up with plastic googly eyes at the three pistols trained on it.

Sam made a sound of amused disgust.

"It looks like nobody's home." Ward glanced around uneasily.

"They should be open," Jason said. "According to their store hours."

She nodded, holstering her pistol and moving toward the rear exit. "I'll check behind the building. There's a parking area back there."

Sam was continuing his sweep of the store floor. Jason stared at the front desk and the door leading to the storeroom.

"I'll check the storeroom."

Sam glanced at him and nodded curtly.

Jason went around the sales desk and craned his head around the doorframe. The room was dark, too dark to safely move around though he could see empty crates and cardboard boxes had been shoved toward the wall. Tall metal shelves were crammed with formless articles.

It sort of looked like a large trunk had been tilted on end and left between two rows of shelves. Something about the outline of that trunk, the way the light from the main floor gleamed on its glossy surface, raised the hair on Jason's head. Was that thing made of glass?

He felt around for a light switch. Failed to find it. He tried the other side of the doorframe and located the switch.

The overhead fluorescent lamps came on with a ghostly buzz, casting a sickly green light over the crammed interior of the storeroom.

Jason stared at the trunk—stared and stared. He couldn't look away. He knew what he was seeing, but somehow his brain could not seem to make sense of it.

This was a replica of the Chinese Water Torture Cell. A device invented by Harry Houdini for his most famous escape. The frame and heavy stocks were made of Honduras mahogany and nickel-plated steel with brass fixtures. The front consisted of a plate of half-inch tempered glass. The apparatus weighed around three-quarters of a ton and held 250 gallons of water. It was relatively small. Only 26 and a half inches wide and 59 inches tall. Too small for the large man jammed upside down into the tank.

Ian Boz's eyes stared in horror through the murky blur of the water still lapping ominously against the glass.

A small yellow and green something flickered at the bottom of the cell. For a crazy instant, Jason imagined it might be a fish. Sanity reasserted itself. Jason knelt and used the zoom on his phone's camera to get a better look without chancing disturbing any crime-scene evidence.

He stared at the screen of his phone. He was looking at a card. A tarot card. A feckless young man in a green tunic was about to step off a cliff.

Jason knew that card. Special Agent Abigail Dreyfus had mistakenly read the description to him in her office the afternoon Boz had pulled a gun on her.

The Fool.

Chapter Twenty-One

Hard to say what was worse.

SAC Reynolds openly laughing at him, or BAU Chief—and current boyfriend—Sam Kennedy trying *not* to laugh at him.

"Abby Dreyfus a serial killer," Reynolds repeated for the nth time, the wobble in his voice barely held in check by what was clearly a will of steel.

Jason couldn't help looking at Sam who, to his credit, looked grave and sympathetic—except for that goddamned gleam of amusement in the back of his eyes. Sam, who usually had all the sense of humor of a marauding grizzly bear, found this funny. In the middle of a fucking homicide investigation, Sam Kennedy found something humorous.

Jason was never going to live this down.

"Abby Dreyfus a *magician*." Reynolds' voice shook again because apparently it was even more ridiculous to be suspected of being a magician than a serial killer.

"I didn't know she was your goddaughter," Jason said. He couldn't quite keep the edge out of his voice. "I didn't realize you'd known her all her life."

"So we heard," Reynolds said. "You thought she was this Andy Alexander, one half of a brother and sister magic act. The brother being this Terry Van der Beck."

"Elle Diamond seemed to recognize her."

But it wasn't just that. It was Dreyfus' odd, seemingly random questions, her strong feelings about magic and magicians, the odd coincidence of her talking about The Fool card before The Fool had shown up at a crime scene, and then finally calling in sick the very day Boz's body turned up. Okay, yes, *granted*, not circumstantial so much as coincidental. A string of peculiar coincidences which, when added up, seemed to mean...something.

Why the hell hadn't he done the intel on Andy Alexander *before* voicing his suspicions about Dreyfus?

Because he'd been so staggered by the discovery of Boz's body with that particular card, he'd blurted all his apprehensions out to Sam.

Talk about The Fool.

Not that he blamed Sam for sharing those concerns with SAC Reynolds. Jason didn't even really blame Reynolds, who'd nearly fallen out of his big leather executive chair, because now that Jason had the full story on Agent Dreyfus, his suspicions *were* ridiculous.

Clearly the situation with Kyser—or whoever his stalker was—had made him paranoid.

Sam's voice interrupted his thoughts. "Putting Special Agent Dreyfus aside for the moment, West was right about the first two killings being linked together. I think we can safely add Ian Boz to the list of our unsub's victims."

Reynolds stopped chortling. "Unsub be damned. I think we know who our budding serial killer is. This crack-brained Van der Beck kid. According to his file, he's got a long history of mental illness and violence." He glanced at the file in front of him. "Highlights include trying to burn his parents' house down when he was eleven and trying to burn his school down when he was thirteen."

Serial killers and fire. He remembered talking to Dreyfus about the symbolism of fire in magic. That was one he could have added to the list. One of the typical warning signs potential serial killers displayed was a love of setting fires.

Reynolds was still reading over the file. "When he was sixteen, he tried to strangle a classmate." He shook his head. "They should have thrown the key away on him a long time ago; unfortunately, it's very difficult to permanently lock anyone in the loony bin these days."

I have a feeling we're not in Kansas anymore, Toto. Although Kansas was probably worse. Not that Jason had any sympathy for psychopaths. They could throw the key away on the Martin Pinks and Jeremy Kysers and Terry Van der Becks for all he cared.

Reynolds added, "Seeing that he's *not* the brother of this Andy Alexander, why is he suddenly so focused on magicians?" He looked at Sam.

Sam said, "I don't know about magic as a performance art, but the occult does attract certain aberrant personality types." He added, "Of course, so does religion."

Jason said, "Magic is an aesthetic exploration of mystery and possibility."

"Is that so? I know it attracts oddballs and misfits," Reynolds said.

Sam said, "You'll make yourself crazy trying to understand why serial killers do what they do."

"Since you're the guy who wrote the book on catching them, I'll have to take your word," Reynolds said. "I have to ask. How many tarot cards are there?"

"He's using the Rider-Waite tarot deck," Jason said. "That's seventy-eight cards altogether, though so far he's sticking to the twenty-two trump cards of the Major Arcana. He seems to be deliberately matching particular cards to his victims. Santos was The Magician, Khan The Hanged Man, and Boz The Fool. It would be hard to predict potential victims based on how a disturbed mind might interpret the cards. But I'm anxious about Elle Diamond. I think she's a good match for The High Priestess."

"Ward's already spoken to Diamond," Sam reassured him.

"Seventy-eight potential victims?" Reynolds stared at Sam.

Sam said briskly, "Not going to happen. He's already devolving. You just have to set the trap and usher him in."

"And how do we do that? You know, this is business as usual for you, but for us—"

"You stick to the plan, Chuck. You join Cheyenne PD and Routt Sheriff's Office for the joint press conference this afternoon in a show of force. Tonight, Van der Beck's photograph will go out over the airwaves on your local TV stations. In both the press conference and the news reports, Van der Beck will hear that law enforcement has taken every precaution to make sure the convention attendees are protected and that the event can proceed as planned."

"And you really think that's going to lure him in?"

"Guaranteed."

Reynolds rubbed his jaw doubtfully. "He'd not only have to be crazy, he'd have to be pretty damned dumb. You really think he's that dumb?"

"He's not dumb. He's megalomaniac. He thinks he's gotten away with murder three times. He's beginning to believe he's invincible. He'll view the press conference and news reports as direct challenges." Sam glanced at Jason. "Look what happened when he imagined West had him in his sights. Instead of fleeing, he went after him. And when he failed to kill West, he immediately compensated for that failure by killing Ian Boz—despite knowing he would inevitably be the primary, if not sole, suspect."

Reynolds nodded, sighed. "Okay. Makes sense. I guess. You wouldn't want to join us for Friday's festivities, by any chance?"

Sam hesitated, meeting Jason's gaze once more. Jason knew what he was thinking. If Sam Kennedy happened to turn up on the national nightly news, it was liable to alert someone paying close attention to the possible location of MIA Special Agent Jason West.

"I'll think about it," Sam said. "I'll let you know one way or the other this evening."

* * * * *

They were just pulling out of the parking lot when Jason's phone rang.

He glanced at Dreyfus' contact info and groaned.

"Better get it over with," Sam advised in the tone of one with a lot of practice at receiving irate phone calls from colleagues.

Jason clicked the Accept button. "West."

"Really, West?" Dreyfus said. "I seem like a serial killer to you?"

"No, of course not. I just..."

"I mean, I'm not a fan of magic, but going around knocking off magicians seems a *little* extreme."

"I agree. I apologize. I really am sorry."

"*I* was the one who guessed that there would be a tarot card at the Santos crime scene. Why would I point that out if *I* was the one leaving the cards?"

"I know. That was partly why I, er, started having doubts. I thought maybe it was a..." He glanced at Sam's profile and cleared his throat. "A cat-and-mouse thing."

Sam made a smothered sound that turned into a cough.

Dreyfus began to splutter.

"Anyway," Jason said quickly. "Aside from thinking you might be a serial killer, I enjoyed working with you."

There was an astonished silence, and then Dreyfus laughed. "Aside from you never wanting to investigate anything that doesn't have to do with art history, I enjoyed working with you too."

"Thanks."

"I guess this is it, then? Are you finished, um, consulting on the Khan case?"

"Yeah. I think I've provided as much insight as I'm able to."

Sam was staring straight ahead. He could have been alone in the car for all the attention he appeared to be paying. Jason searched his soul and said, "Hey, Dreyfus. I think you should probably try to get a search warrant for Elle Diamond's place."

"Really?"

"Yeah. It's a long shot, but...yeah. I think that moving van of hers is probably going to turn up on some of the surrounding security cameras in the Khans' neighborhood."

"Wow. Okay. I'll do that. I'll try, anyway."

They chatted a minute or two more and then said their goodbyes. Jason clicked off his phone.

Sam said, "Nicely done, West."

"Yeah. Well." Jason turned to stare out the window.

Sam reached over and gave his shoulder a squeeze. *Buck up, little buckaroo.* "You can only do what you can do within the confines of the law—which you've sworn to uphold."

"Yes. I know." Jason sighed. He thought it over and said more cheerfully, "Anyway, she's never going to get a search warrant on my say so. I'm the guy who accused her of being a serial killer to her godfather."

Sam's lips twitched. "Possibly not. Shall we celebrate the semi-successful end to your case? How about I treat you to the best steak dinner in Cheyenne?"

"It's a little early for dinner."

Sam gave him a sideways look. "True, but if we get the meal out of the way, I figure we can find other ways to spend the evening."

Jason smiled.

* * * * *

The steak dinner was delicious.

And the preparations for "other ways to spend the evening" were pleasantly underway when Jason suddenly gasped and sat up, brushing Sam's hand aside.

"Jesus Christ."

He must have sounded sufficiently horrified because Sam rolled over, reaching for his pistol. Jason barely noticed, barely noted the dangerous, glittering look in Sam's eyes. Jason's vision was turned inward, seeing the terrifying and inevitable unfolding of events that might be happening in Cheyenne at that very moment.

He said, "It's not tomorrow night. It's tonight."

"What are you talking about?" Sam demanded.

Jason stared at him. "Sam, Friday night is the club's official opening. But there's a private show *tonight*. Tonight, it's magicians only."

Sam searched his face with a hard, blue gaze. "The magicians' club? There's a show at Top Hat White Rabbit tonight?"

"*Yes.*"

"Are you sure? Why would no one have mentioned that? Nobody said a word about a private show."

Jason pressed his fist against his forehead. How the hell had he forgotten? When Reynolds and Sam were discussing their trap for Terry Van der Beck, how had he not remembered then? How the hell had *that* skipped his mind?

"Because they're magicians," he said tightly. "Because their world is secluded, secret, separate." He opened his eyes. "Sam, you've got to believe me. I was wrong about Dreyfus, and I might even be wrong about Kyser, but I'm *not* wrong about this. You think seventy-eight victims are too many? Every magician in Cheyenne is going to be in that club tonight."

Sam reached for his phone.

Chapter Twenty-Two

Dinner for the six p.m. seating was being served, and the first show was already underway when Cheyenne PD and the FBI arrived at Top Hat White Rabbit.

The leggy receptionist from Ted Fields' office gaped as uniformed officers and blue-and-gold-jacketed agents flooded the reception hall. No one even had to say the magic word. She reached beneath the tall wooden counter, pressed a button, and the hidden door in the bookcase swung open.

Jason stepped aside as agents and cops filed past through the narrow doorway. He studied the shelves of the bookcase. *Of Legerdemain and Diverse Juggling Knacks* by John Braun. *The Encyclopedia of Stage Illusions* by Burling Hull. *The Unmasking of Robert-Houdin* by Harry Houdini. *The History of Conjuring and Magic* by Henry Ridgely Evans had a bookmark sticking up.

Jason reached for the book and pulled out the bookmark. A tarot card. The Tower. A tower appeared to have been struck by lightning and was now burning. People tumbled from windows into the black sky, pursued by flames. Jason's heart seemed to tumble with them.

He squeezed past the others filing through the door, jogging after Sam and Reynolds. He caught them up as they reached the dining room.

A woman spoke to the audience from the stage. "At no time will that bullet leave The Maestro's hand until the moment he loads it into the pistol."

Minerva Khan, dressed in what appeared to be a handful of strategically flung diamonds, stood at the end of the stage, smiling out at the packed room. Waiters and waitresses bearing trays of champagne, Oysters Rockefeller, and Brie crostini circulated through the tightly wedged tables and chairs, trying to avoid stepping on anyone's cape or tripping over anyone's sword cane.

Top Hat White Rabbit seemed to be a little more Black Rabbit Rose than Magic Castle. There did not appear to be a membership fee or a dress code, though everyone present was clearly a magician and dressed to the nines.

Minerva broke off her speech as a cadre of police officers mounted the steps to the stage. SAC Reynolds intercepted Doug Devant as he left the bar and came to inquire what was happening.

Jason showed The Tower card to Sam. "He's definitely here. Or was."

"We know we're on the right track, then." Sam took the card and frowned. "What the hell does that mean?"

"A bomb? Fire? At a guess, total destruction of the club and everyone in it," Jason said.

"Christ."

From the stage, a police captain was asking people to move slowly and calmly to the exits.

Jason spotted Ted Fields making his way to the front of the stage. He lifted down Minerva and then The Maestro.

Sam whistled to Reynolds. Reynolds patted Devant on the arm, and Devant, looking deeply shaken, joined the officers directing people to the fire exits. Despite the instructions to stay calm, a few people began to rush. Glasses were spilled, chairs knocked over as guests scrambled to grab their belongings and push through the sea of tables. Officers moved to assist.

Reynolds rejoined Sam and Jason.

"We could be looking for a bomb," Sam said.

Even in the muted light, Jason could see Reynolds lost color. "Where the hell would he get hold of something like that?"

"Explosives, incendiary devices are used frequently in magic shows. Not the real thing, of course, but the principles of putting a device like that together are essentially the same."

Reynolds gave Jason a look of noncomprehension before turning to make his way through the crowd to begin directing his team to search beneath tables, chairs, potted plants, and every other place they could think of.

"Would he stay to watch?" Jason asked Sam. Sam was surveying the crowd, scanning intently for Terry. Every officer and agent had been provided with a photo of Van der Beck.

Sam gave him a quick, distracted look. "He doesn't plan on dying in here, that I can tell you."

There was an unearthly *whoosh* from a few feet to the side. A woman screamed as the black and gold draperies behind the stage burst into flames. A wave of heat seemed to roll over them.

"Move," Sam ordered. His hands locked on Jason's shoulders, and he thrust him into the stream of now panicking people shoving their way back through the bookcase door.

"Sam!" Jason tried to look back over his shoulder. The room was already filling with smoke. He could not see Sam. "*Sam!*"

He tried to push a return path through the wall of terrified people, but that was impossible. No one was about to fall back or give way. The tide of club guests surged forward, carrying Jason with them.

Someone stumbled against him. An older man with a cane. Jason steadied him. Someone knocked into him on the other side. He looked and saw Elle Diamond in a black sequined evening gown. Her blue eyes seemed to reflect the flames now engulfing the stage.

"Don't fall. Don't slip," Diamond said. "Don't lose your footing." She was half dragging an elderly woman in a silver chiffon gown behind her. "Don't fall. Don't slip," She repeated like a mantra.

The crowd lurched forward, and Jason was half-crushed against the edge of the bookshelf, but then he managed to wriggle through. When he reached the entry hall, he realized he could not go back for Sam.

His first responsibility was to make sure everyone got out safely. As agonizing a choice as it was, that had to be his priority.

He stepped to the side and began to help people through the doorway, sometimes bodily hauling them through. Smoke was billowing from the dining room, and the final people stumbling out were choking and coughing.

Jason slipped back through the doorcase—the heat on the other side was like stepping into a sauna. *But it's a dry heat*, he thought crazily.

Only a step or two in, he bumped into someone slim and slight and blonde. Through the smoke, he recognized Detective Ward. She wore a blue silk evening dress and held a wad of colored silk scarves in front of her face.

I thought so. I thought you were probably a member of the community.

"You can't go back in there," she cried hoarsely. And then, "Agent West? Are you crazy? What the hell are you doing?"

"Sam Kennedy is still in there."

"Nobody is in there. We're the last ones out." She planted a surprisingly forceful hand in his chest, driving him backward toward the main entrance and the fresh air.

As they stumbled outside into the cold night, firemen brushed past them, dragging heavy rubber hoses. Red and blue strobe lights cut through the smoky darkness. The shriek of sirens drowned out the sound of voices, the crackle of radios.

The April night was so frigid, Jason felt like he was choking on it. He couldn't stop coughing. Someone in a paramedic's uniform slapped an oxygen mask over his face, draped a blanket over his shoulders, and asked him a bunch of questions he didn't listen to.

Where is he? Where the hell is he? Why doesn't he come? Why don't I see him anywhere?

When he was able to stop coughing, he shoved the mask away and started moving through the crowd. News vans were arriving and more paramedics and more fire engines. The street outside the club was jammed with vehicles and people. Club goers stood in bunches, talking and crying. Some spoke to police officers. Some spoke to reporters.

Sam was nowhere.

Where are you? Don't do this to me, Kennedy. Not now.

Jason ran into SAC Reynolds, who was directing agents to fan out through the streets surrounding the club. "This guy can *not* slip through our fingers," Reynolds was shouting. "I don't care what you have to do. Turn over every lid of every trash can. Check every doghouse, treehouse and outhouse."

"Have you seen Sam?"

Reynolds' face was streaked with soot. He looked at Jason without recognition for a moment, then said, "He went after Van der Beck."

"Went where after Van der Beck?"

"Out through the kitchen into the back alley. Wait. *West!*"

Jason turned and started back the way he had come, ignoring Reynolds' shout, "Special Agent West!"

He jogged down the length of the building, turned a corner, and found a crowd of firemen and cops.

No Sam.

I don't believe it. It's not true. If you let that evil little shit get the drop on you, I'll kill you myself, Kennedy. A sound alarmingly like a sob caught in his throat.

Don't be a dumbass, West. He's fine. He's like those Old West marshals. Too tough to die.

Kennedy, where the fuck are *you?*

Hand resting on his weapon, he continued down the alley, past Dumpsters and stacks of cardboard boxes and mountains of black trash bags. The smell of smoke permeated everything. He heard a faint sound— for an instant he thought it was the mewl of a cat—then a chill went down his spine. He began to run toward the cross street he could see at the end of the alley.

He skidded to a stop as a tall form came around the corner, dragging something along the ground with him.

Jason's heart was still banging in his chest, but now it was with relief.

"I curse you with the power of the demon lords," Terry Van der Beck was babbling through his tears. "You will face the wrath of—"

"Bibbidi-bobbidi-boo to you too," Sam drawled.

"Sam?" Jason called. His voice was almost steady.

"Right here," Sam called back. He sounded as cool and untroubled as if he'd gone for a stroll in the park.

Jason waited, working to control his breathing and his face as Sam dragged Van der Beck along like a sack of potatoes.

"Look what I found hiding under a bush," Kennedy said.

"I see."

Kennedy peered at him. "Okay, West?"

"Sure. Why wouldn't I be okay?" Jason asked tersely, joining the procession. "Just because you shoved me out the door like a goddamned civilian while you—"

"Okay, okay," Sam said mildly. "Let me just drop this off."

And that was, in fact, about what he did. Hurled Van der Beck into a crowd of cops, who delightedly took possession of him. Cameras began clicking, flashes going off in bright white flashes. Sam led Jason by the arm away from the smoldering and soggy club. They ended up in the sheltering alcove doorway of the neighboring building.

"Okay, let's hear it."

The weird thing was, as scared and angry and dying to speak his mind as Jason had been a few minutes earlier, he was suddenly just... tired.

Maybe Sam was right about delayed reaction and PTS and all the rest of it because it felt like a wave had knocked his legs out from under him, knocked him flat on his ass. Everything that had happened in the last week was all catching up with him: the attack in the China King parking lot, the fact that no one could find Kyser, the crazy race through the fun-house and believing he was going to see his young partner shot in front of him, not recognizing the prop gun for what it was, not realizing that

Terry Van der Beck had actually tried to break-in while he was sleeping, thinking Sam might be dead...and way, way, *way* too many dead bodies.

Maybe he *wasn't* cut out for this.

He shook his head.

"Go on."

Jason closed his eyes.

"Hey," Sam murmured, concerned. "West?"

Jason moved his head in negation, dropped his forehead on Kennedy's shoulder. Kennedy's arm came around him.

"Come on, West." Kennedy nuzzled his ear. "Everything's okay. It's just reaction. You did good work tonight."

Oh yeah, and this. Feeling the way I do about you and not knowing where this is going. Not knowing what you really want. If you see a future for it. Never knowing when I'm going to see you again.

But, of course, he couldn't say that.

Jason raised his head. Scowled. "Not exactly teamwork, was it?"

Kennedy said with surprised sincerity, "It was pretty close."

"Yeah?" Jason turned to stare as the cleanup process began on the street.

"You're tired, that's all." Kennedy said. He sounded like he was trying to convince himself.

"Sure."

Kennedy leaned forward to kiss him. "Good thing you've still got a week of sick leave left."

Jason smiled reluctantly.

"It'll be okay, Jason," Kennedy said. "You'll see. Trust me."

* * * * *

So… Déjà vu.

One week later, Jason unlocked the side door that served as his front door and let himself into the small cozy kitchen of the blue cottage on Carroll Canal.

The timers were on, so the house was brightly lit and felt comfortably warm—it also felt very, very quiet.

He and Sam had said their goodbyes at the airport that morning. Sam had been flying to that long-delayed meeting in Seattle. Jason had been headed home. And *home* had never sounded so lonely.

But it had been a very good week. Restful, relaxing. The week he should have had when he'd left the hospital. After Terry Van Der Beck's arraignment for murder, arson and a whole host of other crimes, Sam had taken Jason to see bison in their natural habitat and visit the Wyoming State Museum. Another night they'd had dinner with SAC Reynolds and his wife Anne, and Jason had seen Sam like he'd never seen him before: laughing and relaxed as he and Reynolds shared unflattering and funny stories about the good old days. They had dined with Ruby a couple of nights too, and Jason had come to realize how much Sam loved and respected his mother beneath the amused exasperation. An entire week of just being a normal couple. Cooking and eating and sleeping and talking and, yeah, occasionally arguing, but it had felt right. It had felt real. Like this could be the future.

But not the immediate future.

There was no talk of an immediate future.

Well, that was the reality of their situation—and it wasn't going to change anytime soon. The good news was, he felt newly confident of Sam's feelings for him—and of his feelings for Sam. They could make this work. Plenty of people made long distance work. It wasn't ideal, but it sure as hell beat the alternative.

A white pitcher filled with scarlet-edged roses from his garden sat on the tile of the kitchen counter. His mail was neatly stacked in front of the pitcher. That would be Charlie welcoming him home. He knew without looking there would be half-and-half in the fridge and clean sheets on his bed. He shook his head, but really, it was one of the perks of having sisters either one old enough to be his mother.

The mail was the usual mix of bills—though he paid almost everything online—circulars, a couple of art magazines, a lot of catalogs targeting law enforcement or at least LEO wannabes...and an oversize dark-blue envelope addressed in a familiar cramped hand.

Jason's heart deflated.

"Shit."

No postmark.

What the hell did *that* mean? Hand-delivered?

Automatically, he felt around for a pair of gloves but ended up having to retrieve a pair from his bedroom—yeah, that was the nice thing about dating another agent; you didn't have to explain about the kinky surplus of latex gloves.

He used a paring knife to slit the envelope and delicately pulled out the stiff card.

He stared at it for a long moment.

Okay. Nothing he hadn't seen before, so no need for his heart to thump in his ears like he was in mortal danger.

There was no proof Kyser was the one who had attacked him. Jason still could not recall the details of the attack.

Instinct is just another word for guessing. Right?

But those faces. Those distorted, misshapen shrieking faces...were those supposed to be flames? The whole thing was kind of reminiscent of Arthur Rackham's more macabre illustrations. Or maybe Edvard Munch's *The Scream*.

Good. Keep that professional distance. Analyze. Assess. Don't let this be about you.

Nothing inherently violent or threatening in the colors—black, red, orange—and yet the overall effect was undeniably disturbing. The nib of the pen had gouged the stiff paper in a couple of spots.

Jason drew a breath and opened the card.

It took him a second to realize the text consisted of one phrase copied over and over, the tiny print seeming to thicken and expand with each reiteration.

Where are you? Where are you?

WHERE ARE YOU? WHERE ARE YOU? WHERE ARE YOU? WHERE ARE YOU? WHERE ARE YOU? WHERE ARE YOU? WHERE ARE YOU? WHERE ARE YOU? WHERE ARE YOU? WHERE ARE YOU? WHERE ARE YOU? WHERE ARE YOU? WHERE ARE YOU? WHERE ARE YOU? WHERE ARE YOU? WHERE ARE YOU? WHERE ARE YOU? WHERE ARE YOU?

WHERE ARE YOU? WHERE ARE YOU?

WHERE ARE YOU?

WHERE
ARE
YOU?

Jason West and Sam Kennedy will return in

THE MONUMENTS MEN MURDERS
(THE ART OF MURDER BOOK IV)

Coming Winter 2019

About the Author

Author of over sixty titles of classic Male/Male fiction featuring twisty mystery, kickass adventure, and unapologetic man-on-man romance, JOSH LANYON'S work has been translated into eleven languages. Her FBI thriller *Fair Game* was the first Male/Male title to be published by Harlequin Mondadori, then the largest romance publisher in Italy. *Stranger on the Shore* (Harper Collins Italia) was the first M/M title to be published in print. In 2016 *Fatal Shadows* placed #5 in Japan's annual Boy Love novel list (the first and only title by a foreign author to place on the list). The *Adrien English* series was awarded the All Time Favorite Couple by the Goodreads M/M Romance Group.

She is an Eppie Award winner, a four-time Lambda Literary Award finalist (twice for Gay Mystery), An Edgar nominee and the first ever recipient of the Goodreads All Time Favorite M/M Author award.

Josh is married and lives in Southern California.

Find other Josh Lanyon titles at www.joshlanyon.com.
You can also follow Josh on Twitter, Facebook, Goodreads, Instagram and Tumblr.

Acknowledgments

Thank you to the following people: Keren Reed, Deborah Nemeth, and Kevin Burton Smith.

Special thanks to my official patrons. I'm so grateful to you for your encouragement and support:

Kaitlyn Abdou, Susan Sorrentino, Brian Dulaney, Sabine Biedenweg, Matthew DeHaan

Miki Prenevost, Ingeborg Elisabeth Carlstrom, Maite Suppes, Linda Eisel, Susan Rethoret, Steve Leonard, Scott McCluskey, Audra Rickman, Eyleen Weiss, Andrea Karg, Marilyn Blimes, Alexa Ebanks, Cassie Poe, Nancy Fields, David D. Warner

Carlita Costello, Susan Reinhart, Sophie Wittlinger, Johanna Ollila, Catherine Lievens, Frances Burgess, Max, Kristina Uvalle, wendy oshea, Dalia Cao, Esha Bhatia, Jennifer Vranek, catherine morden, Cynthia Hemme, Karin Wollina, Chrystalla Thoma, Jacqueline Tan

Marie-Claude Emond, Dianalee Rode, Mika Fetter, Kendra Chambers, Peg McMahon, Alison Butler, Carole Lake, Debra Woods, J.H., EL Kinnison, Mary Barzyk, Robin Allen, Karla Ruksys, Susan Wilson, Rachel C Owens, Michelle Kidwell, Susan Lee, Christina Rodriguez, Janet Sidelinger, Stephanie Bogart, Cheryll Athorp, Jason Russell, Delphia Baisden, Amy Schaffer, Andrea Israel

James Kennington, Catherine Dair, Bobbi Lyons, stacy rauch, Joanie Walters, Nancy Schneider, Kelly, Michelle Ivey, Hannah Krajcik, Ha T Nguyen, Nicholas, Natasha Chesterbrook, Shelby P., Juliet Beier, Tracy Goodin, Queenie J. Alexander, Elle P., TRUE Ryndes, Adell

Ina Husemann, Christine Skolnick, BongMate, Jackie Davey, Anne Ystenes, Rebecca Espinosa, Deborah Graham, Marilyn Abbott, Maureen Moss, Emilie, Dan Hoxter, Debra Guyette, Ariel Morse, Alice Viviano, Billie G Ramey, ingrid titus, Christy Duckett, Karen Reck, Jamell Howell, Frauke Franz, Halcyone, Nancy Andrews, Kate Sobejko, Kat Kelley, Denise Dernorsek, Lucas A. O.

Stara Herron, Geo Lofts, Katelyn Sweigart, Jacquelyn Mela, P. W., Madeline Menzer, K Miller, Saule, Brigitte Wissner, Tara Raimondo, Stacie Stanley

RJS, Adrian, Stuart Kelsey, Anika Heike Schindler, Liu Yunjia, P Camarri, Susan Hoffman, Robert Anthony, Indy Melody, crone, Sheila wand, Maia Brown, Annery Marte-McNulty, Bryrose A, Amandine Huntzinger, Tina Burgess, Deb R. Ashley, P Cristie, Lisa Baker, Brian Howard, Joanne Perry, Molly Moody, Amanda Lagarde, Suong Doan, Brooke Hudson, Hanh nguyen, Tina Good, Glee Daniela, Kelly Gibbons, Rizo Pilko, Patricia Mangahis, Tish Lopez, Liz Madrox, Anne Hoffman, Sherry Rivera (MtSnow), Nicole Zeller, Rae S., Wanderlust14, Mike Martinez, Lynne Clifford, Lisa Nicole Gordon, Mandy, Emlyn Eisenach, Anke LÃ¼pges, Jordan Sophia Lombard, Gillian Thomas Edwards, A.R. Foitswagle, Kristin Tomic, wardy, Margaret, sherry lynn, Natasha Snow, Don M, Jann Norman, Eveline Lo, Cris Niccolini, Kate Ellis, Diana Teaman, Sue-Ellen Gower, K Clary Gnine, Marge Cee, Monique Ford, Eirin Elli, Géraldine Zenhäusern, Jo Ann Cerula, Geraldine Austin, Susan McCormick, Loretta J Sharp, Molly Basney, Jennifer Ronca, Jessica Riskedahl, Kaori Ueki, Sarah Wh, karen koijane, Pierre Houle, Tracy Timmons-Gray, Jessica L

Avila, Jocelyn Bissett, Abby Dain, Dianne T. Alice Brewer, Jennie Goloboy, Diana Quilty

Jenna Vance, Barbara grossbaum, Kira, elise ivey, Patricia Davisson, Susan McKenna, Whitney Wilkening, Rosa Nieto, Ame Pourtant, Brynne Lagaao, Philipp Schmidt, Martine DROUET, Jules Wildt

Brenda Snyder, Susanne Birk, Sara Bond, Susan Cox, Monica Navidad, Sowmya B, Annie Tate, Maria MacSmith, Virginia Modugno, Penelope Oulton, Marina, Juli-Anna Dobson, leah j berg, Stephani Kuperschmid, Carmen Carr, Brittany MacDougall, Rohini Karve, Julie Salverian, Cathy Weber, Amy Jarvis, Sarah Guest, Veroluc, Richelle McDaniel, Britta Ventura, Trio Seven, Jennifer Keirans, Michelle Marquez, Lucia V, Vivianne Todd, Miriam NIghtengale, Colette, Elizabeth Hayes, Laura E, Artemis Kaloudi, Marianne Ciaudo, Philippa Howe, Ashi, Joan De Leon, Rebecca Barr, H.L. Holston, CAROLYN ZOE BROUTHERS, W DEC, Sarah Teal, Kari Gregg, Annika BÃ¼hrmann, KM McCormack, Anu, Katherine Smith, Anne Jessica DuLong, Mody Bossy, Lisa Vanessa, kragthang, Rena Freefall, Clare London, Paula Knox, Aic, Jacob Magnusson, Jennifer Collyer, Miwa Nakano, Kevin Burton Smith, Alienor Drasen

Also by Josh Lanyon

NOVELS

The ADRIEN ENGLISH Mysteries

Fatal Shadows • A Dangerous Thing • The Hell You Say
Death of a Pirate King • The Dark Tide
Stranger Things Have Happened • So This is Christmas

The HOLMES & MORIARITY Mysteries

Somebody Killed His Editor • All She Wrote
The Boy with the Painful Tattoo

The ALL'S FAIR Series

Fair Game • Fair Play • Fair Chance

The ART OF MURDER Series

The Mermaid Murders •The Monet Murders • The Magician Murders

The A SHOT IN THE DARK Series

This Rough Magic

OTHER NOVELS

This Rough Magic • The Ghost Wore Yellow Socks
Mexican Heat (with Laura Baumbach)
Strange Fortune • Come Unto These Yellow Sands
Stranger on the Shore •Winter Kill • Jefferson Blythe, Esquire
Murder in Pastel • The Curse of the Blue Scarab
The Ghost Had an Early Checkout

NOVELLAS

The DANGEROUS GROUND Series

Dangerous Ground • Old Poison • Blood Heat
Dead Run • Kick Start

The I SPY Series

I Spy Something Bloody • I Spy Something Wicked
I Spy Something Christmas

Also by Josh Lanyon

The IN A DARK WOOD Series
In a Dark Wood • The Parting Glass

The DARK HORSE Series
The Dark Horse • The White Knight

The DOYLE & SPAIN Series
Snowball in Hell)

The HAUNTED HEART Series
Haunted Heart Winter

The XOXO FILES Series
Mummie Dearest

OTHER NOVELLAS

Cards on the Table • The Dark Farewell • The Darkling Thrush
The Dickens with Love • Don't Look Back • A Ghost of a Chance
Lovers and Other Strangers • Out of the Blue • A Vintage Affair
Lone Star (in Men Under the Mistletoe) • Green Glass Beads (in Irregulars)
Blood Red Butterfly • Everything I Know • Baby, It's Cold (in Comfort and Joy)
A Case of Christmas • Murder Between the Pages

SHORT STORIES

A Limited Engagement • The French Have a Word for It
In Sunshine or In Shadow • Until We Meet Once More
Icecapade (in His for the Holidays) • Perfect Day • Heart Trouble
Other People's Weddings (Petit Mort) • Slings and Arrows (Petit Mort)
Sort of Stranger Than Fiction (Petit Mort) • Critic's Choice (Petit Mort)
Just Desserts (Petit Mort) • In Plain Sight • Wedding Favors • Wizard's Moon
Fade to Black • Night Watch • Plenty of Fish • Halloween is Murder
The Boy Next Door

COLLECTIONS

Short Stories (Vol. 1) • Sweet Spot (the Petit Morts)
Merry Christmas, Darling (Holiday Codas) • Christmas Waltz (Holiday Codas 2)
I Spy...Three Novellas • Point Blank (Five Dangerous Ground Novellas)
Dark Horse, White Knight (Two Novellas)

Printed in Great Britain
by Amazon

24853625R00136